Unrequited Yearning

It was the first time Catherine had ever been in Devlin's room—and the first time she had ever seen him in bed. And though when they were children she had viewed him without a shirt, as a grown man he looked far different—and her feelings were different, too.

Tawny hair covered a muscular chest and equally muscular legs and arms. In his sleep he twisted, the motion pulling the bedclothes to his trim waist. The mat of chest hair tapered to a single line, tantalizing her eyes and drawing them lower until she felt an overpowering urge to slide the sheet aside.

Then he woke from his troubled dream—and shattered her growing one.

"Good night, Catherine," he said coldly. "You will freeze if you do not go back to bed."

It was clear to Catherine now how little Lord Damon Devlin wanted her as a woman or as a wife. As achingly clear as it was how much she wanted him. . . .

The Unscrupulous Uncle

by

Allison Lane

A SIGNET BOOK

SIGNET
Published by the Penguin Group
Penguin Putnam Inc., 375 Hudson Street,
New York, New York 10014, U.S.A.
Penguin Books Ltd, 27 Wrights Lane,
London W8 5TZ, England
Penguin Books Australia Ltd, Ringwood,
Victoria, Australia
Penguin Books Canada Ltd, 10 Alcorn Avenue,
Toronto, Ontario, Canada M4V 3B2
Penguin Books (N.Z.) Ltd, 182-190 Wairau Road,
Auckland 10, New Zealand

Penguin Books Ltd, Registered Offices:
Harmondsworth, Middlesex, England

First published by Signet, an imprint of Dutton Signet,
a member of Penguin Putnam Inc.

First Printing, November, 1997
10 9 8 7 6 5 4 3 2 1

Copyright © Susan Ann Pace, 1997

All rights reserved

 REGISTERED TRADEMARK—MARCA REGISTRADA

Printed in the United States of America

Prologue

Vimeiro, Portugal
August 20, 1808

"Promise me, Damon!" demanded Peter Braxton for the third time.

"Speaking of death attracts bad luck," insisted his life-long friend. "Would you force me to take that chance?"

Graceful despite his agitation, Peter strode rapidly away. He was slender to the point of fragility, as though he might vanish at any moment. But the impression was false. Underneath he was as strong and determined as Damon himself. Damon often wondered how two men who looked so different could be so alike. Peter was six inches taller, Damon two days older. Peter was dark, Damon fair. Peter's restless energy and excessive sensibility contrasted with Damon's leonine power and sober sense. But their minds were nearly interchangeable, so attuned that they rarely had to question each other. If only Peter had not done so now!

"The French are bound to attack soon," Peter reminded him, having circled back before reaching the edge of their camp. "That first skirmish was nothing. They cannot allow us a toehold in Portugal. When the battle starts, I will need all my wits, but I can't concentrate if my mind is distracted, Damon. You know I cannot."

Damon nodded on a long sigh. It had ever been thus.

Peter continued. "So you must promise that if anything happens to me, you will look after Catherine. I need the words, Damon! I know Papa will do his best, but he understands her no better than he understands me."

"Very well. I promise."

The discussion was pointless, for he would have watched over her whatever Peter's wishes. Their families were so close that he had long considered Cat to be the sister his own parents had never produced. Her face shimmered against the night sky as it had appeared the day he left

home, her violet eyes brimming with unshed tears. Though
she had known that buying colors was something Peter had
to do, her acceptance did not mitigate her fear. But she
trusted Damon to keep Peter safe.

A cannon roared in the distance as Damon struggled to
escape black despair. Peter was dead. He still could not
take it in. They had been closer than brothers, closer than
twins for two-and-twenty years. His anguish grew until he
wanted to scream and scream and scream, but a gentleman
could never do something so crass, especially an officer
newly returned from the battlefield.

He sucked in a deep breath, fighting for control. *How
can I go on without you, Peter?* What a tragic penalty for
youthful idealism! And how naive they had been—buying
colors so they could push Napoleon out of Portugal and
Spain through their own strength of will.

His hand shook as he opened his writing case. Twice the
pen slipped from his fingers, ruining a page with inkblots.
Gritting his teeth, he tried again. How was he to break the
news to Lord and Lady Braxton? They were as dear to him
as his own parents. And how could he hurt Catherine so
badly? He had failed her.

Oh God, Peter! Why? His vision blurred as the tears he
could no longer repress gushed down his face.

Seventeen-year-old Catherine Braxton awoke from the
drugged haze she had hidden behind for the last week, determined to get herself under control. Peter would expect
more than this craven escape from the world. She must see
after the household until he returned. Had the news reached
him yet?

Stifling another round of tears, she resolutely summoned
her maid. She had wallowed in grief long enough. She was
a Braxton, daughter of a proud lineage of barons and grand-
daughter to an equally proud line of earls through her
mother. Never again would tragedy overset her.

Memory threatened her resolve, but she was finally
numb enough to examine the facts dispassionately. The
twenty-third of August had been a delightful day—warm

and sunny, with only the mildest breeze. There was no hint of change when Lord and Lady Braxton agreed to go sailing with their dearest friends and neighbors, Lord and Lady Devlin. Catherine was also invited, but had stayed behind to comfort an injured tenant until the surgeon arrived to set the girl's broken leg. She never saw any of them again. A sudden squall capsized Lord Devlin's yacht, killing everyone aboard. Despite all logic, she felt guilty for remaining alive.

Had Peter heard the news yet? Had Damon? Everyone had feared for their lives since the day they had bought colors. Who would have thought that it would be those who stayed behind who would perish?

Someone scratched on the door, thankfully distracting her thoughts.

"Enter!"

But instead of her maid, Uncle Henry Braxton strode into the room, noting her red-rimmed eyes with his usual disapproving grimace. Yet his underlying expression more closely resembled suppressed excitement.

"Troubles never arrive alone," he announced ponderously, making none of the usual greetings and allowing her no time for any. "Your irresponsible brother got himself killed. The barony is now mine."

Catherine's screams echoed all the way to the kitchens, bringing the servants on the run. Her shrieks stopped only when she fainted.

Chapter One

Spring 1816

Hortense Braxton stormed into the breakfast room and glared at her cousin Catherine. "Lazy ingrate! Why Papa allows you to cadge off of us, I do not know."

"Is there a problem?"

"Of course there's a problem! I must wear my pink muslin tonight, but you haven't fixed that torn flounce. Why? It's been a week since that clumsy oaf ripped it!"

It was the first time Horty had mentioned a tear, but Catherine was too wise to point that out. "I will look at it after breakfast," she agreed quietly. "But are you sure you wish to wear that gown? It is becoming a trifle worn."

"What choice do I have?" snapped Hortense. "Papa refuses to buy me a decent wardrobe. He is making me a laughingstock. Even young girls titter behind their fans when I appear. It is unconscionable that my beauty should be so tarnished!"

"Perhaps your new shawl will dress it up," suggested Catherine. "Or cherry ribbons. Which would you prefer?"

"Both!" Horty's expression changed from petulance to calculation. "And change the sleeves. Those puffs make me look a veritable child. Jones can try something new with my hair. It is time to show those cats that they can never hope to outshine me."

"You and your delusions!" Drucilla Braxton scoffed, giving Catherine no chance to reply. "You make a cake of yourself by trying to be a diamond. That old gown is beyond repair. Besides, Cat won't have the time. She must fix the neckline on my new lutestring. I cannot understand how the dressmaker cut it so badly. I'll not look a dowd at Sir Mortimer's dinner. He has houseguests from London!"

"Better a dowd than a courtesan." Hortense sneered. "If you lower that neckline even half an inch, you will fall out of it the first time you breathe. Your antics embarrass us all."

"Embarrassment? Ha! It is rampant jealousy. You are so flat you could rip your bodice right off and no one would notice."

"What shocking vulgarity! Mama should leave you in the schoolroom. You can use the time to review fashion. Slenderness is all the crack these days." She stared her sister up and down. "Perhaps you should try Byron's regimen of boiled potatoes and vinegar. Gentlemen do not like fat."

"Fat! Listen to the self-appointed expert!" Dru's cup slammed onto the table, sloshing coffee across its surface. "I've heard you described many ways, Hortense Braxton, but fashionable was never one of them. Why only yesterday Jeremy Tuggens complimented my maidenly curves, disparaging your imitation of a fence post. And gentlemen have a penchant for blondes. You lose on that count too!"

"So you accept advances from a farmer's son!" Hortense snorted. "Have you no concept of what you owe your position? But this discussion is pointless. Your scandalous neckline will have to wait. As the elder, I have first claim on Catherine's services."

"It is just as well," agreed Drucilla. "If you wear the pink—which makes you look sallow and scrawny—even that rag I wear for gardening will attract Sir Mortimer's guests."

"How dare you?" demanded Hortense, pounding her fork on the tabletop hard enough to dent the wood. She cast a malicious eye over her sister. "But of course! You are upset because no gentleman will look twice at you unless you throw your naked body into his arms."

"Such language!" countered a seething Drucilla.

"What is the meaning of this contretemps?" demanded Lady Braxton from the breakfast room doorway.

"I wish Catherine to mend a small tear on my pink muslin so I can wear it tonight," stated Hortense firmly. "But Dru is being difficult. Can you imagine? She wants to appear at Sir Mortimer's dressed as a lady of the evening!"

"Fustian!" replied Drucilla. "I merely need Catherine to

make a slight adjustment on my new gown, which does not fit as perfectly as it should."

"Hortense, you will wear your white crepe," ordered her ladyship. "You will not appear in colors before you are officially out. I have already spoken to Jones about your hair. She must take particular care with it, for I hope to arrange a match with one of Sir Mortimer's guests. Both are of marriageable age and cannot help but look fondly on such a fine girl."

Calculation appeared in Hortense's eyes.

Lady Braxton nodded and turned her attention to her younger daughter. "Drucilla, there is nothing wrong with your gown. I checked it myself before we left the dressmaker's. You had best spend the day reviewing deportment. You are young yet, and unknown, so any mistake can prove fatal. Use the evening to hone your social skills."

Without giving Drucilla a chance to respond, she addressed her niece. "Catherine, you will plan a picnic for next week. And perhaps a dinner. We must take advantage of this opportunity. It isn't often that we get such distinguished visitors to Somerset. If only we could go to town this Season!"

"Yes, Aunt Eugenia," agreed Catherine.

"And speak to Cook about her blancmange. It was nearly inedible last night."

"Immediately."

"Mary was unacceptably pert this morning. If you cannot keep the girl under control, I will have to turn her off without a character."

"I will take care of it," promised Catherine, motioning Wiggins to remove her plate. This would not be a day she could linger over meals. Mary was a continuing problem. Though she was an outstanding worker, her high spirits left her unable to endure Lady Braxton's abuse in silence. But losing this position would hurt her family.

"I thought I told you to remove that obscene tapestry in the ballroom," complained Lady Braxton.

"Uncle Henry forbade it," Catherine reminded her aunt, shuddering at the desecration Eugenia had suggested the last time the subject arose. The tapestry was not the least obscene, but Lady Braxton hated the Elizabethan decor and was determined to introduce a vivid Egyptian theme. "There is no other hanging that will fit and he refuses to panel that wall. It is nought but rough stone right now."

"Papa is a pinchpenny," grumbled Hortense. "An Egyptian ballroom would be the talk of the neighborhood."

"But not from envy," countered Drucilla. "Chinese is more fashionable these days."

Hortense objected and they were off.

Catherine ignored the argument. Squabbling between her cousins was so normal that it hardly registered. In the early days, she had cringed at every contretemps, bursting into tears when their tantrums destroyed items that her family had prized. Not until she realized that the girls enjoyed hurting her did she learn to hide her pain, but it had been too late to salvage her mother's treasures. The collection of china figurines was long gone. Horty had smashed the oriental vases after Sir Mortimer's son called her a jade. Dru had tossed an entire folio of watercolors into the fire the day Mr. Dawkins rebuffed her. Though physically different, the sisters had identical characters. Both were terrified of spinsterhood, so they threw themselves at every available man. Catherine could do nothing to stop them or even to guide them, for she only lived here on sufferance.

She had endured many changes in the last eight years. The first was the cancellation of her Season. Her father had squandered much of his wealth—including her dowry—leaving the barony on the verge of destitution and herself unmarriageable. Uncle Henry had offered her a home, but it was long before Catherine fully accepted the situation.

At least Uncle Henry understood her aversion to charity and had helped her retain some self-respect. "I have a favor to ask of you," he had said a week after they had received word of Peter's death. It was the first time she had ventured downstairs since the accident.

"Yes?" Catherine looked straight at her uncle, avoiding the empty library wall where her father's picture had always hung. It had already been removed to the portrait gallery.

"You must stay busy if you wish to recover from your

grief," he pointed out after explaining the financial difficulties they all faced. "Eugenia has never run a house this size, and I must cut the staff, which will make the job even more difficult. Can you assist her?"

"Of course," she agreed readily, eager to do anything to pay for her upkeep. The new arrangement also earned the gratitude of the staff, many of whom had resented Lady Braxton's arrogance and petty complaints. Within the month, Catherine had taken sole charge of the manor, allowing the housekeeper to retire. Two servants who had protested using a baron's daughter as an unpaid menial were dismissed. The rest silently conformed to the new regime.

Catherine had been satisfied with the arrangement. Accepting charity from an uncle who was already suffering financial problems would have bedeviled her conscience. She might not like her change in fortune, but work kept her mind off grief and regret.

The next adjustment occurred near the end of deep mourning. She had looked forward to visiting neighbors again, but her fantasies had exploded during another chat with Uncle Henry.

"I truly hate to ask so much of you, my dear," he apologized, pacing restlessly about the library. "But I have a serious problem. Eugenia lacks your training in society manners, for she was not born to this position. Thus her confidence is easily shaken. She has the odd notion that the invitations she received are really meant for you and include her only from politeness. Perhaps you could remain behind until she discovers that the neighbors accept her for herself. Once she learns the truth, you are welcome to join her. It should not take long, for she has it backwards, as you well know. You are included only out of pity for the poor orphan or to show that they do not hold your father's irresponsibility against you."

"They know?" She had not believed that Uncle Henry would make his affairs public.

"Of course. It is impossible to keep secrets from servants, and they freely discuss their masters with others.

You must not pay heed to the talk. Few openly condemn you, for you were not to blame."

Yet she could not forget the shame her father had visited on the family. The last thing she wanted was pity from her former friends. She had readily agreed to remain behind so that Aunt Eugenia could establish herself as the new baroness. As time passed, she found that facing the neighbors was too humiliating. Peter would have called her craven, but she preferred to avoid a world in which she no longer had a place. Instead, she concentrated on running the house and helping the tenants, who had done nothing to deserve their change of fortune. As the family finances worsened, she took on more responsibilities. By age twenty, she did the household mending and was making her own clothes. By two-and-twenty, she was handling much of her uncle's correspondence so that he no longer needed a secretary. It was the least she could do to repay the rising cost of supporting her.

Uncle Henry often thanked her for her assistance. Aunt Eugenia's constitution had weakened until it required all of her energy to participate in neighborhood society, so she appreciated Catherine's efforts. Hortense and Drucilla ignored her unless they wanted help. Sidney, her uncle's heir, was rarely at Ridgway House, having been away at school when his father acceded to the title. More recently, he spent much of his time in town, and she was glad. The grievances he had nursed since childhood made him gloat over her new status as a poor relation. He did everything in his power to demean her.

Thrusting memory aside, Catherine followed her aunt to the morning room.

"We will hold the picnic on Wednesday," announced Lady Braxton once she was settled on a couch. "Cook must surpass herself if we are to make an impression. Oh how I wish we could afford a decent chef! How are we to attract the gentlemen's notice with nought but Mrs. Willowby? Sir Mortimer's cook is so much better."

"Mrs. Willowby does quite well," Catherine reminded her, refusing to mention that Sir Mortimer's cook had worked at Ridgway until Lady Braxton's insults drove her away. It was useless to repine over what could not be changed.

"I hope so," said her aunt with a sigh. "How are we to find husbands for the girls when we must start with such handicaps? Imagine! Only five hundred pounds each for dowries. What lord will overlook that? And they must find lords. It would never do to marry beneath them. As daughters of a baron, it is their right."

"What do you know of these gentlemen?" asked Catherine to divert her from an oft-repeated tirade.

"Everything important. Lord Grey is a baron, his title reaching back hundreds of years. He has two estates and a considerable fortune. Sir Timothy is but a baronet, but he will do to keep Drucilla occupied while we fix Hortense's interests with Lord Grey. She is already nineteen and must wed before she turns twenty or she will be considered on the shelf. That gives us six months."

They turned to planning the picnic, hoping for a warm day, though it was still early spring. Catherine accepted all her aunt's suggestions, her mind on other things. This would be another pointless exercise. Neither Horty nor Dru could bring Lord Grey up to scratch. Her aunt might live on dreams of a wealthy, powerful alliance, but her cousins were not the girls to achieve one.

Damon Alexander Fairbourne, ninth Earl of Devlin, glared at the missive in his hand. Triple disasters had struck his estate, requiring his immediate personal attention.

He shivered. Though he had sold out six months earlier, he had not yet visited Somerset, preferring to address other business first—like assuring the succession; he had pushed his luck far enough. Thus he had accepted invitations to several winter house parties and was now immersed in the London Season. It allowed him to forget his other reason for avoiding Devlin Court. Too many ghosts lived there, for everyone he had loved was gone. Peter's image floated before his eyes as it had done so often since Vimeiro, blotting out the sight of his study. How could he live without so basic a part of himself? After all this time it was still an unanswered question.

But the letter would not disappear.

"Tell Tucker we will leave immediately," he ordered the butler, who had been silently awaiting instructions near the door.

"Yes, my lord."

He scrawled a note to the Marquess of Tardale, postponing the meeting they had arranged for the following morning and crying off his plans to escort Lady Hermione to the theater. Two days to Devlin, three to address its problems—he should return in a sennight. Hermione would understand.

Lady Hermione Smythe. His face softened as he thought of the beauty he had chosen to be his bride. Tall and slender, with blond hair and green eyes, she sent chills tumbling down his spine whenever she entered a room. She would drive away the ghosts. The prospect of a week apart was daunting, confirming the wisdom of his plans. Hermione would preside over Devlin Court with the same graciousness as his mother and grandmother had. His tenants would welcome a mistress who could share their concerns. She would fit perfectly into his life, offering conversation or loving silence according to his mood, her sweet temper guaranteed to make his home the sanctuary it had been in his youth.

But it would do no good to dwell on their upcoming separation. He reread the letter from his steward. Troubles never came singly or even simply. One of the cottages had burned to the ground, injuring the tenant and killing his eldest son. Already the family was behind with the spring planting. To make matters worse, a mysterious illness was sweeping the county's dairy herds, promising bad times for the cheesemakers. Both problems would impact his rents. And the unrest that had plagued England for some years—most recently in the form of the corn riots—had now broken out in the village, as grumbling over dwindling incomes and rising prices turned to violence.

Damon sighed. He should have gone home earlier. Hastings was an excellent steward, but he had been left in sole charge of the estate since the previous earl's death. It was too big a burden.

He considered settling his betrothal immediately so he need not rush back to town, but reluctantly abandoned the idea. Managing the trip with only one overnight stop was already questionable. If he delayed any longer, he would require two. And it might take hours to track her down. She was probably out making calls or shopping. It was what ladies were expected to do when in town, and Hermione always conformed to expectations.

"I will leave immediately," he informed Tucker as his batman-turned-valet adjusted his jacket. "Pack enough for a week, then follow in the carriage."

"Of course, my lord," replied Tucker with a grin. "Don't you fret none. 'T'won't be the first time we up and left in a hurry."

Damon's eyes narrowed as he pushed memory past the years to which Tucker referred, past the disillusionment of war and the devastation of death, to another departure. That had been his last visit home.

Home. His mouth tasted metallic and he swallowed convulsively. He and Peter had bought colors in the spring of 1808, determined to counter Napoleon's move into Portugal. It had been Peter's idea, of course. He had been army-mad since escaping leading strings. That was all that had saved Damon's sanity after Vimeiro. If he had led his closest friend to death, he could not have lived with himself.

Their fathers had protested, but the boys were fired with idealism and an age-old drive to test their mettle on the field of combat. Next to that, the argument that heirs should not endanger their lives did not sway them. After all, a good friend had died while hunting. When the boys remained adamant, Damon's father had accepted defeat, mouthing all the appropriate words, though his disapproving expression belied most of them. Lord Braxton eschewed pretense, condemning them both for willful disobedience, and even threatening to disinherit Peter if he persisted in this folly—an empty threat, as they all knew, for the estate was entailed to the eldest son. Peter hadn't enjoyed the rift, but he understood his parent, having inherited his own passionate nature from his sire. He listened and agreed with many of Lord Braxton's points, but the remonstrations changed nothing. The boys had been of age.

Lord Braxton's diatribe had hurt Damon nearly as much as Peter. The baron was his godfather and was as beloved as his father. That had made Peter's death even harder to bear. Damon had always been the steady, rational one of the pair, expected to protect Peter and prevent rash behavior.

"Master Peter would chastise you for avoiding home for so long," observed Tucker, their long acquaintance under the most trying of circumstances allowing him to speak as a friend and advisor rather than a servant.

"There is no one there to care," responded Damon sadly. "My parents are gone, as are his. His sister married some years ago. I don't even know where she lives now. Under the circumstances, Peter would understand my reluctance."

"Maybe so, but you still have to live with yourself. If nothing else, you can decide what changes must be made before you marry."

Damon's brows shot up. He had never considered the question, but Tucker had a point. The house had been untenanted for years. Was it ready to receive the new countess?

Chapter Two

Damon's curricle threaded the gates of Devlin Court and snaked through the deer park, topping the rise that offered such a spectacular view of the house. His vision blurred. The Court was one of the most beautiful estates in England. Nestled in a valley against a backdrop of forested hills, the Palladian facade added by his grandfather glowed in the warmth of the setting sun. Behind that new front sprawled the Court. Originally built in the E-shape that paid homage to Elizabeth—who had bestowed both land and title on the first earl—it had since been enclosed and enlarged into a sprawling maze of wings and courtyards.

But the sight did not explain his moistened eyes. Nor did his eight-year absence. He had known how it would be. Peter was everywhere—racing at breakneck speed along the stream that traced the valley floor; dodging behind trees in uncounted games; gracefully clearing walls and ditches on his favorite black horse. Damon cleared his throat in a futile effort to choke back a sob. For years he had struggled to banish his agony by thrusting all emotion from his life. It was disheartening to learn that he had failed.

Drawing off the road, he tethered the horses and walked briskly into the woods. What a splendid figure he cut! Major Fairbourne, hero of the Peninsular campaign, a man who had looked death and carnage in the face without flinching. Yet he could not even enter his estate dry-eyed!

"Go away!" he shouted at Peter's lingering image. That quirky black eyebrow rose in silent laughter, but Peter complied.

Other ghosts immediately crowded close—his stern but loving father; his warm, compassionate mother, whose advice and help had extricated him from countless scrapes; Lord Braxton had been as stern as his own father, though more tolerant of his godson than of Peter; Lady Braxton was another he could turn to, particularly with problems he didn't care to confess at home.

Even Catherine glared at him, blaming him for not protecting Peter from the perils of war. After all, he was the elder. He knew better how to go on in the world. And he was always the practical one. Peter had fluttered from interest to interest with butterfly quickness, shedding trouble like a snake shed its skin—and with as little memory of the event. Not that Peter had been a shallow man, merely one filled with *joie de vivre*. It was that quality that had countered Damon's innate sobriety and stultifying common sense, injecting warmth into his life that had also died at Vimeiro. In like manner, Damon's practicality had kept Peter anchored firmly to the earth. They had been opposites, but of the same coin, one man who happened to occupy two bodies.

But such thinking was pointless. Peter was gone. Damon was left with only his own harsh self, untempered by Peter's enthusiasm. These days, he acted only out of duty— to see the war to its conclusion; to marry and secure the succession; to address the problems plaguing his estate. Straightening abruptly, he strode back to his curricle. He was the Earl of Devlin, sole survivor of two once-vibrant families. It was time to start acting like an earl. He would not think of Peter again. It was the only way to carry on.

"Welcome home, my lord," said Wendell when Damon appeared at the door.

"You look well," he replied, though he was shocked at how much older the butler appeared. Doing a quick calculation, he realized that the man was now in his late sixties. Could he still perform his duties? And what of the rest of the staff? Both the housekeeper and the head groom had been the same age as the butler. But he could hardly pension off everyone the moment he returned. And Hermione would have her own ideas about servants. Tucker was right. There would have to be changes.

"Robbie will bring up hot water. He is new since you

were last here." Wendell gestured to a liveried lad who
looked sixteen.

"But well trained, I am sure."

"Your luggage—"

"Will be along shortly. Send Tucker up when he arrives.
And a bath."

Damon headed for his room but halted at the split in the
stairs to gaze at his father's portrait. The eighth earl looked
little like his son, a shock of black hair topping a long face.
Only his tawny eyes glowed with kinship, even more alike
now that Damon had banished all gaiety from his own.
That feline stare seemed accusatory today, and Damon's
cheeks burned.

His father's teachings had always centered on the duty
he owed to his title. Damon had been an only child, the
next in line a third cousin who lived in America. Thus
Damon must guard himself against all peril lest the earldom
pass to unworthy hands. He had lived with that reality from
birth, and it had fueled his father's opposition to buying
colors. Damon's dereliction of duty had meant a painful
parting despite the conciliatory words. If the eighth earl had
lived, Damon's safe return would have brushed all that
aside. Instead, pain clouded his memories.

"Forgive me, Papa," he mouthed silently. "Your fears
were well founded, yet my own point was also valid. If I
had stayed, Peter would still have gone and would still have
died, and I would have lived forever with the conviction
that I could have saved him had I been there." He laughed
mirthlessly. "How stupid! I would not have known, for I
would have been on the yacht that day. Perhaps fate protected me by sending me to war. But enough of the past. I
am alive so everything will be all right. And I will marry
soon, probably at midsummer. You would have liked her,
Papa, for she is very like Mama—golden, beautiful, and
loving."

His sire's expression remained stony. Nothing had really
changed. And why was he talking to a portrait? He was becoming eccentric. Already he spoke with too many ghosts.
It was nearly as bad as talking to trees, which absurdity had
gotten the King locked in a padded room.

Damon quickly mounted the rest of the stairs and was turning left when movement drew his attention to the right. Robbie was entering his father's room. But it was now his, he admitted as the finality of his position registered. He must step into his sire's shoes, and taking over the earl's suite was the opening move. Yet it seemed almost blasphemous. Drawing in a deep breath, he marched down the right-hand corridor.

Damon sat at his father's desk, listening to the steward's droning voice. The library looked strange from this perspective. Instead of his usual sight of the fourth and sixth earls—whose frowning countenances had added the disapproval of all his ancestors to his father's lectures—he now saw books, globes, and a view of the formal gardens and lake. He thrust down the thought that the hill beyond shielded his eyes from the Bristol Channel, wherein lay the bones of his family.

Hastings was detailing estate problems—and there were plenty. The disasters that had summoned him from London were merely the most pressing. "Devlin is not alone in either village unrest or in losing cattle. You should discuss the situation with other landowners, staring with Lord Braxton. He has lost his entire dairy herd."

"I had not planned to call," protested Damon, wanting to never set foot there again. If the ghosts at Devlin had nearly broke him, those at Ridgway House were guaranteed to do so. "There is no one there I know."

"Not even Miss Catherine?" asked the steward in amazement, before recalling his place and snapping his mouth closed. "Forgive me, my lord. I understood that the previous baron's family was close to your own, but she is considerably younger than you."

"I thought she married seven years ago." Shock nearly paralyzed his voice.

"Married? I heard of no such plans, but then I was new to this position when you left, and met the previous baron only once before his own death. We did not discuss his family."

"You are sure that she is still there?"

"Yes, though she does not go about in society."

Damon returned to the business at hand, but his mind raced. What could have happened? He could not imagine her crying off. Did her beau die before her mourning period was over? Yet surely she would have looked about for another suitor. She would never wear the willow.

He fought past the haze that had engulfed his brain after Peter's death, forcing himself to remember. The pain had not even begun to dull when word reached him that his parents and Peter's had been lost in a sailing accident. It had been the last straw for his reason. He had no memory of the days that had followed and had never asked Tucker for the details, but a fortnight later he was on a ship headed for England, with a broken arm and the sort of bruises one acquired in a fight. Also aboard were the army's top officers.

Sir Arthur Wellesley had trounced the French at Vimeiro, capturing their entire force. It should have freed Portugal and driven the invaders from much of Spain, but the arrival of his superiors—Sir Harry Burrard and Sir Hew Dalrymple—guaranteed a protracted struggle. In a move of utter stupidity, the two had negotiated the Convention of Cintra, allowing the French Army to return intact to France, where it was immediately reposted to the Peninsula. Burrard, Dalrymple, and Wellesley were recalled to face courts-martial, but the damage had been done.

Aboard ship, Damon was only peripherally aware of their presence. Still in a fog of grief and despair, his thoughts had focused on the substantial legal business engendered by his accession and on Catherine, whose situation was uncertain after the loss of her family. But he never traveled beyond London, getting caught up in the courts-martial proceedings. Though only a low-ranking officer, he had fought under Wellesley, receiving a field promotion for his efforts. His convenient presence in London demanded that he be called as a witness. By the time Wellesley was exonerated, there was no reason to go home, for Damon had encountered the new Lord Braxton at Brook's.

They exchanged condolences on family tragedy and congratulations on their respective accessions.

"What will Miss Catherine do now?" Damon asked. "Peter was worried about her future."

"And with good reason," agreed Lord Braxton. "But you need not concern yourself, my lord. She will be wed next summer. The betrothal was arranged a sennight before my brother died."

This was news to Damon, though Peter could not have heard before Vimeiro and Damon would have seen none of his friend's letters afterward. "Who is the gentleman?"

"I doubt you know Roderick, my lord. He is a younger son of Sir Arthur Graham, who visited Somerset on business after you had left for Portugal. I met him at the funeral. He seems to be all that is proper, and my brother had already agreed to the connection. He is home in Yorkshire now, for Catherine is still devastated by the loss of her family."

"Of course," agreed Damon, recognizing the understatement.

Now he nodded at whatever Hastings was suggesting. What had happened? And why was she avoiding society? There was only one way to find out—call at Ridgway House and ask her.

Promise me, Damon. If anything happens to me, you will look after Catherine. But he had not. He had failed to carry out a sacred vow. By not keeping in touch with Devlin Court, he had not learned that Catherine's future was still unsettled. Guilt flogged him, joining the ghosts that already berated him.

I'm sorry, Peter! Somehow, I will make up for my negligence.

"Peckland claims that Mrs. Newman has a putrid sore throat," groused Lady Braxton, biting into a scone. "I don't know why he has to bother me with tenant problems. Handling such things is his job."

Catherine mentally shrugged. Her aunt had never grasped the fact that the lady of the manor was expected to look after the welfare of the tenants. Peckland usually brought problems to Catherine. Why not this time?

Lady Braxton finished her scone and sighed. "You will have to see the woman, I suppose. Take her a basket."

"Gladly."

"But don't give her anything valuable. It only encourages sensibility. Peasants should never succumb to so trifling an ailment. They are too lazy already."

Biting back a scathing rejoinder, Catherine left to execute this latest commission. It did no good to brangle with her relatives. They were in a position to make her life miserable. But there were times that silence was difficult.

Lady Braxton's contempt was nothing new. Nor was it unusual for someone in her position. Her father was a prosperous farmer who had been thrilled when Eugenia caught the eye of a baron's younger son. But once she was wed, the girl ignored her family. Hortense and Drucilla had never even met their maternal grandparents, despite living barely twenty miles away. And Eugenia's antagonism had worsened once death had elevated her husband to the peerage. Her background also colored her attitude toward Catherine, for she resented the aristocratic blood flowing through her niece's veins.

Lady Braxton's current ill temper dated to Sir Mortimer's dinner party. Catherine had not attended, of course, but Dru's description of the houseguests matched Eugenia's assessment—except that Lord Grey was in his late forties. Yet the evening had ended like so many others. The gentlemen politely avoided the Braxton sisters. Nor were they interested in attending a picnic, however well planned, claiming that business necessitated an immediate return to town. Word that they had not departed until three days later further infuriated the baroness. She had stormed about like a stoat with a sore paw ever since.

Hortense followed her mother's lead, railing at spiteful gossip, for only a jealous rival could have prompted the cut she received before Lord Grey even made her acquaintance. Catherine made no comment, though she was mortified on behalf of her family. School friends whose older brothers were considered catches had repeated tales about matchmaking mothers and the stratagems they employed. The lower their own social status, the more blatant their lures. She could only conclude that her aunt was worse than the most encroaching mushroom, throwing her daughters at gentlemen with no regard to convention or even good taste.

The Braxton ancestors must be turning in their graves at how far their once-proud name had fallen.

She had tried to convince Hortense that a different approach would work better. "Gentlemen prefer demure innocence and dislike being openly pursued," she warned. "It creates an impression of impropriety that is difficult to overcome."

"What would you know about the world?" scoffed her cousin. "You have never even been out in local society."

"True, but Peter was, and I had many friends at school whose brothers and sisters were in London."

"Ha! Some friends! Have you heard a word from any of them since you lost your place in our world?"

Catherine did not reply, for the question was rhetorical. They both knew she had no relationships outside of the family.

"Quit blathering about things you do not understand," continued Hortense brutally. "There are different rules for town and country. London manners must be restrictive, for one sees the same people every day. But here one must seize the moment else visitors will leave before they can become acquainted."

She had nearly contradicted the falsehood, but protest was pointless, for Horty's manner drove off the very men she hoped to attract. Pushing the memory from her mind, she sighed. Only the present was real.

She met with the cook to go over the day's menus, then visited Mrs. Newman. The woman had suffered a severe inflammation of the lungs during the winter that had left her very weak, so it was hardly surprising that she was again ill. Her real problem was the poverty that had forced her to rise from her sickbed before she was fully recovered. The Newmans could not afford servants, and Lord Braxton had refused to supply one during her winter illness. With four small children at home, she would face the same future. One of the Tuggens girls might be willing to help, but she would have to be paid. Catherine had no money and could not use household funds for something her uncle had prohibited. Compounding the problem, Mrs. Newman was again increasing. Would she survive this time?

* * *

Damon turned his curricle through the gates of Ridgway House and gasped. The manicured park that had rivaled Devlin Court in all but size was now a property on the decline. Weeds encroached on the drive. The estate wall was crumbing where roots had buckled its foundation. Brush grew under the trees, and damaged limbs remained in place, posing a hazard to the unwary.

But overriding his sadness was renewed grief. Memories were everywhere, even stronger than at Devlin—he and Peter playing at soldiers in the clearing, reenacting ancient battles from Hastings to Culloden; Catherine trotting after her twin brothers (as they had always styled themselves), her five-year-old legs unable to keep up with their longer ones; the fence which Peter had cleared at age eight, while Damon had suffered the ignominy of being thrown; a glimpse of the best fishing spot along the stream—Old Wily had kept them busy for years, moving at random between this stretch and the similar one at the Court. The ancient trout was recognizable both by his enormous size and by the distinctive notch on his dorsal spine. Fifteen-year-old Peter finally captured the fish, though his sympathy for so stout an opponent had prompted him to throw Old Wily back. It was the last time they had gone fishing.

Damon shook his head to clear the visions, determined not to allow the past to intrude during this visit. He would not be here at all if Catherine had wed as expected.

"Master Damon!" exclaimed the butler when the earl appeared at the door, but he rapidly recovered his poise. "Or Lord Devlin, I should say."

"You've not changed a bit, Wiggins," said Damon with a smile. "Is Catherine at home?"

If anything, Wiggins became even stiffer. "I believe Lady Braxton is in the drawing room. I will see if she is receiving."

Damon frowned at Wiggins's retreating back. Times had certainly changed since the days when he had run tame here, rarely even bothering to knock. Had Catherine suffered a disfiguring injury that forced her to break off her betrothal? That might explain why she was never seen in company. But he immediately chastised himself for a lurid imagination. This was not like him; Peter was the one with his head in the clouds. Besides, Wendell would have heard of any accident.

"This way, my lord," said Wiggins.

Some things were the same, observed Damon, following the butler across the great hall. The paneling glowed with care—though with the perfectionist Wiggins in charge, that was hardly surprising. The drawing room was exactly as before, the French furniture Peter's mother had installed gracing a room designed by Adam. It had always been one of his favorite places, so soothing that one could not help but relax. The walls were covered with ice green brocade above ivory wainscoting. The custom-woven Axminster carpet repeated the design of the stuccatori ceiling just as the chairs bore the same brocade as the walls. Rose velvet draperies festooned the windows. The one oddity was the pianoforte, which had unaccountably migrated from the music room. Only as he turned to greet his hostess did he note that the upholstery was frayed. A sharper look revealed a poorly mended hole in the carpet, sun damage to both draperies and wallcoverings, and the absence of two Chinese vases that had always sat on the mantelpiece.

The new Lady Braxton was in her early forties, her faded blond hair showing only a slight infringement of gray. Brown eyes were her most notable feature. A beribboned morning gown sported more ruffles than he had seen on the fussiest creation in London, yet did nothing to hide the lady's overindulgence in sweetmeats and lack of all but the most innocuous exercise.

"I vow this is the greatest surprise!" she twittered, waving a pudgy hand in welcome. "We had not heard of your return, my lord. And to call on us the very first thing! But I suppose you have been told how charming my daughters are and had to see for yourself if the tales were true."

"Actually—" he began, but she continued without pause.

"They will be down directly. I doubt you will encounter their like in London, at least not this Season. We will be there ourselves next year."

"I will be charmed to meet them," he replied, having already taken the woman's measure. She might as well emblazon *mushroom* across her forehead. Peter had rarely mentioned his aunt, dismissing her as the family black sheep. She had never accompanied her husband when he visited Ridgway, and now he knew why. "But I also wish to speak with Miss Catherine. Peter would want me to answer any questions she might have about his final days."

"She has long since forgotten this death," announced Lady Braxton airily. "There is no point in reminding her. I won't tolerate another day of blue-devils. In any case, she is out. But here are my daughters. May I present Hortense and Drucilla? Girls, this is our neighbor, the Earl of Devlin."

Damon greeted them politely, but inwardly he winced. Nothing about the elder appeared feminine. She was tall and thin, with a figure much like a mast and a face more closely resembling that of a horse, a forelock of brown hair nearly obscuring her dull brown eyes.

"I'm simply thrilled to meet you!" she simpered, batting her lashes so rapidly that they disappeared in a blur of movement. Latching long, pointed nails onto his sleeve, she leaned closer until he had to step backward to avoid contact.

He automatically responded to her words, unfastening her hand and briefly saluting her fingers before turning away with a suppressed shudder. Her gown was covered with even more ornamentation than her mother's.

But Drucilla offered an equally painful sight. The younger Miss Braxton was short, inheriting her mother's penchant for stoutness as well as her blond hair. She also harked back to the animal kingdom, a round face, bucktoothed smile, short nose, and receding chin giving her a marked resemblance to a rabbit. Another fussily adorned gown emphasized her plump figure, its scandalous bodice threatening to spill its contents into full view.

"I daresay you are enthralled to be home at last," she managed between giggles, thwacking his arm with her fan.

"Come sit by the fire," urged Hortense, giving him no opportunity to reply. She practically dragged him across the room as Wiggins appeared with a tea tray.

"Yes, do," echoed Drucilla, neatly slipping onto the couch at his side so that her sister dropped into her lap. Hortense's squeak of furious surprise nearly sent him into paroxysms of laughter.

"Wine, my lord?" asked Lady Braxton.

By the time he was gingerly sampling an indifferent sherry, Hortense had regained her composure and removed herself to a chair. "Is Lord Braxton available?" Damon asked. "There is some business we must discuss." Both girls immediately straightened. "I wish to learn more about this mysterious malady that has overtaken our dairy herds," he added.

Four shoulders slumped in dejection and Lady Braxton glared. "I will tell him you called when he returns from Taunton tonight. You will visit again, I presume?"

He would have preferred to meet the baron elsewhere, but he still needed to speak to Catherine, so he nodded.

"Have you just returned from France?" asked Drucilla, finishing the question with another giggle. "Tales of your heroic adventures have thrilled us for years."

"I have been back for some time," he said resignedly. "But business has kept me busy elsewhere, most recently in London."

"You must tell us the latest *on-dits!*" exclaimed Hortense, leaning closer in her excitement. She shifted her shoulders so that her low-cut neckline gaped. There was little to see.

Damon complied. It was as good a way as any to pass the time until he could leave. The Braxtons were appalling. At any moment he expected one or both of the girls to tear his clothes off in an attempt to get closer. His nearside arm was already bruised from Drucilla's fan, which accompanied every one of her incessant giggles. Hortense had managed to scoot her chair closer until he could almost feel the breeze stirred up by her lashes. Lady Braxton beamed on the girls as if they were diamonds of the first water, approved by every patroness at Almack's. But given her own lack of taste, he was not surprised.

He finally made his escape, but the hope of exchanging a private word with Wiggins was foiled when the girls insisted on accompanying him outside, gushing ignorant praise of his curricle—which they thought was a phaeton—and of his horses. How much would Catherine have changed after living for eight years with such brazen people? Peter's eyes again castigated him.

Catherine had hardly reached the top of the stairs when Drucilla pounced on her.

"You must help me refurbish this gown," she ordered breathlessly. "He will return tomorrow and I must be ready. Oh, I just know he has fallen in love with me! He leaned quite close and his leg brushed mine three times."

"Who?" asked Catherine, but Hortense's strident voice drowned out her sister's response.

"Ignore her, Cat. She is air-dreaming again. You must add braiding to this pelisse. He will certainly invite me for a walk in the garden, for he could hardly take his eyes off me. I could feel him mentally undressing me as we spoke. It was horridly disconcerting, but one must face facts. He was interested only in me, despite her unbecoming attempt to throw herself into his arms. He was not deceived for a moment."

"Unbecoming! Who was it who practically tore her gown off trying to thrust a nonexistent bosom in his face?"

"Ha! All he could possibly feel for you was pity that so fat a child will be condemned to eternal spinsterhood."

"What is going on?" demanded Catherine, raising her voice above the clamor.

Both sisters broke into excited chatter, from which tangle she eventually deduced that the Earl of Devlin had called two hours earlier. She hardly noticed when the explanations degenerated into another brangle over which of the girls his lordship preferred.

Damon was home. Her thoughts swirled, unable to move beyond that fact for some time. Memories of her second brother washed over her. Damon had always looked after her, providing help, advice, and companionship. Peter had been an exciting playmate, but he was also a dreamer who was unreliable in a crisis, so it was Damon who repaired her doll when its head broke off, Damon who picked her up and comforted her after her pony threw her against a tree, Damon who had consoled her the day her favorite dog was found dead in the meadow, and Damon who banished her fears about going away to school.

And yet he had failed her when it mattered most. Anger stirred. He had sent not one word after Peter's death. She still had no idea how her brother had died. She assumed it was at Vimeiro since that was the date on his tombstone, but even that remained unconfirmed. Nor had he sent a word after their parents' deaths. At first, she had excused his silence, knowing the depth of his own grief. But as the weeks and months passed, she could no longer accept that explanation. All her life they had considered each other's parents as their own. She had grieved as much for Lord and Lady Devlin as for her own family. Yet Damon had said nothing, not even in response to the condolences she had sent. Had he decided to repudiate his childhood? Was his grief so all-consuming that he could spare no thought for her?

She almost wished she could tell him how badly his indifference had hurt. But she was afraid to talk about it. That could only reopen the wounds and resurrect her pain. Not that she need consider such an eventuality. She would not see him, even if he called again. Poor relations were not welcome in the drawing room.

Setting her face into a soothing expression, she turned her attention to calming her cousins' dispute, using the expertise of years to prevent it from turning into a brawl.

Chapter Three

I promise, I promise . . . Damon pulled a pillow over his head, hoping against hope that he could return to sleep, but it was impossible. He had lain awake long into the night, shuddering over his call at Ridgway House. Peter's accusatory eyes hovered long after he closed his own.

The Braxtons were appalling. *Family black sheep* . . . That euphemism covered a multitude of sins, from idiocy to eccentricity to openly criminal. Apparently Peter had applied it to a serious mésalliance. And that was not the worst of it. Once Lady Braxton dragged her daughters to London, Peter's family name would be permanently blackened. The idea hurt as badly as if his own were threatened. But there was nothing he could do—except rescue Catherine. It was what Peter would have expected. Poor Cat. She must have suffered more than he had ever imagined.

I promissse . . .

But I tried to help, he reminded his conscience. He had checked on her welfare after Vimeiro, assuring himself that her future was settled. Everything had seemed perfect. His vow was discharged and he could return to Portugal with an easy mind.

He groaned. Why had he not spoken directly to her? He should have verified that she was coping with grief, made sure that she was happy with her betrothal, and looked up her prospective husband. Peter had not trusted even his father to properly see after her future. But Damon had done nothing, so relieved at avoiding Peter's home that he had accepted the arrangements without question. Perhaps if he had investigated, he could at least have averted the final tragedy and saved her from years with her family when her betrothal ended.

But that led his thoughts to the other puzzle in this mishandled mess. Why had Catherine not responded to his letters? He had written three times—that heart-rending missive just after Vimeiro, another a fortnight later when he learned of the accident, and a note wishing her well when mourning was over and her wedding was due. She had acknowledged none of them. Nor had she sent a single word of condolence over his own losses. He rolled over, frowning. Grief aside, it was unlike her to ignore his existence. She could not have changed that much.

He finally fell into a fitful doze but was unable to rest. Dreams, memories, and nightmares tormented him. Peter urged him to action, berating him for negligence and weeping in frustration.

He groaned, awakening in a cold sweat to furiously pace the room in a vain attempt to wear his body down. Even Peter's father glowered, cursing fate and reminding Damon that he was the only one now in a position to do anything. Giving it up, he rang for Tucker. Guilt would prevent any real rest until he discovered what had happened. He must rectify his oversight if he ever wanted to sleep peacefully again.

What could he do for Catherine? he wondered as he stared out the window. She ought to leave Ridgway House, but where could she go? Devlin Court would not do. Living there would destroy her reputation, and he doubted that Hermione would understand his obligations. In the eyes of the world, they were unrelated. But perhaps Hermione could sponsor Catherine into society. Finding a suitable husband would solve the problem quite nicely. And it should not be difficult. Catherine was not yet five-and-twenty. Her breeding was excellent, her dowry substantial, and her looks well above average.

Damon pulled to a stop before Ridgway House, noting further signs of disrepair that he had missed the previous afternoon. Tucker had heard that the baron was destitute. How had he dissipated his fortune so rapidly? Or had he? Peter had often described his uncle as a miser. Every visit to his brother in twenty years had been to ask for money, even though the man's income was adequate. Perhaps he was deliberately cultivating an impoverished facade to keep his wife fixed in the country. After growing up in the elegance of Ridgway House, he must know how unsuited she and his daughters were.

Damon had chosen to arrive at the earliest acceptable calling hour to assure that Catherine would be at home, but she was not in the drawing room.

"My dear Lord Devlin!" gushed Lady Braxton. "We are delighted to see you again so soon. But then few men are able to forego sight of my girls for long."

He responded formally, but none of the ladies noted his coolness. Wiggins's arrival with a tea tray created a bustle during which Hortense cut out Drucilla for the privilege of sitting next to the earl. Drucilla's glare could have slain armies.

The Braxton women were again gowned in fussy ruffles and ribbons, more ornamented than the day before. But none of them sported the tiniest gem. And that was a glaring omission, for others of Lady Braxton's ilk wore their entire jewelry case when they wished to impress. He could only conclude that they owned none.

Drucilla looked even more like a rabbit today, with her hair arranged in earlike coils on either side of her head and a ribbon tied around her neck like a collar. Hortense had dampened her gown, the clinging muslin proving that her figure was as bony and off-putting as he had suspected. She had borrowed a trick from her sister and now carried a fan which had already twice assaulted yesterday's bruises. Neither girl had the slightest notion of subtlety.

"Will your niece be joining us?" he asked Lady Braxton after accepting a biscuit from the shabby footman.

"Not today. Poor Catherine is suffering a headache." She smiled, but there was a hint of unease in her face.

"Are you attending Sir Mortimer's party next week?" demanded Hortense, her strident voice turning the question into an accusation and offering an incongruous contrast to her furiously batting eyes.

"I doubt it. I still have business in town. Only the problems caused by the Connors fire made this trip necessary."

"Surely you can remain that long. Everyone will be

there," urged Drucilla, leaning forward much as her sister had done the day before.

The results this time were worth assessing, but his appraisal was no different from those he made of the Cyprians outside the opera house, and with the same conclusion—he was not interested. "What is the occasion?" he asked.

"A christening party for his grandson," explained Lady Braxton. "The boy was born only three days ago."

"So Toby is married and now has an heir," he said in surprise. The lad was only two years younger than himself, so was ready for the responsibility, but he had not heard of the nuptials.

"His wedding was a veritable scandal." Hortense snorted. "They wed in much haste barely eight months ago, and now we see why."

"Perhaps not," objected Drucilla, more to irritate her sister than because she believed it—or so it seemed to Damon. "They had been courting for much of the summer. It is unfortunate that the child was born early, but he is reportedly very small and may not live out the year."

"Much you know about it," Hortense snapped. "You have never even seen a babe, so how are you to judge what is proper?"

"Nor have you!" shot back Drucilla. "You are merely jealous because Diana snagged a gentleman you had been making sheep's eyes at." She giggled at Damon. "Her taste runs to tall, thin men rather than powerful, handsome ones." She tried to bat her lashes but only twisted her face into a grimace.

"Girls!" admonished Lady Braxton, a blush staining her cheeks as she turned to Damon. "How is Mr. Connors?"

"As well as can be expected." He shrugged. "Burns are the worst sorts of injuries. It will be several weeks before he has any chance of returning to the fields."

They chatted about neighbors he had known before joining the army and about changes in the area. Damon was merely going through the motions, for Lady Braxton's judgments were so catty that he refused to believe any of her statements. And she could not hide her disdain for the lower classes. Drucilla had reverted to giggling, though he was spared the frequent rap of her fan. Hortense's voice grated on his ear until he was ready to scream, and her simpering was enough to put him off food for a week.

"But Mrs. Carmody's girls cannot hold a candle to my own," declared Lady Braxton, returning to her favorite topic. "You should hear Hortense on the pianoforte, my lord. Such power! Such control! There cannot be another performer like her in the world. No one in town can compare. She will take society by storm when we bring her out. Play that piece by Beethoven, dear."

Hortense smiled and batted her lashes furiously before taking her seat at the pianoforte. This explained why it had been moved to the drawing room. Performances must be a regular part of entertaining.

He grimaced as she hit the first notes, recognizing the piece—barely. It was Beethoven's "*Für Elise,*" though he wondered if the composer would still take credit for it should he hear Miss Braxton's version. Instead of the gentle, flowing tones he had expected, Hortense produced labored, strident sounds in a rhythm Beethoven never imagined, from an instrument that could not have been tuned since Damon left for war. Gritting his teeth, he set his expression to neutrality—any form of a smile was impossible—and endured the longest fifteen minutes of his life. He tried to convince his brain that this was artillery fire. It didn't work. Would she never finish? God help him if she tackled anything longer.

"Lovely, dear," said Lady Braxton, smiling as her daughter finally plowed through the last run. "Did I not tell you how accomplished she is, my lord?"

"You are right. I have never heard the like," he managed, but some of his pain must have shown, for Lady Braxton's smile wavered.

"Drucilla also plays," the baroness announced brightly, "though she is younger so has had less instruction."

Damon almost groaned when the girl pulled out a Mozart sonata. Dear Lord! It was three times as long as the Beethoven piece. But he relaxed once she started. Though she had even less concept of rhythm and expression than her sister, she did have the advantage of speed. Mozart would undoubtedly turn in his grave if he could hear the crashing dissonance imparted to his work, but Drucilla finished in half the time the composer intended. Damon sighed in relief.

"Quite remarkable dexterity," he murmured, then turned his attention to quitting the premises.

Catherine slipped out of the servants' entrance and escaped through the kitchen garden. Escape was not a proper way to think of her behavior, but it was true. She needed some time to herself.

For two days she had listened to Dru and Horty gloat over the Earl of Devlin. His second visit had convinced the hen-wits that he adored them, though they argued frequently over which he would choose as his countess. They repudiated other explanations for the earliness of his second call. Their conceit had survived three years during which not a single gentleman had visited twice, so no warning from Catherine could dull their enthusiasm.

She gave up trying. Time would reveal the truth. Damon could not possibly have changed that much. Besides, Wiggins confirmed that he had called to see Uncle Henry about estate matters. It wasn't his fault that Lord Braxton had remained in Taunton. Damon's failure to reappear supported this theory. He would not return until he knew Uncle Henry was home. But convincing Dru and Horty was impossible. Any hint that the girls were air-dreaming and they would turn on her.

It was the argument over their relative skills on the pianoforte that had finally driven Catherine from the house. Poor Damon. She was appalled that he had been subjected to such torture. It must have taxed his manners to the limit. He had an excellent ear and appreciated good music. Even picturing him within hearing of her cousins made her shudder. That alone would explain his failure to call again.

She wandered across the meadow and entered the tract of forest that was her favorite part of the estate. It bordered Devlin Court and had been a playground for the three of them when they were young. Even after the boys started school, they had spent term breaks at home, only rarely objecting when she tagged along.

She slipped into the clearing that had always been her refuge and perched on her usual rock. The stream bubbled over rounded stones, filling the glade with laughter. Here they had played at knights and pirates. Here she had brought her books to read when Peter and Damon were away. Now she came to think and—occasionally—to dream, for she knew her cousins would not find her. They refused to walk farther than the distance from door to coach unless accompanied by a gentleman.

Where were her dreams now? They had changed as she grew older, modified by time, by maturity, and most recently by her lowered status. The dreams of a dappled gray pony gave way to those of a spirited horse, to life at school, and to her expected come-out. When Peter and Damon bought colors, fear for their safety and disappointment that they would miss her Season moved to the fore, accompanied by prayers that her father would turn aside his anger and accept Peter's decision. For two months he refused, ranting almost daily about his son's intransigence. She now wondered if he had used ire to mask his own fear. But she would never know, for before his temper could cool they were all dead. After the devastation of that summer, she had avoided this spot for a long time, unable to face the memories.

But its tranquility eventually drew her back. Peter was safe for all eternity and Damon had survived. Now her dreams were purely selfish—hopes that Uncle Henry would recoup enough to buy husbands for her cousins, for they would blame everyone but themselves if they faced spinsterhood, and she would be their first target; prayers that she and Sidney would learn to get along, for when he acceded to the title, she would have to share his house; and fantasies that Aunt Eugenia would become worthy of her position before she blackened the family name beyond redemption.

Unwillingly, her thoughts returned to Damon. She had always known that he would return. And feared it. Despite her prayers, a tiny voice inside her head wished that he had perished along with Peter. For the first time, she blessed fate for preventing her from appearing in company. How could she face him? He had forgotten her, repudiating the connection she had expected to last a lifetime. And she would never understand why.

Damon cantered across the park, his eyes taking in none of the beauties of the day. Something was very wrong at Ridgway. Burt, his groom, reported that Catherine never spoke with the neighbors, refused to appear in the drawing room when guests were present, and turned down all invitations. She rarely left the estate, never traveling beyond the village. That was not at all like her. What had happened?

More to the point, how was he to meet her? If she did not greet guests, there was no point in calling again—and he doubted he could tolerate another hour with the Braxtons. Should he send her a letter? But she had responded to none of his previous ones. Burt claimed she was well, according to the Ridgway grooms, and had suffered neither accident nor illness since Damon had left, but he could not reconcile that with her behavior. No one could change so drastically.

She had always bubbled over with enthusiasm and humor, jumping at any challenge. He had often needed to rescue her because she insisted that she could do anything that Peter could—and usually better. Never mind that she was a girl and was five years younger. She had ridden races, jumped impossible fences, climbed trees, fished the stream, challenged Peter at chess—though never Damon, for he could beat them both to flinders—and done a host of other things Lady Braxton would have swooned over. But hiding from the neighborhood and cutting old friends was out of character.

He slowed as he entered the woods, nearly turning aside. Peter was more strongly present here than at any other place on the estate. It had been a favorite playground in their youth. But it was also a place of peace and tranquility that he needed more than anything right now. Picking his way through the trees, he suddenly pulled Pythias to a halt.

Catherine sat on a rock as she had so many times in the past. But this was a different Catherine from the girl he had known, and not just because her gown was several years out of date. Her face was sad, her expression far away. Was she also troubled by memories of Peter?

How absurd! She would have visited this spot hundreds of times over the last eight years. Besides, she was not a girl to dwell on her losses.

But she was no longer a girl, he realized an instant later. She was a woman. Unfashionable as the gown was, it encased an appealingly curvaceous figure. Gone were the blemishes she had struggled with that last year. Instead, those startling violet eyes dominated a heart-shaped face with a smooth, creamy complexion. Full, red lips were set in a frown, but he remembered her sunny smile. Her black hair was unflatteringly pulled back, but its innate curliness could not be hidden and he had no trouble picturing her in a stylish cut. No wonder she never appeared in public. Lady Braxton must know how poorly her own girls would compare, though that could not explain why Cat had not wed years ago. She was beautiful. His fingers tingled with the need to loosen the grim hair arrangement and tear off the hideous gown so he could dress her as she deserved. He thrust the thought aside, guilty over admiring anyone but Hermione—even the girl who was nearly his sister.

"Hello, Catherine," he called softly as his horse picked its way across the stream.

She jumped. "My lord." The cold voice halted him, his surprise turning to pain as she whirled to leave, almost as awkward as the last time they had met.

"You did not used to be so formal," he protested.

"I believe you are trespassing, my lord," she reminded him. "The stream marks the boundary, as you must recall."

"Catherine! What have I done to deserve this?"

She froze, her face twisting into anguish. "How can he do this to me?" Her whisper cracked on the words.

"Do what?" he demanded.

She jumped, obviously unaware that she had spoken aloud. But she pulled herself straighter and raised her eyes to his. "Not one word," she choked, tears shimmering on her lashes. "I don't even know how he died!"

"My God!" Damon dismounted, tethering Pythias to a

tree. "I wrote that night. It was the hardest letter of my life. And I wrote again a fortnight later when I heard of the accident."

"I never got them," she insisted.

"I wrote, Little Cat," he repeated, reverting to his childhood address. "How could you believe I would ignore your pain?"

Her shoulders slumped. "Perhaps it was the shock. No one spoke of them after the first couple of weeks. But I recall neither letter. I made all sorts of excuses for you, but finally decided you had excised the past from your life." She broke into wracking sobs.

He pulled her close, battling his own tears as he allowed her to cry into his jacket. Never in his darkest hours had he expected this. He had considered himself her brother for all of her life. She must have felt abandoned indeed. No wonder he had never received a response. It sounded as though she had collapsed for some time after the accident. And who could blame her? He had always considered her more sensible than Peter, but she was capable of the same intensity as her brother. It was a fact he sometimes forgot.

"Forgive me," she begged at last. "How could I become such a watering pot after all this time."

"There is nothing to forgive. The uncertainty would prolong your grief." Why had she not asked her uncle for the details? he wondered, but it did not seem appropriate to question her actions. "Come and sit down. What do you wish to know?"

"Everything," she replied so naturally that he might have been fifteen again, describing Eton to a breathless ten-year-old—in this same spot.

"There really is not much to tell." He sighed, his face falling into a frown as he cast his mind back to those idealistic first days in Portugal. "We landed on the coast just north of Lisbon. There was a minor skirmish almost immediately, but it resolved nothing and we all knew there would be a larger battle soon. But the French badly underestimated our forces. Wellesley—or Wellington as he is now styled—is a master of tactics, not only winning, but capturing the entire French force."

"Then why did the war not end?"

He grimaced. "It was not Wellesley who negotiated the terms of surrender. Burrard and Dalrymple arrived the next day. Understanding nothing about Napoleon, they allowed the French to keep their weapons and return home. Both were court-martialed and relieved of their positions, but the damage was already done."

"How did Peter die?" she asked directly, returning his mind to the point. It did no good to remember how many friends had suffered and died due to the incompetence of two men.

"It was in the first charge," he replied sadly. "The only comfort is that he died instantly, taking a bullet squarely between the eyes. I doubt he felt a thing." His voice trembled, but she did not seem to notice.

"W-was he all right afterward?" she asked, almost apologetically. "There have been so many tales of desecration and pillaging on battlefields."

"Rest easy," he commanded, again fighting tears, for the reality far exceeded anything she could have heard. "I saw him go down. The moment there was a break in the action, I sent Burt to bear him back to camp. You may remember Burt."

"Of course. His cousin Ned is one of our footmen."

"There is nothing more I can add. Rather than wait for word from home, I arranged to dispatch the body here— and was ultimately glad to have done so, for only you were left by the time the notice arrived. How did you survive so much grief?"

She turned bleak eyes toward his face. "I don't know. I recall little after I wrote you, so I suppose I slipped into shock. By the time I recovered, the funerals were over and Uncle Henry had taken care of everything else. I should have known that you would not have forgotten us, but having no memory of that time, I assumed that there was nothing to know."

"Did you really write me?" he asked suddenly.

"Of course. The evening of the accident. You must have gotten it!"

He shook his head. "Not a word. It hurt."

They stared at each other for over a minute.

"This is very odd," she said.

"Not really." He shrugged. "The vagaries of war. We lost some ships in the early days. I suppose our mail was on them."

"How cruel can life get?" she murmured rhetorically. "Not one word from you since Peter's death."

"But surely your uncle reported meeting me in London!"

She raised her brows. "When was this?"

"Early November. I came back to deal with all the legal business engendered by my parents' deaths. I was planning to come down to see you, but frankly I was dreading having to face the ghosts here, so when I met your uncle in town, I turned coward and rejoined my regiment. He assured me that you were well. But I sent you a message."

"Saying what?"

"Repeating my condolences and congratulating you on your betrothal." But even as he spoke, cold settled into his stomach.

"What betrothal?" Shock widened her eyes.

"Lord Braxton said that you had accepted the hand of Roderick Graham just before the accident."

"I have never heard of such a man. I have certainly never been betrothed. I was not even planning to come out until the following Season. You know I was barely seventeen that summer."

"What is going on here?" he demanded sharply.

"I have no idea. Why would Uncle claim that I was betrothed? Unless he expected to arrange something. There was no money for a Season. But why would he even try? No man wants a girl without a dowry."

"Nonsense! Your dowry was settled when you were a child."

"You have been away a long time, Damon. Papa could be quite the charmer, as I am sure you recall. He was also quite good at obscuring truth. When my uncle inherited, he discovered that there was no money. Even my dowry had disappeared. He would have done what he could to arrange my future—not out of goodness, of course, but to save himself the expense of keeping me. Whatever gentleman he hoped to convince must have refused."

"Perhaps," he agreed, though not believing it for a moment. The dowry had been there. And nothing would convince him that Peter's father had been hiding indebtedness. He knew the man too well.

"You think I'm exaggerating, don't you?" she observed sadly. "But you did not know everything. Even Peter didn't. How could you when you were both gone most of the time? I do not know if it was gaming or bad investments, though I suspect the latter. And Papa was not the sort to flaunt poverty. He would have continued as before, wearing a prosperous face and hoping that he could turn things around before the truth emerged. But he did not have time."

Her words pulled Damon up short. Was it possible that he was less knowing than he thought? But either way, he must take care of Cat.

She continued, showing no sign of noticing his preoccupation. "But Uncle Henry is not the sort for pretense. He decreed that the only hope of recouping Papa's losses was to tighten our belts. And it has worked, though it is unlikely that my cousins will enjoy London Seasons any time soon. Hopefully they will not have to wait until they are on the shelf like me, for they have already had a difficult time adjusting to penury. We have fewer servants than they would like and smaller wardrobes. I help where I can, but there is no point pretending that all is well."

"Why do you not go out more?" he asked.

She shrugged. "There is no point in embarrassing my family. Poor relations are not accepted as equals. I do not wish to endure that. Even worse, there are those who might pretend nothing had changed. That is as good as a slap in the face to my aunt and cousins. It was difficult enough for them to come to a neighborhood where they were unknown. Things would only have been worse if I were seen to be the reason people included them."

"After nearly eight years, such an excuse can no longer be valid," he reminded her.

"Then perhaps I am a coward," she admitted angrily. "I

cannot face the change in my own status. Is that what you wanted to hear?"

"Of course not! And I don't believe it."

"Believe it, Damon. There are days when I want to scream in frustration, but we can only play the cards we are dealt. It does no good to swear at the dealer. When things get too bad, I come here. It is wondrously soothing to my spirits. Now enough of me. What have you been up to these last years? I hear you are quite the hero."

"Not at all," he disclaimed. "The real heroes are all dead, so when the government needs to trot someone out as an example, they must choose some poor bastard from the living."

"You did not used to be so cynical."

"War changes people, mostly for the worse. I do not wish to discuss it." He paced restlessly around the clearing.

"Very well." Her words were conventional, but he could hear the pain at what she could only interpret as another rebuff. Before he could formulate an explanation, her face cleared and her eyes lit with mischief, sending a *frisson* of warmth through his heart that the Cat he remembered still lived. "Uncle Henry got back last night. And my cousins will be out this afternoon. You can call on him without running the risk of another musicale."

He chuckled. "Still looking out for me, Little Cat?"

"Unless war has destroyed your hearing, you cannot have enjoyed it, however much you praised them."

"How well you know me. But praise? They must lack understanding of the English language. I merely agreed with your aunt that I had never heard the like. And you must agree that Drucilla shows great dexterity."

"You have become a rogue!"

"Hardly. Merely displaying manners in the face of trial. Is there nothing you can do to discourage them?"

"No. They must prove that they are proper ladies by demonstrating their accomplishments. Since neither can set a stitch without knotting every thread in their sewing baskets or paint even the simplest picture well enough that they can identify it themselves the next day, they must rely on music. Be thankful they don't sing. Even Aunt Eugenia cannot pretend their voices are acceptable."

Damon shook his head. "How is Wiggles?" he asked, naming the puppy he had given her before leaving for war.

Her face softened. "He is fine, though I no longer have him. Aunt Eugenia cannot abide animals, so the Newmans have taken care of him since we heard about Peter. I still see him often. He has become a wily herd dog, helping Sam look after his sheep, though he reserves most of his affection for me."

"And Lady Jane?" he asked, referring to her mare.

"Gone. Uncle Henry sold the stable as soon as he learned how bad finances were."

She straightened, putting an end to his questions. "I must go, for there is much to be done today. Do you wish to call on Uncle?"

"Not yet. I must see how Mr. Connors goes on." And he needed some information before he faced Lord Braxton. Too many things didn't add up. They could not all be passed off as coincidence.

Catherine nodded. "Please convey my greetings to Mr. Connors and wish him a speedy recovery. I doubt I can visit him for several days. Mrs. Newman needs help."

Damon raised a brow and she explained. "I will arrange care," he offered. "It is the least I can do." Peter would be appalled at such neglect.

Thanking him, she disappeared into the woods.

Chapter Four

Catherine climbed into bed, finally able to relax. Aunt Eugenia had ordered a fancy dinner and cleaning of the public rooms for a party she was planning the next evening. Wiggins had said nothing as they supervised maids and footmen, though both knew it was wasted effort. This would be another in a long line of entertainments that were not held. Few people were willing to endure recitals at the Braxtons', so they usually found excuses to turn down invitations.

Dru and Horty had been equally annoying, demanding endless help with their wardrobes and creating petty chores to relieve their irritation at Damon's absence. They had eagerly overdressed to attend a village fete celebrating the nuptials of Major Kersey's grandson. When the earl did not appear, their disappointment surfaced as bad-tempered demands on Catherine, though it was obvious why he had stayed away. One of their quarrels revealed that both had sent word to Devlin Court that they would be attending. While they had been searching for him in the village, he had been in the clearing.

Pressing her face into the pillow, she reviewed that meeting. Damon had changed in eight years. Instead of a youth on the verge of adulthood, he was now a powerful man, hardened in ways she could only imagine. As usual, his tawny curls raged in longish riot around a broad face whose amber eyes and flat nose had always reminded her of the lion in one of her picture books. But the face had aged. Browned by the Spanish sun, it now bore lines about his eyes that hinted at incessant squinting to discern distant movement of the enemy. And it bore other lines—from grief and pain?—across his forehead. His body was as solid as ever, but instead of comfort, it now radiated strength, and something else. Anger?

But she had dwelt on the subject longer than was prudent. It had been good to see him again, but she wished she had not. It recalled all that she had lost. Normally she was content with her lot, but once in a while something happened to illustrate just how far she had fallen. Even this room and this bed irritated her tonight, though it had been years since she had last noticed her surroundings. She now lived on the nursery floor in a room last used by her grandmother's companion.

She could not recall the change. It had occurred while she was immersed in grief. Her aunt blamed the doctor, who had recommended a break with anything connected to the past—or so they claimed. She knew the real reason was to remove the poor relation from one of the best rooms in the house. And she could hardly expect to live with the family. But at the moment it was difficult to appreciate a room no better than that occupied by her aunt's maid.

Sleep still would not come and she finally admitted that she was deliberately focusing on her position in a futile attempt to ignore Damon's revelations.

He had set her mind to rest about Peter, and for that she was grateful. She had often been plagued by visions of her brother lingering in agony or hopelessly disfigured. Battlefield tales appalled her. She heard of men who had been blown to bits and others who had died slowly and painfully of gangrene or infection. Afterward, she suffered hideous nightmares in which Peter met a similar fate. Stories describing how scavengers stole uniforms, weapons, and even teeth from the dead kept her awake for weeks. Knowing that Peter had died cleanly and had been removed to Damon's keeping even before the battle ended was a great comfort. She only wished that she had learned those details years ago.

It was Damon's other claims that shocked her. A betrothal. He could not have invented that story. Nor was he the sort who would misunderstand a vague comment. Once Uncle Henry mentioned it, Damon would have pried loose every detail. If he believed the betrothal was a settled fact, then he must have been told so. But why would Uncle Henry lie about so momentous a subject?

She frowned and again shifted position, staring morosely at the ceiling. It was possible that Uncle Henry had exaggerated. He was prone to doing so, something Damon might not have known. Henry had once bragged about selling her father's best hunter to a Quorn member, boasting for days of the astute deal he had made. It turned out that Lord Graylock had only expressed an interest in looking at the horse, ultimately deciding that it did not meet his needs.

Perhaps something similar had happened with Damon. Her uncle had been trying to arrange a betrothal and, as usual, was a little too sure of success. The more she thought of it, the more certain she became. Uncle Henry had exaggerated, but Damon would have believed that everything was settled. And perhaps it was better that he had. Thinking all was well at home, he could have concentrated on his duties. It might even have contributed to his survival.

Having explained that situation, she was left with the lesser questions. Why had no one told her of Damon's letters? It was hard to accept that she had been so grief-stricken that she would not remember. He was the one person whose condolences would have soothed her. And it was even harder to accept that all the letters had been lost at sea. He had written twice, as had she. Four ships could not have gone down in the space of a month. And Uncle Henry had not mentioned meeting him in London. She would not have forgotten that. The trip had occurred long after the accident and at least a month after she had emerged from her deepest grief. She had joined the family for dinner the night of his return, listening to his descriptions of all that he had done in the city, including excruciating details of the people he had met, but there had not been a single word about Damon.

It could not be oversight, she realized. For some reason the Braxtons had decided to sever the connection and must have destroyed the letters. There was no question that they were gone. About six months after the accident, she had gone to the attic to find a more comfortable chair for her new room. A bundle of letters sat atop an old table, their thin coating of dust proving that they were recent. She had thumbed through them, noting that they were condolence letters for her parents and brother. Over the following weeks, she read and reread them, touched by the compassion addressed to her from people she had never met. She had not mentioned finding them. Her aunt wanted her to put the past behind her and believed that never broaching the subject was the quickest way to do so. After a while, Catherine had put the letters away and moved on with her life.

Hands shaking, she lit a candle and dug into her battered desk. The bundle was still where she had pushed it all those years ago. At the time it had seemed important to keep this memento of her former place in the world. Carefully turning over each letter, she verified that there was no word from Damon. And now that her suspicions were raised, she could think of at least a dozen others who should have written.

Other puzzles nagged at her mind. She had never questioned the statement that her dowry had been lost along with the rest of her father's wealth. The shock in Damon's eyes could not have been feigned. Of course, her father would hardly advertise a penchant for poor investments. But what if the dowry still existed?

She shook her head over this sudden resurrection of an old dream, put out the candle, and crawled back into bed. Ever the romantic, she had spent too many days picturing herself with a husband and children. It was a fantasy that she had deliberately discarded after the accident, for it did no good to dwell on what could never be. And it still could not, she reminded herself brutally. Even if the dowry existed, she never met eligible males. And even if she did, she was now firmly on the shelf. She had never appeared even in local society, for she had not yet been out when her parents died. Within the month she would be five-and-twenty, an ape-leader in anyone's book.

Firmly casting aside nonsensical hopes, she set her mind to planning the morning's activities. The linen inventory should have been done a month ago; several sheets needed mending; Hortense had torn the flounce on another gown— really, that girl must learn to move more gracefully; it was past time to prune the rose arbor—she would speak to Wye about it, for there was still enough grounds staff . . . On that thought, she finally drifted into uneasy slumber.

"How could you!" demanded Peter Braxton. Blue eyes glared as blood oozed from the hole in his forehead, running down to drip off the tip of his aristocratic nose. *"You promised! You promised to take care of Catherine for me!"*

Damon opened his mouth to reply but no words emerged. He tried to raise his hand, but it refused to budge.

"How could you!" He had been wrong. It was not Peter who faced him, but Hermione, her voice vibrating with approbation. "You promised to be back in a sennight, but you have already been gone for eight days. How can I face society when you have abandoned me?" Tears dripped from her chin to feed an ever-widening pool on the floor.

Again Damon tried to speak—without success.

"How could you!" It hardly surprised him when his accuser again changed. "You could have discovered the truth anytime merely by contacting your steward!" charged Catherine. "Instead, you condemned me to a life of slavery." Fury burned in her eyes, but before he could open his mouth, she vanished.

Two figures wrestled on the ground, suddenly visible through a break in the mist.

"His duty is clear!" gasped Peter, applying a hammerlock.

"To return to London!" insisted Hermione, twisting to pin his bare shoulder to the ground.

"A vow is a vow!"

"Even an implied vow!"

They sprang up, leaping toward Damon, who was still frozen in place—tied to the mast of his parents' sinking yacht.

"Cad!" Hermione charged, slicing his cheeks with nails that extended three inches beyond talonlike fingers.

"Liar!" hissed Peter, pressing the point of a sword against Damon's throat.

"Help!" shrieked Catherine.

Three heads swiveled. She was rapidly sinking beneath the waves, helped to her doom by a flock of chortling Brax-

tons, whose flapping ribbons kept them hovering above the water as they dropped a pianoforte onto her head.

Peter's sword severed Damon's bonds, but Hermione threw herself into his arms and dragged his lips into a passionate kiss.

"You promisssssed . . ."

Damon clawed his way into the air. Where was he? Heart pounding in terror, he peered through the gloom, finally identifying his room at Devlin Court. Dawn filtered through a crack in the draperies.

He sagged back onto the mattress and pulled the coverlet tightly around his shoulders, suppressing a shudder. That had been a bad one, though not his usual nightmare.

Frowning, he tried to recall the details, but he was too wide awake. They were already fading into oblivion. Hermione had been there. And Catherine. Were they fighting? But that made no sense. His obligations to Cat would not affect his relationship with Hermione. Unless they were fighting the Braxtons. There had been something about the Braxtons he was sure. But that made even less sense. Perhaps the dream was a warning. If the Braxtons were desperate enough, they might pose a danger. Shaking his head, he rose to greet the day. Long experience had taught him that sleep was impossible after one of his dreams.

Lady Braxton was alone in the morning room, so Catherine plunged in before she could lose her nerve.

"Aunt Eugenia, why did I never see the condolences that arrived after my parents died?"

"You did, dear. We read them together and then I left them for you to look at later. But when the doctor suggested we remove all traces of the past, I put them in one of the attics. You may have forgotten."

"You are right that I remember nothing of that time, though I went over the letters later. But that is not what I was asking. The packet was incomplete and I wondered where the others were put. Lord Devlin's letters were missing, among others."

"You are mistaken," insisted her aunt coldly. "There was

no word from his lordship. He was undoubtedly too caught up in the war to consider what was happening at home."

"You forget yourself, madam," stated Catherine just as coldly, shocking the woman into silence. "My father was Damon's godfather. My brother was his closest friend. And his parents died in that same accident. Nothing was capable of distracting his attention at such a time. But I am not speculating. He wrote immediately after Peter's death and again after receiving word of the accident. And he never got any of my condolences. He spoke with Uncle Henry in town two months later, sending me a message which I also never received. Why?"

"It is pointless to discuss ancient history," declared Lady Braxton. "But what makes you believe such fustian?"

"I ran into Damon when I was out walking yesterday. He told me."

"Then he lied to cover up a lapse of manners. It was what he should have done, of course."

No gentleman would behave thus. Catherine started to point that out but thought better of it. Even if her aunt knew of the letters, she was obviously unwilling to discuss them.

"Who lied?" demanded Hortense, appearing in the doorway with Drucilla.

Catherine cringed at the sight of her cousins. Both had modified their gowns to be more eye-catching. Dru's neckline would be scandalous even in London ballrooms and seemed ludicrous on a country morning gown. Horty had embellished a walking dress with red and black ribbons placed to attract the eye to her less-than-abundant charms. They both wore a startling amount of makeup, looking like little more than Cyprians. For the first time, Catherine felt ashamed to be related.

"Lord Devlin," replied Aunt Eugenia.

"So you have been sneaking off to see his lordship!" exclaimed Drucilla, storming across the room to slap Catherine's face. "How dare you try to cut me out?"

"Cut *you* out!" shrieked Hortense, poking Dru in the ribs. "There is nothing to cut. I am the eldest and the only one he is interested in. You are nought but a schoolroom infant making a cake of yourself by trying to act like a lady."

"Ignorant fool!" shouted Drucilla, whirling to face her sister while Catherine put a hand to her ashen face. "No lord as well set up as Devlin would look twice at a flat-chested beanpole like you. You should have seen him grimace while you were plodding through your music!" She turned back to Catherine. "And don't get your hopes up, Cat. All he could ever want from a penniless servant is dalliance. Or are you already his latest mistress?"

"Drucilla!" snapped her mother. "A lady does not speak of such things."

"And whores should not be allowed in our house!" Dru pointed out, glaring at her mother. "It is time to decide what to do with our cousin. Either make her live and eat with the other servants or send her to play fetch and carry for Great-aunt Alice out in Cornwall. She should not be allowed to interfere with my gentlemen friends."

Catherine paled even further at the venom in Dru's voice. "You mistake the situation. I merely ran into him while out for a walk. Of course he stopped to greet me. He was my brother's best friend and was with him when he died."

"It is improper for you to be conversing with any gentleman," intoned Lady Braxton. "Drucilla is right. Your position might lead him to make improper advances."

"Exactly," agreed Hortense. "And it is not good for Lord Devlin's attention to stray. It would interfere with concluding my marriage contract."

Drucilla took umbrage.

"Enough, girls!" barked Lady Braxton when their squabbling degenerated to hair-pulling. "I do not wish to hear another word. Catherine will avoid Lord Devlin by remaining in the park. Leave the tenants to Peckland," she ordered. "You will have plenty to do in the house. I had to turn Mary off this morning."

Catherine wisely refrained from admitting that she had met Damon in the park, thrusting down distress at the thought of never seeing him again. It was better for her peace of mind to avoid him, for he was a bitter reminder of all that she had lost.

* * *

Lord Braxton was glaring at the estate books when his wife entered the library.

"We must do something about Catherine," she began without preamble. "The chit is doing her best to destroy our girls' marriage chances."

"What is this?"

"You know that I am well on the way to arranging an alliance with the Earl of Devlin."

"Do you actually believe he can stomach either of them?" he scoffed, throwing his usual reticence aside. "He is a gentleman."

"Of course. Which is why he will offer for Hortense. His honor demands it."

He stared a moment. "I see. Up to your old tricks, aren't you?"

She ignored the comment. "Catherine deliberately sought his lordship out yesterday to play on his sympathy. And she is painting us in a false light to turn him against Hortense. Why, she even accused me of stealing letters that he claimed to have sent her some years ago!"

Braxton paled. "What tale is this?"

"She insists that the earl sent her several notes shortly after her parents died and even sent a message by you that she never received. All false, of course. I put every letter aside and gave them to her."

"Of course you did," he concurred, frowning in thought. "As to the message, it is true that I met the earl in London some years ago. He sent general greetings to the family—you know how one does. If I did not mention it, I can only remind her that other things pressed heavily on me. I was still reeling from the knowledge that my accursed brother had squandered the family fortune."

"But what are we to do with Catherine?" she wailed, again ignoring his words. "She has never liked us. I fear Sidney is right. She resents her reduced status and is only waiting for the chance to stab us in the back. Destroying this alliance would be a perfect revenge."

"That is simple enough. I will send her to Braxton Manor for the summer. The household needs supervision. She can see that the place is being properly kept up. That should give you ample opportunity to snag the earl. The settlements may be just what we need to pay off some pressing debts."

"What a suitable place for the girl!" exclaimed Lady Braxton. "Let her molder there forever."

"Are you prepared to take over her chores?" he asked maliciously. "There is no money for a housekeeper."

She sighed. "You are right, of course. But it is time she learned her place. When she returns, she must move into the housekeeper's room.

Chapter Five

Damon pulled his curricle to a halt in front of Ridgway House and frowned. His back was crawling the way it always did before a battle. Peter whispered warnings in his ear as he had so often done in Spain, but this time he could not distinguish the words.

Lord Braxton had invited him to join a dinner party after which the neighborhood gentlemen would consider the dairy herd problem, but he saw no other arrivals. Turning the ribbons over to Burt, he hesitantly plied the knocker.

"Good evening, my lord," intoned Wiggins, motioning Ned to take Damon's hat, driving coat, and gloves.

"Am I early?" murmured Damon.

"Not at all. You will be dining *en famille* tonight."

"Does that mean that Catherine will join us?"

"She is no longer at Ridgway, my lord." Despite the wooden face, Damon detected a warning tone. Wiggins had always had a soft spot for both himself and Peter, often extricating them from potential trouble.

His goose bumps doubled as every hair on his body stood to attention. Fragments of his morning nightmare returned, including an incongruous image of a pianoforte. Danger thickened the air, but he could not question Wiggins further, for they were no longer alone.

"How wonderful that you could join us, my lord," gushed Lady Braxton, bustling across the great hall. Her evening gown was even fussier than her daytime wear, every square inch bedecked with ribbons, lace, and ruffles. Matching bows dotted a head covered in girlish ringlets. She simpered, multiplying her chins.

"My pleasure," he replied dutifully, even as his mind was working out Wiggins's warning. It increased his sense of urgency. Braxton's lie added credence to the notion that they might actually try to compromise him. *Never!* he vowed, already plotting strategy.

Lady Braxton tried to maneuver Drucilla away while he spoke to Hortense, adding to his suspicions. But he had a powerful weapon in the rivalry between the sisters, a weapon he intended to use.

"That is a lovely gown, Miss Drucilla," he said with a smile that kept the girl at his side. He allowed his gaze to rest on her abundant charms, making her blush and bringing a spark of malicious pleasure to her eyes. Her bosom swelled as her breathing accelerated. Would she pop out of that scandalous dress before the evening ended?

"Thank you, my lord." She giggled, leaning closer to improve his view. "So pretty a compliment from one who must be London's finest dresser will surely turn my head." Her fan smacked the bruise on his arm and he nearly winced.

"Of course I must also commend your own elegant attire," he said with patent untruth as he turned his eyes to Hortense. Her white gauze was so encumbered with bows that she resembled a ribbon counter in a linen draper's shop. The only thing that might have increased her vulgarity was a king's ransom in jewels. It was too bad that neither of these dim-witted chits could explain the loss of the Braxton fortune.

"Really?" she choked, batting her lashes and simpering foolishly, though her harsh voice destroyed the picture she was trying to present.

"Would I lie?" he asked outrageously. "I have not seen two such visions anywhere in London." That, at least, was true, though hardly flattering.

They edged closer, jockeying for position until he feared that Hortense's rapidly fluttering lashes might catch in his cravat. At least Drucilla could no longer put any power behind the shortened thrust of her fan.

He pushed credulity as far as he dared, flattering first one lady, then the other, until their tempers were near the explosion point. It would not do to actually have them tearing each other's hair out—or his—but as long as each believed he might succumb to the charms of the other, he would be safe. Drucilla brushed her bosom against his arm while Hortense fanned his ear with her lashes. His skin crawled. War strategy was easier, both to design and to implement.

Dinner was tedious, with indifferent food and boring conversation. It was the first time in years that he had met the baron and he wondered at the changes. Braxton was thinner, his gray hair and cadaverous face making him look twenty years older than when he had acceded. Unlike his family, Henry dressed conservatively, making few concessions to current fashion. Drucilla and Hortense continued to vie for Damon's attention, their manners deteriorating as the meal progressed. Lady Braxton's eyes raised new danger signals. He could almost hear her thoughts—should she pursue her original scheme or might Drucilla make a more welcome spouse? He glanced at Wiggins and relaxed a trifle. At least he had one ally, not that he could count on much actual help from that quarter.

He breathed a sigh of relief when the ladies retired to the drawing room. Not giving Lord Braxton time to assume whatever role he had been assigned in this farce, he launched a discussion of the disease that was Braxton's excuse for inviting him, soliciting the baron's thoughts and hanging on his every word. Unfortunately, the man had not the slightest knowledge of the subject, his ridiculous assertions making it difficult to keep a straight face. Only Damon's long absence on the Peninsula allowed him to credibly pretend to take the baron's words to heart. He managed to stretch the conversation for over an hour despite Braxton's growing irritation. But finally they had to join the ladies.

"Will you be staying at Devlin, my lord?" the baron asked with patent disinterest as they approached the door.

"Eventually," admitted Damon. "This trip was in response to the Connors fire, but I will be returning to London in another day or two."

"So soon?"

"I must be there when my betrothal is announced. My fiancée would be upset if I missed the ball."

Braxton nearly choked. "I had not heard that you were betrothed."

"Naturally not. The public announcement will be made on Friday and will appear in Saturday's papers."

Lord Braxton dropped the subject, unable to miss the steel that underlay Damon's statement.

He had not meant to declare his intentions so openly, though it was nought but the truth. But claiming the betrothal as fact might depress the pretensions of this very vulgar family. Poor Peter would turn in his grave if he could see how low the barony had sunk.

"Lord Devlin is betrothed to a London miss," stated Lord Braxton when they entered the drawing room.

"What?" Lady Braxton paled alarmingly.

"Who is she?" demanded Hortense.

"Why had you not mentioned her earlier?" asked Drucilla with a pout.

Damon spent several minutes fending off questions. "You will learn all when we make the announcement public," he repeated for at least the tenth time, anger clear in his voice. He recovered his address and continued. "But I know that you will like her. Such charming ladies cannot help but become her closest friends. I count on you to introduce her around the neighborhood."

Though pique lingered in all eyes, the girls replied with unexpected grace and Lady Braxton offered congratulations. Damon breathed a sigh of relief. His words were blatantly false, of course, for he could not imagine Hermione in the same room with these two, but with such a scheming mother they would not remain problems for long. It was only a matter of time before Lady Braxton settled on a new victim.

He kept a pleasant expression pasted on his face through the purgatory of another musical evening, wishing he could dispense with manners long enough to leave. But at least he had successfully diverted whatever plot Lady Braxton had devised.

While these congratulatory thoughts occupied one corner of his mind, the remainder was pondering Catherine's absence. Wiggins was always very precise in his choice of words. *She is no longer at Ridgway* could only mean that she had been packed off elsewhere. Why? If Lady Braxton feared competition for her daughters, Cat would have left years ago. Likewise, if she feared Cat might interfere with a plot to compromise him, why would the lady wait for a week after he arrived before sending her away? It was only after their meeting that anything had happened despite his asking after her during both visits. The Braxtons must fear that she might reveal a secret—something beyond their apparent poverty. What were they hiding? It must be serious if it justified the expense of banishing her.

The insidious idea grew, seeming impossible at first but refusing to go away. Suppose Lord Braxton was trying to harm Catherine. It appeared ludicrous on the surface, but there were too many oddities to ignore the possibility. The first was Braxton's lie that Catherine was betrothed. She had denied the story, though the baron had sworn that her father had approved it. When sorting conflicting statements, Damon would believe Catherine over her uncle any day. She had a sense of honor worthy of a gentleman.

Then there was the poverty at Ridgway House. Everyone agreed that they lived in straitened circumstances. Yet the estate had always been productive. Peter's father had been a devotee of Coke's agricultural experiments, hiring an innovative steward and working with him to increase yields. Peter had a generous allowance, and plans had already been underway for Cat's come-out in London. Peter had heard of no reverses. Lord Braxton had frequently scorned those who let greed tempt them into disastrous investments, stating that he was satisfied with the limited but guaranteed returns he received from Consols. He had never been a man to take risks, so why was his fortune suddenly gone? Surely his successor had not recklessly gamed it away!

The excruciating music finally ended and Lady Braxton suggested they adjourn to the conservatory to admire a rare tropical plant that had bloomed just that morning. Hortense grabbed his proffered arm, but Drucilla could not take the other. She had to listen to her mother praise her mutilation of a Bach prelude. The two women fell into step just behind him.

"Over here, my lord," urged Hortense when they reached the end of the hall. She pulled him into the room, her enthusiasm setting off alarms in his head. Lady Braxton's voice ceased as the door clicked shut. Hortense turned a predatory smile on him and reached up to caress his face.

"Harlot!" he hissed, knocking her hand into a thorn-encrusted branch. "You know not what you are asking."

"I will take my rightful place in society at last," she gloated.

"What a stupid wench!" he returned, shoving her bodily into the thorn tree when she tried to throw her arms around him. "I wouldn't allow you near society's servants let alone its members. If you persist in this farce, you will spend the rest of your days locked in a tower without even a maid for company."

"There you are, my lord," exclaimed Wiggins, interrupting Hortense's gasps as he stepped out from behind a potted palm. "A messenger just arrived from Devlin requesting your immediate return."

"Thank you, Wiggins," replied Damon, heart still pounding from his narrow escape. "Will you summon my curricle?"

"It is already waiting."

"You will give my regrets to your parents," Damon said to Hortense, who was glaring at both of them. "I fear my wife will not be visiting you after all," he added for her ears only. "I cannot allow her to associate with vulgar trollops." She looked ready to explode, her fingers already curving into talons.

Striding away just ahead of Wiggins, he noted without surprise that Lady Braxton and Drucilla were nowhere in sight, but Lord Braxton was headed for the conservatory. After a brief farewell, Damon followed Wiggins to the door.

"If there are repercussions, come to Devlin," he murmured to his old protector. "I will leave word with Wendell to look after you until we can arrange something."

He was still furious when dawn crept through his window. Another sleepless night had provided more than enough time to ponder the very fishy smell emanating from Ridgway House. If Braxton had been engaged in deception for eight years, there must be a tremendous amount at stake. And Catherine was caught in the middle.

Burt had gleaned more information from his cousin Ned. Cat had assumed the duties of housekeeper shortly after Peter's death and had accepted responsibility for more and more chores in the years since, becoming little more than a slave. No one knew why, but she had been abruptly packed off to Braxton Manor at noon. He did not like the timing, particularly since the official reason—inspecting the caretaker staff at the baron's ancestral estate—did not jibe with her hasty departure. The first anyone had heard of her impending journey was shortly after Lord and Lady Braxton had met in the library. Even more disturbing was the news that she was expected back within the month. Was Braxton's plot reaching a critical point?

He shivered, his face assuming a forbidding expression that his troops would have recognized. He could not sit by and see Catherine abused. It was time to fulfill his vow to Peter, starting with exposing Lord Braxton. That meant investigating every incident since he had left home—the sailing accident, her father's affairs, and Braxton's financial standing before and after assuming the title. Ringing for Tucker, he ordered his curricle.

Catherine's head hit the side of the badly sprung coach, waking her from a fitful doze. A week of constant travel over appalling roads had left her exhausted, miserable, and confused. Marginal inns hadn't helped, but her growing anger kept her from sliding into despair.

Why was she here?

"Eugenia needs a change of climate," had been Uncle Henry's first words when she entered the library in response to his summons. "Her constitution demands a more bracing locale. I suggested Braxton Manor, and her doctor agreed. She and the girls will make the trip next month, but I want you to leave immediately to open the house."

"Of course," she had responded automatically. "But there is much to do here. Would it not be better if I waited until a week before they leave?"

"Not in this case. The manor needs repairs. The steward is busy with the spring planting so you must supervise the work."

"How many rooms will you wish to use?"

"The house is so small that you may as well open everything. Sidney will spend at least part of the summer there, and Eugenia will want to entertain our old neighbors. Hire sufficient staff—though no excess; the budget will not allow waste. And you needn't concern yourself with the journey. I will send outriders to handle all arrangements."

"Very well," she agreed, hiding her astonishment at his uncharacteristic generosity. It would have been less surprising if he had dispatched her on the stage.

They had spent the next half hour discussing repairs, leaving her barely fifteen minutes to pack before the coach arrived to carry her to Cumberland. Not until she was away did she have time to think. Then more and more questions arose. Why was she here?

Her uncle's orders were patent nonsense. In eight years at Ridgway House, he had never once considered returning to Braxton Manor. She knew from her father's description that it was small, derelict, and barely livable. He had originally offered it to Henry to prevent the very vulgar Eugenia from blackening the family name in society. Lady Braxton would never agree to revisit so isolated a place. Catherine could still recall her aunt's joy at leaving the ancestral pile far behind. Uncle Henry disliked strife, capitulating to his wife whenever she made a stand. And Dr. Mumford would never send Lady Braxton to Cumberland for her health. He had often declared that no climate was more beneficial than the coast of Somerset. So what was Henry's purpose?

She conjured up many possibilities, each more ludicrous than the last. The only one that made any sense was that her aunt had demanded her removal to facilitate trapping Damon into marriage. Catherine had heard enough hints to deduce that Eugenia had engineered her own wedding. But while Uncle Henry might have agreed—soley to keep the peace—he would never have condoned the expense of sending her so far away. Nor would he have considered the even more expensive notion of opening and staffing Braxton Manor. Regardless of the true state of his finances, the man was a nipfarthing, even begrudging the cost of putting quality food on the table when they entertained. If he needed to get her out of the way, he could have locked her up in Ridgway—or in a nearby cottage if he feared the servants might support her. So why this very costly journey?

The carriage finally turned along a heavily rutted drive and crept to a halt before an aging manor house. The outside appeared dark, damp, and dingy, a perfect setting for a gothic tale of ghostly horrors.

Her reception was even worse than she had imagined and lent credence to Henry's claim about the work that was needed. The staff consisted of an elderly woman, a fifteen-year-old maid, and an even younger groom who doubled as a footman. The woman sent the groom to fetch the steward, then gave Catherine a brief tour of the manor.

It was obvious who had last lived there. Structural maintenance had been ignored in favor of garish decorating. The intended style was indecipherable, for the rooms contained a little of everything, as cluttered as her aunt's gowns. But the deplorable state of the house was not the worst news. She had gone to her room to change for dinner, her spirits sagging after an interview with an openly antagonistic steward. When she tried to go downstairs, she discovered that her door was locked with no sign of a key.

"His lordship thinks you need a little holiday," reported one of the outriders when she rattled the handle. His unpleasant laughter echoed along the hallway.

Dear Lord! That explained the steward's attitude. Uncle Henry must have ordered that she be incarcerated. But why? Panic set in.

She checked the window. At any other time, the view would have been spectacular—forested mountains cradling a narrow valley through which a river tumbled in wild abandon. But today she saw only the thirty-foot drop to the ground. There was not even a ledge to offer the chance of reaching an unlocked room.

She whirled as the door opened, but hope died in an instant. Her two burly jailers blocked the entrance, watching in stone-faced silence as the timid maid set a full coal scuttle by the fire and placed a dinner tray on the table. At least she would neither freeze nor starve. But how was she to keep madness at bay with no occupation?

By morning she had cried herself dry but still had no explanation for her predicament. Somehow she must escape and get word to Damon. He could discover what was going on. With that in mind, she began to cultivate the maid, requesting assistance with her hair and dress so the guards would allow the girl to stay.

Chapter Six

"What a devil of a coil," murmured Damon as he turned down New Bond Street. His frown made him conspicuous, other gentlemen's expressions conveying either weary boredom or hearty cheer.

It was a warm day and a remarkably clear one. A brisk breeze had pushed the usual haze of smoke and coal soot to the east, leaving the sky a brilliant blue. Bond Street was crowded with colorfully dressed ladies and equally colorful dandies. A flower cart filled the air with a heady scent, footmen raced by on errands, and two girls exclaimed over hats in a window. Acquaintances chattered as though they had been separated for weeks rather than hours, exchanging scandalous *on-dits* and enthusing about the day's social calendar. Hawkers pushed their wares, shouting above the noise. Horses and carriages rattled over the cobblestones, the confusion made worse when a horseman cantered past.

But Damon was oblivious. Only the tiniest corner of his mind knew where he was. Shock deadened the rest.

"How could he do it?" he asked rhetorically, deaf to greetings from Mr. Caristoke and Lady Wormsley as his feet automatically threaded the crowd. "How can he sleep?"

Approaching Bruton Street, which would lead him home, he sidestepped two ladies exiting a modiste's shop and blindly turned the corner, unaware that he had just cut Lady Hermione in front of at least fifty members of the *ton*.

"What can I do?" The question that had kept him awake much of the night still plagued him. And there were no easy answers. His life was suddenly in chaos. Every time he reached a decision, guilt raised new doubts that thrust him back into uncertainty.

Bruton Street emptied into Berkeley Square. He crossed

the central garden, pausing a moment under the plane trees
as his face twisted in pain. His plans lay in ruins. Even
worse, his life was a mockery. He had always conducted
himself according to the strictest principles of duty and
honor. Yet it had been a lie.

Honor. He snorted as he climbed the steps to his town
house. No matter which course he chose, honor would suffer. Not that anything would change. What was one more
infamy when added to years of disgrace?

Duty. Who had the strongest claim? The ghosts again
stood before him—Peter, his accusatory stare burning into
Damon's soul as he condemned him for negligence, selfish-
ness, and ignoring a solemn oath; his godfather, face twisting in pain as he admonished Damon for failing to keep
Peter safe and bemoaned Catherine's fate; Hermione, reminding him that his courtship was too far advanced to
withdraw, her smile recalling the evening he had spirited
her into the garden and swept her into a scandalous embrace that society would deem utterly compromising if anyone knew about it; Peter's mother and his own, who had
always believed the best of him; and Catherine in tears as
she asked about Peter's last days. He had not told her that
Peter's final thoughts had been for her future.

And sitting in the center of a gigantic web that trapped
all these faces in its sticky coils was the present Lord Braxton. Damon shuddered. How could a gentleman conceive of
such wickedness?

The first blow had struck at Doctors' Commons. He had
arrived in London at dusk, leaving the knocker down to
avoid callers. When the records office opened the next
morning, he was already waiting at the door. An eager
young clerk helped him locate the thirteenth baron's will. It
read very much as he had anticipated—bequests to the servants and to a couple of distant relatives; a sizable jointure
to his wife that would assure her independence; a dowry of
ten thousand pounds for Catherine, along with guardianship
arrangements until she was of age; and the remainder going
to the fourteenth baron.

Damon almost missed the codicil. It was dated two days
after he and Peter had joined their regiment, but its provi-

sions were so incredible that he stared at it for an hour before the reality sank in.

He could hear Lord Braxton dictating it, his harsh voice unable to hide his pain. That same voice had flailed them from the moment they had revealed their commissions. The accusations again rang in his ears—heartless, irresponsible, undutiful, dishonorable. Damon shook his head, staring at the paper in his hands. The baron would have destroyed the codicil when his temper cooled. It was too obviously the product of anger and grief. But there had been no time. Two months later, he was dead—without learning that Peter had already perished.

Damon read the provisions one last time, though they were already engraved on his heart. The solicitor had died less than a week after reading the will. It was conceivable that no one but the new baron knew the terms. Certainly Catherine seemed not to. Even an honorable and strong-willed man would have been tempted. Henry Braxton was neither.

He must have conceived his plot immediately. The man he had named as Catherine's betrothed did not exist. Nor did the lad's father. Neither were listed in Debrett's *Baronetage of England,* a book Braxton may not have known existed at the time—the first edition had been published only a few months earlier. Not that deceit was anything new for the current baron. Damon's secretary had uncovered several old tales about the fourteenth Lord Braxton. In his youth, he had been suspected of fuzzing cards, though no one offered proof and his winnings were never outrageous. Others had accused him of stealing small but valuable objects from their homes. Damon had long known that Braxton was susceptible to pressure, but that kind of cowardice often made men sneaky and vicious toward those weaker than themselves.

What had Catherine suffered during eight years as housekeeper and whipping boy for her uncle's family? Peter's eyes again glared at him. He had vowed to look after her, but had not done it. Now he faced an impossible decision. Catherine must wed within seven days or her unscrupulous uncle would get away with massive fraud.

That was what had kept him sleepless. He downed a glass of brandy and settled into the chair in his library. Catherine was at Braxton Manor, practically on the Scottish border—he had just learned the estate's location from the old baron's man of business. It was a five-day trip, even on horseback. Could he find an acceptable candidate for her hand, convince him to wed her sight unseen, obtain a special license in the appropriate names, travel to Cumberland, convince Catherine to marry a total stranger, and finalize the nuptials in one week? Of course not! The only solution was to wed her himself.

He ran a hand through his hair and poured another brandy. His chest felt as if all the dead from Waterloo were piled on it.

How could he turn his back on Hermione? It was not just the dishonor. He suspected he was falling in love with her. She was beautiful, refined, talented, and as conformable as any man could wish. Nor was she an empty-headed ninny like so many young ladies. But regardless of his own feelings, society expected a declaration. His attentions had been marked to the point of indiscretion. If he failed to come up to scratch, her reputation would suffer—badly. How could he do that to her? Even if she understood his reasons, he could hardly expect forgiveness. And he wanted to marry her, devil confound fate! Was it fair to Catherine to wed under those conditions?

Yet how could he condemn Peter's sister to slavery? The Braxtons were already treating her badly, and that would only get worse. The baron would never keep her at Ridgway, for she would be a constant reminder of his sins. He might find her a post with someone else or turn her off without a shilling. More likely, he would sell her to some elderly lecher who would pay for the privilege of debauching so tasty a morsel.

Damon swallowed bile at the picture his mind had painted. He had promised to look after Catherine and had never quite shaken the belief that dragging those fateful words into the light of day had killed his closest friend. Could he live with himself if he added to his sins? Frustrated fingers again raked his tawny mane, his mind sidetracked for a moment by the thought that it was past time for a haircut. Agonizing over fate was pointless. The decision had been made the moment he saw the codicil. All his raving for two days had been nought but a desperate attempt to deny the inevitable. But why? Damon Fairbourne eschewed emotion. He left that for Peter. No matter what he did, he would be labeled a cad. No matter what he did, one of the women would get hurt. Catherine's claim had precedence.

He paid one last visit to Doctors' Commons, packed a few essentials into his saddlebags, and left at first light. This could not possibly be worse than what he had faced in Spain and Belgium.

"There was a gentleman askin' for a night's shelter," whispered Brigit as she set Catherine's dinner tray on the rickety table by the fireplace.

"Did he give his name?" she murmured, showing interest only because the maid was her sole visitor. Communication on any subject was preferable to her unproductive thoughts. They spoke softly to hide their conversation from the guard, for he demanded silence.

"Somethin' Devil. Soames sent him away."

Devlin! Somehow Devlin had discovered that she was imprisoned here and had come to rescue her. But she thrust the thought violently aside, knowing that it was unlikely and refusing to allow hope to grow lest disappointment make the coming days even worse.

But she was tired of doing nothing, tired of enduring days of fear and nights of despair. Whether Damon was in the village or not, it was time to escape.

"Have you heard why I am here?" she whispered.

"No, miss. Soames don't talk to no one, and Gordy is right nasty."

"Then I must investigate for myself. Are you sure you can get me out?"

"Yes, miss. Gordy is on duty now. He's drunk most of the time and always demanding more, so adding laudanum to his ale should be easy. Our brew's bitter to begin with. Soames takes his place 'bout midnight. Once you sneak out

of the house, you can get to the village in half an hour. I
gots a cousin who will loan you a horse."

"We shall see. I want to leave as soon as possible, but
you must come with me. There is no telling what they
would do to you when I am gone. It will be impossible to
hide your part in this."

Brigit shivered, fear creasing her face. But after a moment's thought, she straightened her thin shoulders and
nodded. "I'll do it, miss. But that means you can't leave
until later. They would miss me in the kitchen if I don't
show up for supper."

Catherine frowned, but had to agree. "There should be
no pursuit if we are lucky." Actually, she could not see how
to avoid one. When Soames found Gordy, he would check
her room. Even a relocked door and a bolster in the bed
would not fool him. But she did not want to scare Brigit
more than necessary.

She deliberately turned her thoughts to planning, working out the details of her escape. Once she was free, she
would summon Damon. He would know how to find the
answers and would know what to do with them. Life had
not really changed so very much. Always he had been there
to pick up the pieces and make everything right again.

Two hours later, they were slipping through the trees that
flanked the drive. Each carried only a single bundle. How
far could they get before morning? Borrowing the cousin's
horse would not do with two of them, and she lacked
money for even a short stagecoach journey—assuming she
dared show her face in the village. Was Damon still at Devlin Court? Perhaps she should send letters both there and to
London. But how were they to avoid detection until he
could come for them?

Damon strode restlessly along the stream that tumbled
past the rear of the village inn. His reception at Braxton
Manor had eliminated the last doubt that he was doing the
right thing. If Lord Braxton was so desperate that he would
lock his niece away in the wilds of Cumberland, what
would he do later on?

No one had seen Cat since her arrival. The villagers had

watched a carriage enter the estate a week earlier, supposedly bringing Lord Braxton's secretary to check the books. Some hoped that the house would be reopened, for the secretary was still there and had brought two servants. Sidney was of an age to marry. He might move into the manor like his father before him.

Turning aside a wealth of anecdotes about the miserly Henry and the prankish Sidney, Damon had visited the manor, posing as a weary traveler whose carriage had broken down. Few estates would refuse to house a lord in such circumstances, but Braxton Manor had done so. And the man who had answered the door resembled a pugilist rather than a butler or footman. A maid had peeped furtively around a corner, curiosity battling fear in her eyes. The sight pushed his own fears several notches higher.

So what was he to do? If he did not find Catherine soon, all his efforts would go for nought. Should he try to break into the house? The groom at the village inn claimed that the manor contained a prisoner, attributing the tale to his cousin, who was the estate groom.

A movement caught his eye on the far side of the stream. He squinted into the darkness, wishing clouds did not obscure the moon. Two figures were slipping from tree to tree, heading for the bridge that would give them access to the road. He would not have paid them much heed except that the land across the stream belonged to Braxton Manor.

Circling away from the water to mask his own movements, he headed for the bridge, then crouched behind a large shrub so he could see. A female stepped out on the drive and walked boldly toward the village. He would have shrugged and left, but she was obviously looking for something. After peering around, she motioned and was immediately joined by Catherine.

Damon let them cross unmolested, then followed them away from the village.

"Catherine!" he called softly when they were half a mile down the road.

She jumped, started to run, then turned as if she had finally identified his voice. "Damon?"

He caught her as she swooned, tears already escaping

from her eyes. Easing her onto the ground, he smoothed the hair back from her forehead as he had done so often before. How many times had he extricated her from scrapes? At least this one was not her fault, though the poor girl appeared to be at the end of her rope.

"Who are you?" demanded her companion, whirling to smack him across the back with a dead branch.

"A friend," he insisted, wincing. "I won't hurt her." He pulled out his handkerchief. "Will you wet this in the stream?"

The girl stared suspiciously, eyes darting between Catherine and Damon. "You's that devil fellow who come to the door."

"The Earl of Devlin," he corrected. "I came to free Miss Braxton. Once we revive her, she will introduce us."

She stared a moment longer, then accepted his handkerchief. The stream was barely six steps away.

Catherine woke with a cool cloth pressed against her forehead. For a moment she could not remember where she was, but as an arm shifted her into a more comfortable position, she opened her eyes to see Damon's face less than a foot from her own. She burst into tears.

"Shh . . . Everything will be all right, Little Cat," he murmured, drawing her against his coat to muffle the sound.

"They locked me in my room with a guard in the hall," she cried. "And I don't even know why!" Another wave of fear intensified her hysteria.

"It's all over. No one can hurt you now," he promised, stroking her silky hair with his free hand.

Tension flowed out with her tears as it had always done when her lionhearted brother took charge. She was safe. At last. Damon could fix anything.

Damon? "What are you doing here?" she demanded, sitting up as the improbability of his presence registered.

"I came to marry you."

Head spinning, she sagged against his arm as black spots threatened to blot out the world. Surely her ears were playing tricks on her. This could not be real.

"Please don't swoon again," he begged after muttering

what sounded like imprecations. "This is not the best place to revive you."

She giggled. They were sitting on a pile of leaves on a mountainside in the middle of the night. "Of course. This is a dream. That's why nothing makes sense. A wicked ogre spirited me away. In another minute my fairy godmother will materialize—or is it wizards who do that? You are really Merlin in disguise."

"This is no dream, Little Cat," vowed Damon, shaking his head. "More of a nightmare. Can you stand?"

The question brought all the terror flooding back. "We must get out of here," she begged. "What is the time?"

Damon pulled out his watch. "Nearly eleven."

"Dear Lord! We've only an hour. Soames will relieve Gordy at midnight and discover that I am gone."

"He checks your bed?" Anger turned his voice to granite.

"Not that I know of, but Gordy is unconscious, so Soames will be suspicious."

"Right. Who is this?" He nodded to her companion.

"Brigit—the maid who helped me escape. I could not leave her there to bear their anger."

"Of course not, but this complicates matters. I brought only one horse with me. He cannot possibly carry all three of us."

"My cousin gots a horse I can borrow," spoke up Brigit. "At least as far as Brampton. There's another cousin there to leave it with."

"Excellent. Go get your cousin's mount, Brigit. I will collect mine. Catherine, you stay out of sight. Will you be all right alone?"

"Of course." She had recovered her composure and set aside her fear. With Damon in charge her escape would be no different from an afternoon riding party.

Damon took one look at Brigit's sorry beast and sighed. "Catherine, you will ride with me. How far is it to Brampton?"

"Ten miles, my lord," spoke up Brigit.

He tossed Catherine in front of his saddle, then swung up

behind her, setting a pace as fast as he guessed the other horse could sustain.

"Do you know why Uncle Henry ordered this?" Catherine asked once she had described her sudden journey and week-long incarceration in words that made him want to call the baron out and thrash her jailers to within an inch of their miserable lives.

"Yes, but it is complicated," he admitted. "Your uncle has been cheating you for years. He must have feared exposure when I returned, so he panicked and sent you up here. I want to deal with him, Catherine, but can only do so if I am your husband. Bringing him to heel will require more legal status than I have as a family friend."

"So your proposal is only a crusade against injustice," she said with a snort.

"Of course not!" His arms tightened, pulling her closer to his chest and noting that Brigit was avidly taking in every word he said. "We have always been friends, Cat. Most couples have far less going for them when they wed."

"Do you really wish to marry me, Damon?"

The plaintive voice slashed through his conscience, but it was too late to change course now. He looked into her eyes and lied, thankful that the darkness obscured his expression. "You would make me the happiest of men if you will accept my hand."

"Very well, Damon. I will endeavor to see that you never regret this." She burrowed her head into his shoulder and relaxed.

"Thank you, Cat. We will visit the vicar first thing in the morning."

She sat up in surprise. "Now?"

"I've a special license with me. If I am to deal with your uncle, there is no time to waste. And it will protect you from pursuit. Once we are wed, Braxton's thugs will no longer have any power over you."

"I see."

Catherine snuggled back into his arms, comforted by the words. His proposal was not a spur-of-the-moment quixotic gesture. He must have gone to London for a license before following her to Cumberland. Dear Damon, always doing whatever was necessary to fix her problems. She need never be unhappy again. Life would pick up where it had left off eight years ago. She slept.

Everything went smoothly, though it took far longer to reach Brampton than Damon had expected. The town was in the next valley. Dawn broke as they plodded wearily down the last slope.

Brigit's cousin was the innkeeper. Though surprised by their arrival, he accepted his cousin's horse and confirmed that he had a post-chaise for hire.

The vicar was also shocked at the early hour, but he agreed to marry them after a few private words with Damon. They returned to the inn to find Soames quizzing the ostler. Less than a minute after confronting Damon, the man mounted his horse and headed north.

Chapter Seven

Two days after arriving in London, Catherine stood at her window, idly watching the crowd clustered around Gunter's confectioner's shop across Berkeley Square.

It had been an exhausting journey. Soames had hardly ridden out of sight when Damon bundled her into a coach with a basket of cheese and rolls. That set the pattern for the succeeding days. He insisted they start at dawn, then pressed forward with hardly a pause until well after dark. Aside from their brief hours of sleep, they matched or exceeded the speed of the King's mail. But she had no idea why he was in such a hurry.

The past three weeks seemed more like a dream than reality. She had agreed to her uncle's request without thought, trained into unquestioning obedience by eight years of servitude. Her incarceration and escape had left her terrified for the future. But Damon had appeared out of the dark, sweeping her into his arms and marrying her in the best fairy-tale tradition. Relief had driven away despair. But now that the numbness had worn off, relief appeared premature.

Damon seemed more distant now than during the years when she believed he had forgotten her. He had not consummated their marriage. He was rarely at home, ignoring her when he was by shutting himself in the library. Aside from his brief explanation for proposing, he had told her nothing. Nor had he introduced her to anyone in town. She did not even know where to buy clothes or how much she could spend. Such neglect put her firmly in her place—a slave who had been sold to a new master. The details of her food and housing may have changed, but she still had no control of her life and no respect from her owner.

Even Brigit had changed. Catherine was training her as a

lady's maid and would have welcomed the conversation they had shared on their journey, but the girl was so intimidated by Damon's London servants and the wonders of the city that she seldom opened her mouth.

Catherine, too, found the servants haughty. They obeyed her orders, but slowly and in so condescending a fashion that she could only conclude that they disapproved of her. So far she had not assumed control of the household, though she must do so soon if she hoped to win acceptance as Countess of Devlin. At the moment she felt as much as prisoner here as at Braxton. Again she sighed. It was time for a frank talk with Damon. Now that she was recovered, they needed to discuss their respective duties, and she must assume her place as his wife.

Damon slammed out of his solicitor's office. The current Lord Braxton was an even lower form of life than he had thought. A complete accounting of Catherine's inheritance would be impossible. Braxton had kept all the records himself, making little effort to keep her funds separate from his own.

Damon shook his head over the revelations of the past week. He had written to his country solicitor before leaving Brampton, enclosing a copy of the thirteenth baron's will and ordering him to see Lord Braxton immediately—in person—to announce Catherine's marriage and demand all records. That had been a canny strategy, for Harte arrived before the report from Catherine's jailers, giving Braxton no time to destroy proof of his perfidy. Braxton knew his gamble had failed. He fled to the Continent that very night. It was Harte's one error. The solicitor had not believed that the baron was cheating, so he did not bring the authorities with him. By the time a quick scan of the books had revealed the fraud, he was gone. Harte had apologized profusely, though in truth, Damon did not rue Henry's escape. Bringing him to trial would tarnish the Braxton name that had long been both proud and honorable.

Now Damon faced the enormous chore of straightening out his wife's finances. Braxton had diverted much of the income into his own pockets, making a complete recovery impossible. It would take a long time to trace all the missing cash. Fury engulfed him as he drove his curricle back to Berkeley Square—and a hefty dose of guilt that his negligence had allowed the situation to remain undetected for so long. It was a fault he could never fully rectify.

So far he had kept his return to London a secret. It had seemed reasonable to address Catherine's affairs before plunging into the social rounds, so he had delayed announcing his marriage. Catherine could not face society alone and he was too busy to help her.

But he recognized the lie the moment he put it into words. In truth, he could not face Hermione. He knew his delay was worsening the damage to her reputation, for the longer society considered them on the verge of betrothal, the bigger the scandal that would result when the truth emerged. And the news was bound to leak out. He owed her an untarnished reputation. He must prove to the world that she was not responsible for his defection. The only way was to continue his friendship, but it would take time, even if he started immediately. The first step was braving her anger to explain what had happened.

Tomorrow, he promised. *Or maybe the next day.* Circling the cluster of carriages in front of Gunter's, he berated himself. He was a coward in more ways than one. He had been ignoring an even worse problem than Hermione—consummating his marriage. After a lifetime of accepting Catherine as his sister, he could not force himself into her bed. Somehow he must come to grips with their new relationship. She was his wife and deserved his respect and support. Yet he could hardly talk to her. The gulf of the past eight years loomed wider every day. His experiences had left their mark, turning him into a grim, cynical shadow of the man she had known, but she was unaware of the change, still treating him as the protective big brother. Yet she must also have changed. Her life in thrall to her uncle's family could not have been easy. Death would have marked her as well. It was something they must discuss, but he did not know where to begin.

Time! Where was he to find the time? He must straighten out Cat's inheritance, introduce her to society, and rescue

Hermione's reputation. All were pressing problems requiring his entire attention.

He handed the ribbons to a footman and headed for the library, his frown suddenly vanishing. Why had he not thought of it earlier? Before Catherine could greet the *ton,* she must have a new wardrobe. It was unlikely that she knew much about current styles—or about members of society and their interminable rules. A chaperon would solve both problems and leave him free to tackle his other chores. He penned a note to his cousin Louisa, then returned his mind to business.

"Mrs. Collingsworth," announced the butler, ushering that lady into the drawing room.

Catherine looked up in surprise. This was the first caller since they had arrived in London. Mrs. Collingsworth was a middle-aged lady with fading brown hair and squint lines around her brown eyes that hinted she might be shortsighted. But her gold-striped poplin morning gown and bronze pelisse were exceedingly elegant, making Catherine feel dowdy and inadequate in her ancient wool round gown. She pulled the dignity of her new position around her like a shield, determined to conduct herself properly.

"Welcome, madam," she said, noting that Tom was already setting a tea tray at her elbow. Was such anticipation normal for a London staff, or was the lady invited? No one had bothered to inform her.

"Please call me Louisa," begged Mrs. Collingsworth. "It is how Damon always addresses me, the dear boy."

"Was he expecting you?" she asked uncertainly.

"Of course. He asked me to call on you today. I am his cousin, as you probably know."

"I didn't."

"Isn't that just like a man! They never make things easy." She snorted inelegantly, but her eyes were busy scrutinizing Catherine. "He claimed you would need guidance while augmenting your wardrobe and making your bows to society."

"I certainly do," she agreed, relaxing. "I feel like a fish out of water despite my breeding."

"Breeding is the key, of course, but only experience prevents mistakes. We will start with your wardrobe. I hope this gown is not indicative. With due apologies to your modiste, it simply will not do for London."

Catherine smiled. "I should not expect it to. I made it myself three years ago, and I must admit that it is one of my newest. I doubt anything I own is suitable, but I have barely recovered from the rigors of travel so have made no attempt to shop."

Louisa set her half-finished tea onto a table. "Come along, then. We've more to do than I expected. The sooner you have proper attire, the sooner you can venture out. And you've little time. Your marriage announcement will be in the papers tomorrow."

"Tomorrow?" Catherine gasped. Why had Damon told his cousin and not his wife?

"Yes. Let us pray Madame Celeste has something already made up that you can wear in the morning, for you will be amazed at the number of callers."

Her mind in chaos at the prospect of greeting crowds of strangers when she had never even entertained friends, Catherine swallowed. "You will help me, I hope."

"Of course. Now come along. We haven't a moment to waste. Oh, congratulations, my dear. I should have offered them sooner. I see I was wrong in questioning Damon's intelligence these past months. You will make him a charming wife."

Catherine meekly followed Mrs. Collingsworth to her carriage and allowed the woman to shepherd her into Madame Celeste's elegant salon. The modiste was a voluble Frenchwoman, whose eyes gleamed at the news that they needed an entire wardrobe.

"*Magnifique!*" she exclaimed, whisking Catherine into a fitting room where she was poked, prodded, and measured to within an inch of her life. Louisa followed, nodding agreement to Celeste's every suggestion as bolts of silk, muslin, gauze, and crepe were draped across Catherine's shoulders. Two assistants dashed in and out with more offerings. "*Très bien,*" murmured the modiste, tossing a shimmer of satin around Cat's neck. "Observe what *violette* does to madame's eyes. *Très élégante!* And the rose silk to emphasize her creamy complexion, *n'est-ce pas?*" she added, shaking out another wave of fabric.

"Lovely," agreed Louisa. "I knew you could help. This will be her first foray into London society, and the right clothes will mark her as a diamond."

"Naturellement."

Catherine wondered if Louisa was paying attention, for she ordered gown after gown, many embellished with expensive lace or intricate embroidery—morning, afternoon, and evening gowns, walking dresses, carriage dresses, riding habits, pelisses, bed gowns, dressing gowns—enough to make her head spin. Fashion plates flashed before her eyes until they all looked alike. Which would flatter her figure? Was she tall or short? Fat or thin? She could no longer remember.

"This is too much," she protested when Celeste bustled off to a storeroom, bursting with energy as though her tiny figure encased the power of a thunderstorm.

"Nonsense, child!" said Louisa. "These are merely the basics. It will take at least a fortnight before you know what else you will need. The Season is at its peak, as you must know."

"I don't. I have lived secluded from even country society for eight years."

"You poor dear. No wonder this seems so confusing. But you will come about very nicely. These gowns will see you through a basic schedule. You will want to decide your social calendar before your next shopping excursion. Do you prefer balls? Soirees? *Al fresco* events? Theater? One cannot wear the same outfits too often. Nor can one appear rumpled in public. There is logic to frequent changes, you will discover. It is far easier to don a new gown than to stay in your room while your maid removes wrinkles so that you can stand in a dress you sat in all morning."

Catherine groaned.

"Now you enjoy a nice cup of tea while Celeste finds something you can wear today. I will return shortly." With that, Louisa slipped out of the fitting room. A servant deposited a tea tray on a table and bustled out without a word. Catherine suddenly found herself alone.

Too dazed to do more than wonder what Damon would say to such profligacy, she let her mind drift until a burst of laughter caught her attention. She knew that voice.

Catherine poked her head out of the curtained fitting room. "I was right. It's Edith Spencer—or was."

The blonde in the hallway gasped. "Catherine!" Ringlets danced and blue eyes widened. But the welcoming smile quickly faded to a frown.

"Pardon my forward tongue, Lady Peverell," begged Catherine formally, her face burning in embarrassment. "I forgot that you had dropped the acquaintance when my fortunes reversed."

"I?" Shock blazed in Edith's eyes. "After you refused to answer my letters, I could only conclude that you had turned your back on the past."

Cat muttered one of Peter's favorite oaths under her breath. "Can you step in here for a moment? There is no need to broadcast this imbroglio to the world."

Edith sent Celeste's assistant to her own fitting room and joined Catherine. "I know that look," she began, lowering her voice to a whisper at Cat's gesture. "What happened?"

"You are the second to claim authorship of letters I never received. You sent two shortly after the spring term ended, and I responded to both. I wrote twice more after my parents died, but never got a reply, so I assumed that you could not accept my demotion to poor relation."

"I wrote the moment I heard of their accident," swore Edith. "And four more times over the following six months. At first, I thought you were too grief-stricken to reply, but finally accepted that you were cutting all connections."

"Absurd, but who can blame you? I suppose you never received my congratulations to your marriage, either."

Edith shook her head. "What is going on?"

"I don't know, though I suspect my uncle is responsible. All mail is delivered to him for sorting, and outgoing letters go to him for franking, so it would be easy to censor my correspondence. But this is no place to talk. Call on me tomorrow—Devlin House in Berkeley Square."

"You are staying with the earl?" asked a shocked Edith.

"We were married last week, but until the official announcement appears, it might be better to keep that quiet. I must figure out my uncle's game."

Edith nodded and slipped out to attend to her own fitting.

"Voilà!" exclaimed Madame Celeste, hurrying in with her arms full of gowns. Louisa fluttered behind. "Two afternoon gowns, an evening gown, and this!" She held up her trophy with a triumphant flourish—a rose silk ball gown with a beaded bodice, vandyked hem, and lacy overskirt sparkling with diamante. "They were made for Lady Dancy, but she is *mauvais ton* and can do without." She lowered her voice to a conspiratorial whisper. *"Entre nous,* her bill is too long unpaid." Tossing the ball gown over Catherine's head, Celeste kept up a continuous stream of words, giving her client no time to reply. *"La parfection, n'est-ce pas?* Or will be *momentanément.* We tuck here and tighten there. *Tiens!"* Another tug straightened the overskirt, and Celeste beamed. Catherine stared in awe at her mirrored image. Even the unflattering hairstyle could not detract from the sparkling cloud of the elegant ball gown— or the shockingly exposed bosom that peeked over its bodice.

She frowned. "Is this not too low?" The last thing she needed was to imitate the vulgar Drucilla.

"Non, non, non!" insisted Celeste. "You are married, *n'est-ce pas?* It is *parfait,* and quite modest."

"Even young girls wear lower gowns," added Louisa. "You've nothing to fret about."

"Very well." Catherine bowed to their superior knowledge.

It was another hour before the gowns fit to Celeste's satisfaction. Relieved that daytime wear was more demure, Cat admitted exhaustion and suggested they go home.

Louisa was outraged. "What of gloves?" she demanded. "And hats? And slippers! You cannot appear in bare feet with your hands and head uncovered. Nor can you be mismatched." She waved a wad of fabric swatches, one for each gown they had just ordered.

"Of course not," agreed Catherine gamely.

And so began a round of other shops. Catherine was quickly disabused of her suggestion that white or black went with everything. The *ton* knew Damon was wealthy. Did she wish them to believe he was also miserly? Each gown must have its own accessories. Gloves, stockings, slippers, shawls, parasols, bonnets, and a host of other trinkets piled in their carriage. The footman packed the boot full, then started on the interior. Catherine entertained a vision of herself and Louisa perched on the roof, fighting to hold on to still more packages. She was numb with exhaustion by the time she exited the last shop.

"What are you doing in town?" demanded a male voice.

She nearly tripped. "Hello, Sidney." It had been a year since he had last visited Ridgway House, and the time had not been well spent. His face was sallow, with lines of dissipation already showing around his mouth and eyes though he was barely three-and-twenty.

"Has Papa decided to come up to London at last?" he asked almost fearfully.

"Of course not. I am here with my husband."

Shock removed the last vestige of normal color from his face, leaving it a sickly yellow that clashed with his elaborate clothing—an extravagant cravat, hugely padded sky blue jacket, and tight silver pantaloons hugging legs that had been improved by false calves. Or so she assumed. Sidney had never been anything but skinny.

"Married?" he choked, then recovered his usual sneer. "To whom? The gardener's son?"

"To an old friend recently returned from the army," she responded, loath to reveal Damon's identity. Sidney would discover it in the morning, but she could more easily deflect his unpleasantness when she was not so tired.

Sidney relaxed. "Of course. But how selfish to leave Mama and the girls in the lurch. This must have been sudden."

"Not particularly," she hedged. "Did Uncle Henry forget to inform you of my plans?"

For an instant, Sidney's face revealed terror, and she wondered what he had been up to. Had he been off on some secret adventure that he wished to keep from his parents?

But his expression quickly reverted to normal. "The housekeeper's wedding was hardly worthy of notice." He shrugged. "I expect he rejoiced at not having to pay your keep in the future."

"Perhaps."

Louisa bustled out of the shop. "I believe that is everything, Catherine. It is more than time we returned home." She spotted Sidney and frowned.

"Louisa, this is my cousin, Mr. Braxton. Sidney, my husband's cousin, Mrs. Collingsworth."

They exchanged frosty greetings, and Louisa hurried Catherine into their waiting carriage.

"Your cousin? That is unfortunate. Many look him askance and some will not receive him," she warned once they were under way.

"I am not surprised, for I have spent the last eight years living with his family. Is it merely his vulgar manners or has he done something to draw censure? We had heard of nothing."

"His manner is unpleasant, though I would not describe it as vulgar. But his friends are not gentlemen."

"Would you be more specific?"

"There are hints of violence against those who cross them. And their habits pass beyond acceptable bounds." She blushed. "You would do well to avoid him, relative though he is. Damon would not wish your reputation to suffer from the association."

"No," agreed Catherine, wondering if Damon knew the details that Louisa was too delicate to describe. She did not wish his reputation to suffer from the connection, either.

In his youth, Sidney had been a problem whenever he visited Ridgway House. Damon and Peter usually welcomed Catherine's company but refused to include the whining, sniveling boy in their activities. Though Sidney disliked all three, his hatred fell hardest on Catherine, in part because she could ride harder, jump higher, fish better, and climb trees faster than he despite being hampered by her skirts. And she was smarter. The high point of Sidney's life had been the day she dwindled to being his poor relation and servant.

*   *   *

Catherine never found a good time to discuss Sidney with Damon. As usual, he was gone all day, returning only for dinner before shutting himself in the library. She could hardly talk about her cousin in front of the servants, who still considered her an interloper. When she had asked Damon what he spent so much time on, he claimed he was dealing with her uncle. The short, sharp retort precluded further conversation. And so she was left to wonder why he had married her. The question had grown in the week since their wedding until it dominated her mind.

Heart pounding in fear, Catherine bolted to the floor. What had awakened her? No one was in the room. Deciding that it had been a dream, she was returning to bed when the sound came again—an agonized shout.

She pulled on a dressing gown and hesitantly approached the communicating door leading to Damon's room. It had not been opened since their marriage and she hated to break the implied taboo, but she could hear groans from the other side. Taking her courage in her hands, she entered her husband's bedchamber. Damon thrashed about in his bed, murmuring indistinguishable words that occasionally rose to incoherent shouting.

She stretched her hand to awaken him, but froze as disturbing sensations tumbled down her spine. He was unclothed—at least the portion that she could see. Tawny hair covered a muscular chest and equally muscular leg and arm. He twisted, the motion pulling the bedclothes to his trim waist. The mat of chest hair tapered to a single line, tantalizing her eyes and drawing them lower until she felt an overpowering urge to slide the sheet aside. Licking suddenly dry lips, she shivered—and not with cold. He had changed since she had last seen him without a shirt. No longer a young man who exhibited the promise of strength, now he radiated power. Again she shivered, remembering his strength and gentleness the summer he had taught her how to swim.

He groaned, reminding her why she was here.

"Damon!" she called loudly, grabbing his arm to shake it. She had to repeat the call twice before he finally opened his eyes.

"Little Cat?" he murmured weakly. "What happened?"

"You were dreaming."

He forced his fingers through his tangled hair and sighed. "Forgive me for waking you."

"Does this happen often?" She sank into a chair near his bed and pulled her dressing gown tighter against the chill air.

"Not as much as it used to." Her concern must have shown, for he managed a weary smile and patted her hand. "Don't look so horrified, Cat. War leaves scars that take time to fade."

"It was not the glorious adventure you expected when you bought colors, was it?" she said softly.

He shuddered, though she could see the effort he exerted to control it. "Not even close. So many friends lost."

She squeezed his hand, which unaccountably remained in her own. "Would it help to talk about it?"

"I doubt it."

"Are you sure? There were times—like when Charlie died—that discussion eased my sorrow. You should know. You were the only one who took the time to listen."

"Ah, Charlie. He was the best of dogs, wasn't he, Cat? But I cannot burden you with such horror. Waterloo. Badajoz. So much blood." His face turned blank as he slipped back into memory. "And that sack! How did we lose control so badly? My God! The waste of it all. I lost a close friend at Toulouse. Was there ever a more useless battle? Napoleon had abdicated two days before." He shivered, blushing as he noted the position of the bedcovers and quickly replaced them. His embarrassment surprised her, sending warmth into her own cheeks.

"Didn't the same thing happen at New Orleans?" she murmured.

"True, though I wasn't there. That one missed by over a fortnight. We must find some faster way to transmit news. Such carnage is unacceptable." He sighed.

"Is that what keeps you from your rest? The waste?" she asked.

"Not really, or at least not entirely. I don't know what it is. Perhaps if I can figure that out, the nightmares will fade. But there is no point discussing it now. Good night, Catherine. You will freeze if you do not go back to bed."

The curt dismissal hurt, but she was wise enough to understand that he had disclosed too much. Damon had always been self-sufficient—except with Peter. She bade him good night and left.

Yet sleep eluded her. She had never before seen Damon unable to cope. All her life, he had been almost godlike—knowledgeable, capable, and efficient, accomplishing his goals with little fuss. She had, as usual, expected him to sweep away all her problems and restore her to a life of peace and happiness. The realization hit hard. She had been merely existing for eight years, knowing in the back of her mind that eventually Damon would come home to rescue her from her menial life and return her to her rightful place in the world. Even these last days had passed in limbo as she waited for him to finish his business and forge her a dazzling place in society as his wife.

How childish! Her fists clenched. She had wasted too many years waiting for someone else to make her happy. Ultimately, the responsibility was her own. She must carve a place for herself in the world and take control of her own destiny, starting with the callers that would arrive in the morning. She would prove herself worthy of London society. And perhaps there was something she could do for Damon. It would be a novel experience to resolve one of *his* problems.

Chapter Eight

"Bloody sharp!" swore Sidney Braxton, adding several more colorful expletives as his fists clenched.

A ball of paper bounced off the grate and landed on the hearth, where it slowly unfurled. Why had Skinner demanded repayment of his loan? It was not in arrears, and the moneylender must know he could not lay hands on any cash until next quarter day. He was already living on tick.

His mood worsened when he picked up the morning *Post* to discover that Catherine had married the Earl of Devlin. His mother's last letter had raved about the earl's attachment to Hortense and their expected announcement. A well-breached brother-in-law would have been perfect, but Catherine must have interfered. How had she cut out his sister? She was an impoverished ape-leader with one of the sharpest tongues he had ever encountered. But the connection might still do.

An hour later Sidney's determination hardened when a note arrived from his solicitor. "Due to unexpected financial reverses, your quarterly allowance has been canceled." He again swore. That explained Skinner's demand. How did those plagued cent-per-cents know of losses even before the principals?

"Good! You are wearing the sprig muslin," Louisa exclaimed from the breakfast room doorway. "But your hair will never do." Allowing no protest, she summoned her own maid from the hall and swept Catherine up to her room.

"This is ridiculous," Catherine muttered as Angelique attacked her head.

"Not at all," countered Louisa. "Appearance is everything. If you look like a dowd, your credit will suffer."

"Patience, Louisa. Brigit lacks experience, but she is intelligent and talented. Tucker is teaching her about fabric care, she is learning about fashion as quickly as I am, and she has been experimenting with hair. In another month she will do as well as your own maid."

"You haven't got a month," stated Louisa brutally, meeting her eyes in the mirror. "You have two hours. Hire a hairdresser to teach her. I cannot risk my own reputation by sponsoring someone who will embarrass me. And I cannot believe you want to hurt Damon. If you wish, I can make arrangements for immediate instruction."

"All right. And thank you." She cringed at the notion that her mistakes would reflect badly on Damon, though she knew it was true. One of the lessons hammered home during her school days was the importance of appearance. First impressions were difficult to change. Already the day loomed as a terrifying challenge.

"Is your cook prepared for callers?" asked Louisa when Cat's hair was nearly finished. "There will be dozens."

Would her marriage really cause such an uproar? But she did not argue again. Normally she was too insignificant to elicit a second thought from society's denizens, but that very characteristic worked against her now that she had married a wealthy earl. It was the first time she had considered Damon in that light, and she found the label oddly intimidating.

"Damon told Simms last night," she reported. She had wondered at the time why he had bothered.

"Good. He will have everything in order then."

Dear Lord, she was unprepared for society. How could she hope to avoid censure? "A school friend is calling soon," she said, praying that she had not committed some dreadful solecism by issuing the invitation.

"Who?"

"Lady Peverell, wife of Sir Isaac. We attended Miss Grimsby's Academy for Young Ladies together."

Louisa nodded. "An unexceptional lady. And I am delighted that you attended so prestigious a school. I believe Lady Ingleside and Lady Sommersby were also graduates of Miss Grimsby's."

Catherine frowned. "Lady Ingleside was born Sarah Havenworth, wasn't she?"

"Yes, her father was Viscount Havenworth of Kensington, heir to the Earl of Marwood."

"She was two years ahead of me. I cannot place Lady Sommersby. Perhaps she married since my father died. I lost track of society after that."

"She was formerly Lady Elizabeth Drakeford, second daughter of the Marquess of Crossbridge—his principal seat is Renfrew Castle in Nottinghamshire, but he owns at least a dozen other estates. Her mother was his second wife, youngest daughter of the Earl of Crewes. Lady Elizabeth wed Lord Sommersby in July of 1810 in spite of her parents' ambivalence to the match. He is merely a viscount with only one estate, though it is lucrative enough. There were rumors about bad blood between the families, but no specifics. Speculation over the wedding did not cease until their daughter was born ten months later."

"Beth Drakeford." Catherine choked back a laugh. It sounded as though Louisa had memorized Debrett's. "She was always determined to get her own way—and often in trouble because of it. Again, I did not know her well, for she was two years younger than I, but we usually got along."

"Excellent. Angelique will speak to Monsieur Henri about training Brigit. He is an outstanding *coiffeur*. I do not expect him to take her in hand himself, of course, but I am sure he can recommend someone. I will return before the first callers arrive. At least if you attended Miss Grimsby's, I needn't fret over your training." Without waiting for a response, she whisked her maid out of the room. Catherine stared at the mirror. Her glossy black hair had been twisted into a knot atop her head, from which curls escaped to frame her face. For the first time in years she looked fashionable. Smiling, she sought out the butler to issue instructions for refreshments.

"You look marvelous," exclaimed Edith a few minutes later. "Of course, you always were the prettiest girl in our class."

"Hardly. You cannot have forgotten Serena."

"Her cutting tongue destroys her beauty the moment she opens her mouth. She would still be a spinster if her parents had not arranged a marriage. I heard she did not exchange a single word with him until after the settlements were signed. But tell me what happened. You could have knocked me down with a feather when I heard you were the Countess of Devlin. Not that you won't make him the perfect wife—I always hoped you would wed him, to be honest; you seem so well suited, but he was in town until recently with nary a hint of his plans."

"It was rather sudden," admitted Catherine. "Though we have been friends forever, I had always considered him a brother."

"Your brother's best friend," agreed Edith.

"And a neighbor and part of our family."

"So tell all!"

"I don't know the details, but the timing has to do with my uncle. He has been scheming for years, though I cannot imagine why. You already know that he censored my mail, cutting me off from all acquaintances. I have lived very secluded since my parents died."

"There was something else rather odd," said Edith. "I only remembered it this morning. Miss Grimsby read me part of the letter in which your uncle announced that you would finish your last term at Miss Marian's School for Girls so that you could enjoy your cousins' support during so sad a period."

"That is preposterous!"

"I swear it. She showed me the page."

"My cousins never attended Miss Marian's or anywhere else. In any case, they are years younger than I. Uncle Henry canceled my last term because there was no money for tuition."

"But it had already been paid," pointed out Edith. "And you know Grimsby never ever refunds tuition. I doubt she would do so even for a royal."

"Another way to cut me off from the world," murmured Catherine. "The only reason I can imagine is that he absconded with my dowry. Heaven knows the estate is in dire enough straits that he probably needed it."

"Or perhaps he was jealous of your looks or breeding," suggested Edith. "I have met young Mr. Braxton and cannot like the fellow. Are his sisters any better?"

"Worse." She described them as positively as possible. "So one cannot help but feel sorry for them. If only they would not try so hard. But their mother goads them into overstepping propriety and Uncle Henry's pinchpenny ways make them frantic to leave home."

"You are too softhearted, Cat, and always have been. I suppose you went out of your way waiting on them. They undoubtedly took horrid advantage of you."

"Somebody had to do the work, and my aunt is unwell."

"Or lazy. Or terrified that you would outshine her own girls, which sounds inevitable."

"She can hardly worry about such fustian now. Besides, I did not really mind. I had nothing better to do with my time. But enough of me. Tell me about yourself. Is Sir Isaac the man of your dreams?"

Edith laughed. "Actually he is, though I hardly knew him when we wed. It was a match my parents pushed. But I have come to love him dearly and we have three delightful little girls." She described her family at length, eliciting a great deal of laughter over her children's antics, for Edith unfashionably spent considerable time with her offspring each day. "But what are your plans? I will be attending the opera tonight with Isaac's grandparents, but perhaps we will meet tomorrow."

"Louisa is taking me to Lady Bristol's rout tonight, but we have not discussed other invitations. Frankly, I am terrified. After living secluded for eight years, I fear my manners will prove sadly lacking. And I know nothing of current *on-dits*."

"That is easy to rectify. Brummell lost an enormous sum at Brook's last night, this following an even bigger loss at Watier's last week. Everyone is speculating about how long his current losing streak will last. He has won and lost several fortunes over the years, but his luck has never been as consistently bad as this Season . . . The Duchess of Wobur-

ton—she is the haughtiest high-stickler I have ever met
aside from certain Almack's patronesses—publicly cut
Lady Barnes yesterday for daring to suggest that her
spoiled brat of a son deserved his recent expulsion from
Eton. The lad is now bedeviling the tutors at Harrow,
though bets favor him being sent down before long break.
The last time he was in London, he released a monkey in
Astley's that sent one of the horses plunging out of control
and caused a near-riot in the theater . . . Jeremy Crenshaw
maneuvered Letitia Armstrong into the garden at Lady
Debenham's ball last night, keeping her there for half an
hour. She returned looking thoroughly kissed. If there is no
betrothal by tomorrow, she will have to rusticate awhile
and pray a juicier scandal draws society's attention before
her reputation is irretrievably shattered."

"How did you learn about Brummell so early in the
morning?" demanded Catherine. "I thought gentlemen remained at the tables until dawn."

"My maid, of course. One of her duties is keeping me
apprised of gossip."

"Brigit knows no one."

"She will. Servants derive their consequence from their
masters, so they have a vested interest in keeping you *au
courant*. But your first job is to learn the position of everyone in society. There are some that you must never contradict. The Almack's patronesses form the core of that group.
Even though you are already wed, you need their goodwill
and a voucher to maintain your status. Two others who can
make lethal enemies are Lady Beatrice and Lady Debenham. Both are insatiable gossips. Though Lady Beatrice is
the more spiteful of the two, either can destroy you. They
know everything and hide nothing, for they are locked in a
long-standing struggle for power. Lady Beatrice has been
the most feared gossip in London for at least thirty years,
but she is getting old and Lady Debenham is determined to
dethrone her."

"Whatever happened to 'Judge not that ye be not judged'
and the Golden Rule?"

"Never in the polite world," Edith reminded her. "The
rules here were created by sterner folk. Breaking them in-

vites instant, and often permanent, censure—which can os-
tracize you completely. Another person you cannot afford
to antagonize is Brummell. Whatever his financial problems, he is still a powerful arbiter of fashion whose disdain
could ruin you. And of course you must always watch what
you say about the Regent. With travel reestablished to
France, the government fears that radical ideas will take
hold here, so Prinny is even touchier than usual of criticism. Unfortunately, he invites all too much of it with his
growing girth, continued flirtations, extravagant spending,
and hatred of his wife."

Louisa returned, followed by Simms bearing a more
elaborate tea tray than Catherine had used for herself and
Edith. Two footmen carried in cakes and biscuits. Within
minutes, Simms was announcing the first callers. Edith departed soon afterward. By the end of the first hour, Catherine's head was throbbing, with so many names and faces
swirling inside that she despaired of ever sorting them out.
Often she thanked Miss Grimsby for her much-criticized
insistence on practicing social skills long after everyone
seemed proficient. Though Catherine had not touched a tea
tray in eight years, she automatically moved through the rit-
ual. Even conversation was not difficult this day. She had
only to repeat that she and Damon had known each other
all their lives, then agree that the dear boy was hopelessly
impetuous to have married her out of hand. So romantic—

Conversation buzzed as the crowd broke into small
groups. She heard further speculation of Brummell's losses,
the duchess's cut, and Miss Armstrong's indiscretion. Others wagered on expected betrothals, condemned a group of
pranksters for introducing a very dead sheep into Lady
Horseley's drawing room just before a card party, welcomed the opening of a new modiste shop, and offered a
dozen reasons for Lady Montgomery's sudden retirement
to the country.

"Colonel John Caldwell," announced Simms.

"Colonel Caldwell." Catherine greeted him with a smile
and handed him a glass of wine. He was taller than Damon,
his red uniform jacket a perfect foil for dark hair and gray

eyes. And he had the same slender build as Peter, which gave her a pang.

"Lady Devlin." He bowed over her hand. "As one of Damon's closest friends, I must berate him for keeping you a secret."

"He was a bit precipitate," she agreed. "However, we have known each other forever."

"So I understand. You were Peter Braxton's sister, were you not?"

"Yes." She thought she had controlled her voice, but he must have seen something in her face, for his own suddenly twisted in remorse.

"Forgive me for reminding you, my lady. He was a good man and one of my better officers."

"Do you command his regiment now?" she asked, making the connection to a name in one of Peter's letters. Caldwell had been a captain when Peter and Damon bought their own commissions.

"No. I have spent the past four years on Wellington's staff and now split my time between a recently inherited estate and London. If the duke turns his hand to politics, I may leave the army to join him."

"Interesting. I would love to hear more of it sometime when we can actually talk."

"I look forward to it. Damon has chosen well," he concluded as Simms appeared in the doorway. Smiling, he joined a group of gentlemen near the window.

"The Marchioness of Tardale and Lady Hermione Smythe," announced Simms, escorting the ladies into the room.

Catherine poured tea, wondering why Simms's wooden voice had sounded even more so and why the buzz of voices was suddenly muted. Though she exchanged conventional greetings, she felt very much at a disadvantage. Lady Hermione was at least seven years her junior, yet appeared far more poised. Even her looks were intimidating—green eyes in an oval face framed by blond curls. Every movement was graceful, from her seductive walk to the way she handled a teacup, so it was no surprise that she attracted every male eye. But the impression of elegant perfection was shattered when the girl opened her mouth, for she was unpleasantly arrogant.

"Such a sudden marriage," she said contemptuously with a pointed look at Catherine's waistline. Her mother had already moved on to converse with Lady Sefton.

"Hardly. We have known each other all our lives," Catherine explained yet again.

"I'm sure you have."

Catherine was shocked into silence by the hard, suggestive tone and the unexpected attack. Several gentlemen drifted closer, staring avidly at Lady Hermoine. The girl's eyes glinted with triumph before she turned a pitying look on her hostess.

"I wonder why he married you," she murmured so softly that no one else could hear. "It certainly wasn't out of affection." With that brazen thrust, she sauntered to the far corner of the drawing room, a procession of young dandies trailing in her wake.

But not everyone approved of her performance. The group by the window pointedly ignored her. Lady Sefton's eyes narrowed. And the dowager Lady Castleton ushered her goddaughter away fully three minutes early.

Damon strode down St. James's, enjoying the cool air after an hour of sparring in Jackson's overheated rooms. The exercise had been welcome, but his problems again clamored for attention. His solicitor's latest report exposed more irregularities in the Braxton affairs. The baron had steadily diverted funds, though whether they went for his own vices or Sidney's was hard to tell. And it was irrelevant. Either way, the money was gone.

"Good day, my lord."

Damon stared at the young dandy who had addressed him. "Mr. Braxton."

"Welcome to the family," the cub said outrageously. "Though it would have been more seemly to inform me before announcing the event to the world."

"I would have expected your father to tell you," commented Damon, sidestepping to continue on his way.

Sidney shrugged. "The past is unimportant, but we have business to discuss."

"Indeed?" Had young Braxton known of the codicil? Not until Sidney paled under his glare did the earl lead the way into Brook's to search out an empty room.

"My father recently suffered a temporary reverse of fortune," began Sidney baldly, skipping the usual polite chatter. "Unfortunately, he did not tell me about it until I had incurred obligations beyond this quarter's allowance. You cannot wish to see your wife's cousin immured in prison, so I trust you will make me a small loan—only enough to tide me over until quarter day. I have investments paying dividends in July that will more than cover the amount."

Damon adopted the expression he had long used to cow errant troops. "Your father's reverses are neither temporary nor undeserved. I don't know what he told you, but he has spent eight years embezzling my wife's inheritance. Though I doubt you knew the source of your funds, I would be a fool to throw good money after bad. Your father has already fled to avoid prosecution. I suggest you visit your man of business and solicitor to discover your circumstances. When you fully understand your position, we can talk." Without waiting for a response, Damon headed for home, leaving an open-mouthed Sidney behind.

Chapter Nine

Catherine dismissed Brigit, then checked her hair again. Monsieur Henri's assistant was an excellent teacher. After only one lesson, her maid could produce an acceptable evening coiffure. Rose ribbon threaded an elaborate mass of ebony curls. The rose ball gown caressed her figure, its low neckline baring creamy shoulders set off by a diamond necklace Simms had produced from the vault. Catherine had hesitated to wear such finery to a rout, but Louisa declared it suitable. Many guests would move on to one or more balls.

Louisa had better arrive soon, Catherine decided, already too nervous to think straight. Though routs were the most innocuous of evening entertainments, she was terrified of doing or saying something wrong. If only Damon could accompany them! But she immediately thrust the thought aside. She must quit leaning on others, for only she was responsible for her fate. Even if she had not already reached that conclusion, breakfast would have made it clear. In a moment of panic, she had begged Damon's escort. His refusal had been gruff to the point of rudeness. She had not seen him since, for he was dining at his club.

His attitude did not bode well for the future. Perhaps he was annoyed that she had awakened him from his nightmare. Or was he having second thoughts about their marriage? It would hardly be surprising, for she was feeling the same. She barely recognized her old friend, and his silence was digging an ever-widening gulf between them. Their former camaraderie had disappeared under his years of war and her years of deprivation. She no longer fit into his world, a fact that he must have discerned. Why had he married her? *It certainly wasn't out of affection.* What had Uncle Henry done that could only be rectified by marriage?

And if it was that bad, how was she to spend the rest of her life as his neighbor?

"Enough!" she snapped. If she worked herself into a frenzy, she would never survive the evening. Picking up a reticule, fan, and shawl, she descended to the drawing room.

"Be very careful," Louisa expostulated one last time as their carriage approached Lady Bristol's town house. "You must always watch your tongue, but on your first outing, the tiniest *faux pas* can ruin you. Serious conversation will not do in public—at least until your credit is well established."

"Of course," agreed Catherine wearily.

"And mind your manners. There will be no dancing tonight—oh dear, we must call in a dancing master. You cannot know the latest steps."

"Too true."

"That continental style of waltzing has even been allowed at Almack's despite being wholly scandalous. And the quadrille is but four years old. Have you mastered the cotillion?"

"Yes. And country dances, minuets, ländlers, reels, and several others."

"Minuets are rarely performed now, and new variations on country dances appear every year. How awful that your uncle did not keep you *au courant*."

Catherine suppressed a description of the Braxton household. Even being his daughter would have made no difference. Her cousins knew fewer steps than she.

They finally arrived at the door, joining the lengthy queue to greet their hostess. Catherine's jitters abated, allowing her natural charm to surface. The rooms were crowded, but that proved to be a blessing, for she spoke with only a few people at a time. The same tales were bandied about that she had already heard, making it easy to hold up her end in conversation.

"Gracious Heaven!" exclaimed a purple-draped dowager, rapping a fan on Catherine's arm to assure her attention. "Did you ever see two people more perfectly suited?" She nodded to a stiff, unsmiling gentleman in an impeccable blue velvet jacket, who was ponderously addressing a haughty young lady clad in white muslin.

"They will undoubtedly make a match of it," agreed another dowager, whose primrose gown emphasized her sallow face. "This is the third time this week he has paid her particular attention, and His Grace is much too proper to raise expectations without paying his addresses."

"Just so." The ladies moved off and Catherine raised her brow.

"The Duke of Norwood," explained Louisa. "After ten years of seclusion, he is considering a second wife. It would appear he has settled on Lady Emily Sterne."

"An appropriate name," Catherine quipped, drawing a censorious glance for her unappreciated sense of humor. She bit her tongue and turned her mind to surviving the evening.

"Congratulations, my dear," said a middle-aged matron swathed in a heavily embroidered pomona green gown and matching turban. "I always claimed you two were made for each other. It has been far too long since I have seen you, for your uncle accepted none of my invitations."

"He cut most of my parents' friends, Lady Hawthorne," admitted Catherine. The baroness lived on the other side of Taunton, but had always been close to her family. "I know little that has happened in recent years. How is Meredith?"

Lady Hawthorne immediately launched a detailed description of her daughter's wedding, adding tales of her two sons, their wives, and her seven grandchildren.

She had been truly cut off, reflected Catherine with a pang. The world had moved on but she had not. It would take time to catch up.

"But this is not the place for a coze," declared Lady Hawthorne at last. "You must call and tell me what you have been up to these past years."

"I would be delighted."

"Ah, Lord James!" she called to a dark-haired gentleman. "Have you met Lady Devlin?"

An odd look flashed across his face, but it disappeared before Catherine could identify it. He was a handsome man with wavy black hair impeccably arranged above startling silver gray eyes. Equally startling was his dress. Catherine was accustomed to skin-tight knee-smalls—which were still *de rigueur* for Almack's and Court. Both Sidney and Damon favored pantaloons—the long-legged garment made popular by Brummell that was likewise tight-fitting to show off a gentleman's muscular physique. But Lord James was wearing Cossack trousers that ballooned from his waist to be gathered into a tie at his ankle. Above these he exhibited the close-cut coat, elegant waistcoat, and intricate cravat that confirmed him as a dandy.

"Catherine, this is Lord James Hutchinson, fourth son of the Marquess of Wythe, and a most amusing gentleman. James, may I present Lady Devlin, daughter of my dear friends, the late Lord and Lady Braxton."

"Another beauty to grace Mayfair's drawing rooms," he murmured, bowing elegantly and smiling with great charm. "Are you a hothouse orchid or a hardy rose? I will soon know."

"You flatter me, my lord," she said as Lady Hawthorne slipped away. "I am but a transplanted country daisy, likely to wilt in this odd environment."

He laughed. "I wager not. But tell me how you caught the eye of Lord Devlin. You cannot accuse me of prying, for you must know that it is the most astonishing *on-dit* today."

"As long as it is only for today. There is really nothing to tell. We have known each other all our lives. His estate borders my father's and he was my brother's closest friend."

"Was?"

"Peter died at Vimeiro." She quickly erased the frown that had accompanied the words. She *must* learn to control her face.

"My apologies for raising a sad topic, my lady."

" 'Tis long in the past."

"I am glad. But you should not let Mayfair intimidate you, for you can never be a daisy. Your eyes glow like dew-touched violets against a shimmering fall of black velvet. Most unusual, and very vivid. You will have every gentleman in London at your feet."

"How absurd you are!" she blurted before she realized where she was and blushed. "Forgive me. That was not at all mannerly."

"Perhaps it pressed the bounds, but only barely. It was honest, and therefore refreshing." His amused chuckle soothed her fears. "Will you be attending the Wharburton Masquerade tomorrow?"

"I believe so."

"You will save me a set, then. Or perhaps two." His beguiling smile sent shivers down her spine. Sparks danced like diamonds in his silvery eyes.

"If you like."

Louisa rejoined her and Lord James took his leave.

"A delightful gentleman, though I suspect he is a confirmed flirt," Catherine murmured, enchanted in part because he had laughed with her. Most gentlemen made a point of appearing bored.

"But never beyond the bounds. His attentions can only increase your credit, for he singles out only those ladies who exhibit both beauty and charm," replied Louisa.

"We meet again, my lady," intruded a voice.

"Colonel Caldwell."

"Do call me Jack," he begged. "As your husband's closest friend, such familiarity is unexceptionable, as Mrs. Collingsworth must confirm." He smiled at Louisa and winked. "You are a delightful feast for the eyes tonight, madame."

"And you are a rogue," Louisa charged, rapping his arm. "But he is right, Catherine. You need not stand on formality."

"Very well, Jack. And since we are casting off convention—at least in part—perhaps you can answer some questions for me. Damon refuses to discuss the war, but I would like to know more of Badajoz and Waterloo."

"This is hardly the place for such a discussion," he protested.

Catherine felt herself flush as Louisa's admonitions returned to mind. She started to apologize, but he must have seen her disappointment for he overrode her words.

"All right, but only briefly." He led her toward a less

crowded alcove where they could talk without being overheard.

"Thank you. I suspect Damon has not yet put the memories behind him. I cannot help him do so unless I understand what he suffered."

"I can appreciate your concern. I might have gone around the bend if my wife had not taken me in hand after Waterloo. That is one battle I will not talk about, but Badajoz was bad enough. Damon won a field promotion for his heroics that day, though it is not a memory any of us recall with pride. The slaughter was sickening. We had to send wave after wave of decent young men toward a breach in the wall, then helplessly watch them cut to shreds. The bodies were piled ten and twenty deep in the ditch below. Damon finally managed to lead his troops over the top, but it was a bloody business."

"Perhaps it is better that Peter died at Vimeiro. His reason might have snapped had he survived."

"I doubt it. There was a core of steel beneath his flights of fancy that would have seen him through. In some ways he was stronger than any of us."

"Because he so easily forgot unpleasantness?"

"Precisely. It is a useful attribute in wartime. As was his cheeriness."

"Thank you. I would like to meet your wife."

"You will one day, but she is not in town this Season. We anticipate an heir in July."

"Congratulations."

The colonel switched to *on-dits* as another officer approached. Catherine acknowledged the introductions, then excused herself. He had given her much to ponder, though this was hardly the place for it. She joined a sarcastic dissection of Brummell's gaming habits, then moved on to a conversation about the Duchess of Woburton. It wasn't until she sought the retiring room half an hour later that the evening began to go sour. Two young ladies were already talking when she entered. Both ignored her after a glance confirmed that they had not been introduced.

"It is scandalous, of course," agreed one. "One wonders

if he is truly a gentleman. Mama is still trying to decide whether to cut him when they next meet."

"But it cannot be his fault," claimed the other. "Papa is certain that he was trapped. Nothing else would account for his behavior. He is one of Wellington's heroes, after all. But who can blame him if the girl deliberately compromised him? Honor would demand marriage."

"Was there a compromise?" asked the first breathlessly.

"There must have been," declared her friend. "What else would force him to wed an unknown when he was already betrothed to Lady Hermione?"

Catherine caught her breath.

"While it is true that he had been living in her pocket, there was no formal betrothal, though Mama heard that a meeting had been scheduled to work out settlements. Of course, his courtship was far enough advanced that he was committed. Even a deliberate compromise would not prompt a gentleman to act the jilt under such circumstances. The most grasping harpy must agree that he was unavailable. That is why Mama is in such a coil."

"Your mama is right—to a point. I have it on the best authority that Lord Devlin had already spoken to the marquess. But why would you expect the girl to behave with honor? Only a compromise could have turned him from Lady Hermione, and it must have been spectacular. Papa does not believe that anything short of an interesting condition would have done the trick."

"Unless he discovered that Lady Hermione is not the sweet miss she pretends. We all know what a cat she can be."

"True. Devlin has had a lucky escape. But enough. Mama will expect me to return. She is determined to introduce me to Lord Wilkington—not that I can abide so debauched a man. But he is wealthy."

The girls left, leaving Catherine in a state of paralysis. So Damon had been betrothed to the lovely Lady Hermione. It explained the girl's antagonism and might also explain his neglect. What it did not explain was why he had married her. It was a decision he had made before traveling to Cumberland, for he had carried a special license issued in her name. What had Uncle Henry done?

She returned to Louisa. The last of her enjoyment fled when Lady Hermione joined a group less than ten feet away. The girl stared at her for a moment before deliberately turning her back. Catherine's blood ran cold at the cut, though she could hardly blame her. Damon's jilting was already having an effect. Lady Hermione was not the center of attention she had been that morning. Few were talking to the girl and the only gentleman by her side was Lord Millhouse, a notorious libertine who Louisa claimed must be avoided at all costs.

Five minutes later Sidney drifted by, deliberately snubbing his cousin. Eyes sparkled as they had not done after Lady Hermione's slight. Catherine had to fight to keep her face in order as her name echoed from all sides.

"Catherine!" Lady Ingleside bustled up, her enthusiasm blunting the speculation. "I was amazed to hear of your marriage until I remembered that Devlin was your brother's closest friend," she said once the greetings were over. "It was a shame Peter was killed. He was always such a carefree gentleman. I still remember the last time he called on you at Miss Grimsby's. I never laughed so hard in my life. We all miss him."

"Yes, but at least Damon survived. Did you ever set up that school for the tenant children that you were planning?" The question neatly diverted the conversation from Peter. She had sometimes suspected that Sarah Havenworth had harbored a *tendre* for her brother.

"Yes. My husband agreed. We started with only six students and are now up to forty."

"I envy you. It is something sorely needed on my father's estate. He would have approved the idea—in fact, we had discussed it that last summer—but his death left everything to my uncle, who has no use for innovation."

"There was nothing you could do?"

"No, though I try. Between higher prices and lower yields, times have been quite bad for our tenants. Even the weather has conspired against them."

"Ah, yes." Sidney sneered, coming up behind her. "Tenants. Does Devlin know about all the time you spent with Joshua Barton last winter?"

"Damon would never mind," countered Catherine. She would have said more, but Sidney had already faded into the crowd. Lady Hermione had also moved on, she noted in relief. She turned back to Lady Ingleside. "Poor Josh. He had a terrible time of it. He is only eight and full of energy, so you can imagine his chagrin at being tied to his bed with a broken leg. I helped look after him for two weeks. But you can see what I've had to contend with. Sidney mimics his father, disapproving all contact with tenants—or anyone else he considers an inferior being."

"I have a cousin like that. Just once I would like to change him into a servant so he can understand that they are also human and deserve a little respect."

"I wish you did not have to claim kinship with Mr. Braxton," added Louisa. "He does not like you one bit."

"He never has, but there is nothing I can do about it. Would that one could choose one's relatives!"

They discussed family black sheep briefly, then she and Louisa took leave of Lady Bristol and returned home.

Lady Hermione drifted down the stairs into Lady Stokeley's ballroom, making sure her movements were as seductive as possible. She hated routs, for few of the interesting gentlemen attended. But now that she was at the ball, the attentions of her court would soon heal her bruised spirits. She was the Season's Incomparable, the subject of more poetry and the recipient of more flowers than anyone else.

But only Mr. Meldon awaited her at the bottom. She suppressed a shudder, but could not refuse him a set.

Half an hour later she was near tears. Her court had deserted her. Millhouse had accosted her at that awful rout. She had danced only the one set—and Meldon hardly counted, for he was nought but a younger son with no prospects. But when Mrs. Bassington sniffed before deliberately turning away, Hermione's irritation turned to fury. Stalking across the room, she sought out the one gossip who might help her.

Lady Debenham's eyes were cold when Hermione confronted her, but the girl was not cowed. "You must help me, my lady," she begged. "I am being unjustly punished for the crimes of others."

"Explain!"

"I did nothing to Lord Devlin beyond accepting his proposal of marriage," she lied. "Yet people are adding injury to the insult he paid by jilting me. You've no idea what I've been made to suffer. Lady Devlin openly gloats over stealing him away—and I harbor no illusions how she did it. Mr. Braxton, her own cousin, confirmed at Lady Bristol's rout this evening that Lady Devlin had conducted a lengthy affair with one of their tenants, a Joshua Barton. Is there any doubt that I am her innocent victim?"

"None." Lady Debenham's eyes gleamed.

Damon pocketed his winnings and rose from the faro table, offering his seat to one of the onlookers.

"One can hardly blame him for spending his evenings at White's. I would do the same if I had been trapped into wedding a chit who was no better than she should be," slurred a young gentleman considerably the worse for wine. He stared at Damon, making it clear to whom he referred.

"Don't exaggerate, Meldon," suggested his friend.

"I don't. She's been carrying on with one of her tenants—a Joshua somebody—and has been bragging about how she trapped a lord into marriage so she could account for an interesting condition." He inhaled a pinch of snuff and violently sneezed, staggering into a chair.

Damon started forward, but Colonel Caldwell grabbed his arm. "Laugh!" ordered Jack. Damon complied, though the sound seemed false to his ears.

"Drink can befuddle even the keenest mind," observed the colonel after his own peal of mirth. "Though I would like to know who is embroidering tales so maliciously, Mr. Meldon. I have never in my life heard such fustian as the drivel you are spouting. The tenant Lady Devlin spent her time with was an eight-year-old boy with a broken leg, as you would know if you had actually attended Lady Bristol's rout. Perhaps you should apologize before the lady's husband challenges you."

Meldon blanched. "Beg pardon, my lord," he mumbled. "Must have heard wrong."

Damon nodded curtly and turned away. "Go home," advised Jack softly. "I was at the rout until half an hour ago and know his claims for lies, but it will be easier to discover who started such stories with you absent."

"You don't believe them, then?"

"Of course not. I've too much experience with malice not to recognize it. This has all the hallmarks of deliberate calumny." He stared unblinkingly, making Damon feel a worm, for the insinuation did not fit Catherine's character. But he had not seen her in years.

He paused just outside the gaming room, on the verge of returning, but a new burst of speculation changed his mind.

"It cannot be wholly false. She fled the rout as soon as the tale emerged."

"True, and though the details may be exaggerated, the basis is probably not. Where there is smoke, one usually finds fire."

"No wonder her family kept her away from London all these years. She sounds little better than a lightskirt."

"Too true. I got it from one in a position to know," injected a third voice. "The woman has no shame!"

Damon turned on his heel and strode away.

Catherine was nearly ready for bed when Damon slammed into her room. At his sharp gesture, Brigit left.

"Well, Cat, it seems you have been making a spectacle of yourself," he charged.

"What are you talking about?"

"The story is all over town that you have been playing fast and loose with one of your tenants and bragging about trapping a wealthy lord."

She glared at him. "And you prefer to believe baseless lies instead of asking for facts. How you have changed!"

"I heard plenty of facts," he retorted, repeating the tale Meldon had told and the other comments he had overheard.

"What can I say? 'Tis obvious you have already judged me guilty." A single tear escaped and she turned sharply away.

Damon froze, the tear shattering his anger. "What happened?" he asked gently.

"How should I know? I was talking to Lady Ingleside about the school she started for her tenants some years ago when Sidney appeared and asked if you knew how much time I had spent with Joshua Barton. I shrugged him off. You must know that Sidney disdains even talking to tenants, let alone helping them."

"Is Joshua Robert's son?" asked Damon.

"Yes. He broke his leg in January."

"That was all?"

"Of course. You must have expected the rest of the charges. Everyone is convinced I must have compromised you. I have said nothing beyond confirming that we have known each other since birth. What else can I say? That you married me to foil some unscrupulous plot by my uncle?"

"I am sorry you were subjected to such unpleasantness," he said wearily. "I wish I *had* anticipated it, but I am not that conversant with London society. I expect it will blow over."

"Not until I fail to produce the suspected child."

"What?"

"How else am I supposed to have trapped you? It would help if you actually escorted me," she suggested, weariness making her voice sharper than she had intended. "That would at least deflect the charges that you were unwilling."

"All right. It might also deflect your cousin. I turned down his demand for a loan today, which probably explains his spite. You realize that he worded his comment to foster the notion that you were dallying with Joshua."

"My God! It never occurred to me. But why would it do so to anyone else? Lady Ingleside and I discussed both Josh's age and his leg immediately after Sidney left."

"Then why would this tale spread—unless Sidney did it."

"I suppose so. He has always hated me, and he has never been that enamored of you, either, as you must recall. But there is little we can do about that."

"But if he is piqued, he may try again. You must be alert so you can prevent further trouble."

She agreed, though he was being naive if he believed Sidney would confine his comments to personal confrontations. Sneaky innuendo to third parties had always been his way. And the gossip would not die any time soon.

She should have asked about Hermione, but she was too tired. Why had Damon married her if he was betrothed to another? Why had he pursued Hermione if he had wanted to marry Catherine?

Despite her weariness, sleep did not come quickly.

Chapter Ten

"That gown is very becoming, my dear," trilled Louisa as she entered the drawing room.

"Thank you." Not that it made much difference. Society's views would be shaped by other factors—like Sidney's spiteful tongue. She was already feeling its effects. The servants were clearly hostile this morning.

"Now you must be careful today," warned Louisa as they climbed into her carriage. "Lady Beatrice takes great pleasure in pillorying anyone who does not follow the rules."

"Can we not visit someone else?" begged Catherine. The last thing she needed was to face a disapproving dowager who would have heard every word of Sidney's lies.

"Of course not. This is her at-home day. If I do not produce you, she will conclude that you are afraid to face her. That would be worse than anything else you could do. We must prove that these tales are false."

Lady Beatrice pounced on Catherine the moment she walked through the door. "So you actually dare show your face in public," she declared with a snort.

"I have done nothing of which I need be ashamed," Catherine countered steadily, though her knees were knocking and black spots whirled before her eyes. "It is unfortunate that I am related to Sidney Braxton, but that is hardly my fault."

"You deny affairs with your tenants then? At last count your list of liaisons had reached two-and-twenty."

Catherine forced herself to laugh, fully aware that fourteen listeners hung on every word. "My, how a tale can grow when watered by malice. I wonder how many people are aware that my uncle's estate includes only eight tenant farms. But that is irrelevant. Even Sidney did not accuse me of such impropriety. He merely implied such by mentioning that I had recently spent considerable time with Joshua Barton."

"So you admit it." The malicious eyes gleamed.

"Absolutely—four hours a day for nearly two weeks." Gasps filled her pause and one lady moved to stand between her daughter and Catherine. "Poor Josh broke his leg just after Christmas. He had just celebrated his eighth year and does not take confinement well. Mr. Barton had been laid up much of the fall with injuries, so his wife had to accept a job as the baker's assistant in order to make their rent. I helped care for Joshua until her sister arrived. My cousin considered my assistance deplorable, of course. He would sooner die than speak to such lowly creatures despite deriving much of his income from their labor."

Faces slipped into shock, laughter, and other emotions for several seconds before their owners regained control.

"Poor boy," murmured one lady.

"Did he recover?" asked another.

"Certainly. So small a thing as a broken leg would not keep Josh down for long. He is back to climbing trees and getting into mischief. Last month he tried to ride a neighbor's cow and was pitched into the stream, breaking his collarbone."

"Why would your cousin imply a different relationship?" asked Lady Beatrice bluntly, her ancient eyes boring into Catherine's as though she would drag her soul out for examination.

"I dislike speaking ill of others, but he has treated me as a lower form of servant ever since my parents died. For some reason, my marriage has caused him distress." She shrugged.

Lady Beatrice frowned. "Why would he care?" Her voice had sunk to a conspiratorial whisper.

"His mother hoped to catch Lord Devlin for one of his sisters," she murmured back. "Perhaps he shared that delusion."

"Idiot!" she said before turning her attention to another guest. Catherine sipped tea as gossip swirled around her. The ordeal could have been worse. London's chief gossip seemed to believe her, though one could never know what really went on inside that lady's head. She hoped her impressions were correct. Though Lady Beatrice was a formidable foe, she could make an equally formidable ally.

"Lady Debenham," announced the butler.

"My dears, did you hear?" Lady Debenham asked even before she received a cup from her hostess.

"I suppose you finally got wind of the Higby affair," scoffed Lady Beatrice.

"That is unworthy of anyone's notice," snapped Lady Debenham in return. "Lord Seaton was caught *en flagrante* in Lady Oakridge's bed last night—by her husband. A duel is unavoidable, for she has not yet produced the requisite heir."

Her voice was drowned out by the sudden buzz of conversation, though no one missed the flash of fury that crossed Lady Beatrice's face.

"The tale must be exaggerated," the gossip scoffed.

"Hardly." Lady Debenham's eyes were triumphant. "I got it from my maid, whose brother is the head footman at Oakridge House. His lordship's threats carried to the servants' quarters. I am *amazed* that you did not know of it."

Catherine could swear that Lady Beatrice gnashed her teeth.

"You would think that Lord Seaton had more sense than to conduct an affair with so recently wed a lady," observed Lady Cunningham, shaking her head over the gentleman's rashness.

"It does not say much for the lady that she would endanger Oakridge's line, even if he is so long in the tooth that she can hardly find him appealing," denounced Mrs. Bassington.

"Girls have no sense of honor these days," declared an elderly dowager. "In *my* day—"

"How were they so careless as to be caught?" asked Lady Cunningham, overriding the reminiscence that continued in the background.

"They haven't half a brain between them," declared Lady Debenham. "How else can one explain conducting the affair in Oakridge's own house."

"Scandalous indeed!"

"Perhaps they wanted to be caught," suggested Lady Beatrice. "If they are that lacking in wit, they may think that killing Oakridge in a duel will be acceptable. But Seaton would have to flee the country."

"And it would hardly improve their situation," Mrs. Bassington reminded everyone. "He is still married, even though his wife has avoided town for three years."

"I heard she prefers the country."

"Isn't it interesting that her neighbor Sir Rudolph has likewise eschewed London?" The insinuation in Lady Beatrice's voice sent shivers down Catherine's spine.

"Surely you are not suggesting that Seaton wishes to wed Lady Oakridge!" snapped Lady Cunningham once the last young innocent took leave of Lady Beatrice and departed. "That man cares for nought but himself and has no intention of confining himself to one lady."

"True," agreed Lady Debenham.

"But his behavior is incomprehensible," complained Louisa. "He knows the rules. A lady must provide an heir before she consents to dalliance. And it is in very bad taste to conduct a liaison in her own home."

"Perhaps it was retaliation. Alvanley claims Seaton and Oakridge had words at Watier's last week, and we all know Seaton's skill at seduction."

Speculation continued for some time. Catherine said nothing, but she was appalled by the casual attitude toward infidelity. Did all gentlemen keep mistresses? Did ladies really take lovers? It was a notion that had never occurred to her. What were Damon's thoughts on the subject? She shivered. He had spent little time with her since their marriage—which was still unconsummated. Who was he seeing in the meantime?

Louisa finally rose to depart, much to Catherine's relief. They were barely out the door when the conversation changed.

"I am surprised you would receive so scandalous a girl," observed Lady Debenham, censure clear in her voice.

"And I am shocked that you would fall for the lies of that notorious young Braxton. Lord Devlin has a fine wife and is well rid of the scheming Lady Hermione," declared Lady Beatrice.

"You cannot know her well if you believe her to be scheming," declared Lady Debenham hotly. "She is all that is sweet and pure."

"Thus speaks her father's second cousin. An impartial observer must conclude that she drove Devlin away, which is no more than she deserves after her behavior last Christmas. He cut her very publicly a fortnight ago—as even you must admit, for you were there!"

The remaining callers joined the fray as Louisa and Catherine exited the house. They made four other calls, but the conversation was the same. Lady Oakridge's indiscretion provided something to discuss while they were present, but every drawing room took up Sidney's malice the moment they left.

Relieved to be home again, Catherine decided to spend the afternoon reading. But Damon was entertaining Colonel Caldwell in the library, their conversation preventing any intrusion.

"I still do not understand why you married Catherine," declared the colonel. "Not that she isn't a delightful young lady. I suspect she will make you an excellent wife. But you have always been honorable, Damon. How could you break trust with Lady Hermione?"

It was precisely what Catherine wanted to know.

"Poor Hermione. I know I damaged her reputation, Jack," admitted Damon sadly. "But much as I cared for her, I had no choice. An earlier vow took precedence."

"What?"

"I promised Peter that I would look after Catherine. I thought I had done so until I returned home. Then I discovered that not only was she unwed and in an untenable position, but her uncle was scheming against her. The only way I could counter his plots was to marry her. Unfortunately, I have not had the opportunity to explain the situation to Hermione. She must hate me by now, and who can blame her? Sometimes I hate myself."

Catherine heard no more as she stumbled up to her room and threw herself across the bed. Damon cared not one whit for her, she admitted, breaking into tears. That explained his shock that she was unwed. His proposal was just a quixotic gesture prompted by some absurd promise he had made to Peter. But promises would never bring happiness.

"Peter, you fool!" she raged, pacing the room in rising anger. "You have doomed us all." Damon was already ruing the loss of Lady Hermione. No wonder he had not touched her. How could he when he loved another?

Damn all honor! It too often forced people into dishonor. How could men be so stupid? One of her schoolmates had been abducted by a fortune hunter. In the name of honor, the girl's father forced her to wed the culprit though she despised him. The village chandler had spent several months in debtors' prison, unable to pay his suppliers because his three biggest customers had repeatedly ignored their bills— honor demanded they pay gaming debts first. And now honor had trapped her into marrying a man who did not want her.

The Wharburton masquerade was like nothing Catherine had ever imagined. Lady Wharburton had swathed her ballroom in blue and white, draping quantities of silk over walls and ceiling to imitate ocean waves and froth. A huge statue of Neptune that Lord Wharburton had acquired in Italy dominated one corner, while lesser marbles with ocean connections sat on pedestals and in alcoves. Cunningly wrought sea creatures twinkled in the light cast by hundreds of candles that were doubled by the huge mirrors that graced one wall.

Catherine paused at the top of the stairs, fear paralyzing her feet. Her first ball was nerve-wracking enough without the rumors, and the decor wasn't helping. She felt as though she were drowning. Breathing was difficult. Inside her gloves, her hands were clammy.

Her temper was not improved when Damon immediately crossed the room to speak with Lady Hermione, abandoning his wife at the foot of the stairs. He would have done better not to escort her at all than to declare his preference so publicly. Despite the distance and the swirling crowd, Catherine could see the longing in his eyes and the triumph in Hermione's. Voices buzzed in speculation. Turning away, she began an animated conversation with Lady Sommersby, hardly aware of what they said.

Damon's eyes devoured Hermione as he approached her. Her costume depicted Aphrodite's birth from the sea foam, making her one with the room. Diamonds threaded her blonde hair, sparkling in the candlelight like sun on the waves.

"Good evening, my lady," he said with a smile. After hearing how she had cut Catherine, he was determined to prevent any further problems. At least that was what he told himself, but as he gazed into her green eyes, he was overcome by regret that she would never be his.

She stared in disapproval, then started to turn away.

"Don't cut me, Hermione," he begged.

"Why should I not return the favor?" she snapped, though her face retained its social smile. "There are just as many witnesses."

"What are you talking about?"

"The cut you delivered on Bond Street two weeks ago today, my lord. It was bad enough that you returned to town without a word, but did you have to humiliate me so publicly? People were speculating about what I had done to you even before yesterday! You have ruined me."

"Dear God! I had no idea. And I never meant to hurt you."

"Then you go about your business oddly, sirrah!"

Damon reddened, guilt over his negligence and cowardice badgering him again. "Let me do what I can to prove the rumors wrong," he begged. "We can get some lemonade and discuss it without an audience." She nodded, so he led her out of the ballroom. As expected, the refreshment room was nearly empty.

"I did not intentionally cut you," he began once they had moved into a quiet corner. "I had received some devastating news and was in too much shock to notice anyone."

"Perhaps it was inadvertent. And there would have been no scandal if that were all. But it wasn't. Why did you lead me to expect a declaration and then abandon me?" she asked bluntly.

Damon shrugged. "I had no choice."

"No choice?" she mocked. "I saw no one holding a pistol to your head."

"None. It was a vow I had made to her brother before his death. How could I honorably renege?"

"How could you honorably court me after making such a vow?" she retorted.

Damon sighed. "I thought that she was already married. It was a shock to discover otherwise, for there had been no hint of it before I returned home. And you must know the decision was the most difficult I have ever faced."

"If you are seeking absolution, you won't get it. You could at least have warned me," she reminded him. "Learning of it from the morning paper is more than anyone should have to endure."

Abashed, Damon groaned. "I was obviously not thinking clearly," he admitted. "I had meant to call on you, but I have been so busy that there was no time."

"You are either a liar or a coward," she charged.

"Forgive me, my dear," he begged, raising her hand to his lips. "My actions were inexcusable. I freely admit it and can only plead shock, but I want to repair as much damage as possible. Your reputation will only recover if we are seen to be friends."

"To say nothing of yours," she murmured, eyes narrowing in calculation. "Yet a public feud must hurt us both. You owe me restitution, and you will have to dance very hard to convince the gossips. I will expect a truly heroic effort."

"Thank you."

She turned watery eyes to his. "But I do not know how I can face the future. There is no one who can replace you."

She might as well have stabbed him.

Catherine saw Damon and Hermione leave the room and fought to maintain her composure. Nothing would be gained by showing how badly his preference hurt. Marriage had been a mistake, she now admitted. If only he had not rushed her to the altar so quickly! Even a week of thinking about it would have shown her that this was a hopeless mésalliance. He had changed too much from the young man he had been, and he made no pretense of caring for her beyond the brotherly affection he had always shown. It was an omission that should have shouted warnings, but she had been too terrified and confused to listen. And it was too late to do anything about it. What would Peter think if he could see the misery caused by one misplaced vow?

Pushing thought aside, she turned her mind to enjoying the evening, though reminders of her precarious position were never far away. Lady Beatrice greeted her with pointed cordiality that prevented any cuts. Lady Debenham had done the same to Hermione. The battle lines were drawn, and she felt trapped in a tug of war with no way to escape. It stretched her nerves even further.

She had not yet seen the dancing master so had to refuse many of the sets. Louisa whispered constant admonitions in her ear. Damon retired to the card room after dancing with Hermione, pricking her again with his public disdain.

A tall, blond cavalier with light aqua eyes led her out for a country dance. The color was odd enough that it triggered a memory.

"Lord Rathbone?" she asked hesitantly, then blushed at her forward tongue. And more. She had entertained a girlish *tendre* for the handsome lord with the twinkling eyes the summer he had visited his friend Toby, heir to Sir Mortimer. She had been sixteen at the time.

"Peter Braxton's sister!" he exclaimed, his mouth curving into a delighted grin. "There cannot be another with eyes that precise shade of violet. You have become a beautiful woman, my dear." His voice stroked her like the softest velvet.

"How can you tell with my face covered by a mask? You have certainly mastered the art of flirtation, my lord," she riposted with emphasis on the formality.

"Not with you, it would seem," he said mournfully. "That disapproving frown confirms that you still haven't forgiven me for stealing a kiss in Sir Mortimer's apple orchard."

"You should not revive ancient history," she objected, cheeks flaming. "Especially where you might be overheard. I've enough trouble with rumors as it is."

"Very well. Anyone who knows you could never suspect you of misbehavior. This tempest will blow over. For now, we will agree that you are a very proper lady-in-waiting who is not subject to the wiles of even the canniest cavalier. But I cannot ignore the most delectable lady-in-waiting in the room or people will assume we are lovers." His eyes caressed her face and neck, stopping to admire the full bosom swelling above the tight bodice of her Elizabethan costume.

Heat rose from her toes to the ends of her hair. Rathbone was still as much a flirt as he had been at age eighteen, though his delivery was smoother and a lot more conceited. But it was not only his admiration and suggestive repartee that prompted her blushes. After eight years catering to her aunt, she felt uncomfortable dressed as another form of servant. It enhanced the irrational feeling that she did not really belong here.

"Forgive me," he begged when she did not respond. "You are newly arrived in London and not so very different from that lass I insulted all those years ago. I must have lost all my usual address. Perhaps we should begin again—as friends. Damon is a lucky man."

"Do you remember him that well?" she teased, relaxing now that his expression had changed from a leer to an easy grin.

"Of course. I live most of the year in town, so we often meet. He could not always get home—as you must know—but his duties frequently brought him to London. I was sorry to learn of your brother's fate, Lady Devlin, as I wrote at the time. He was a good friend, as lighthearted and carefree as myself."

"Thank you." So Rathbone was another whose letter had disappeared. How many others had she inadvertently cut by not replying to their cards of condolence?

He misunderstood the annoyance that must have shown on her face. "Enough of sadness. If I promise to behave, will you drive with me in the park tomorrow? I have not seen Toby in a couple of years and would like to hear about his heir."

"I would be delighted . . . to relay news of your friend," she added firmly.

He laughed as he twirled her down the line.

Not all of Catherine's partners proved as congenial as Rathbone. Sidney commandeered her hand for a cotillion, whisking her onto the floor without giving her a chance to refuse. Nervousness already overset her, for it was eight years since she had last executed the intricate steps of the dance, and the figures had changed slightly in the meantime. Sidney did not improve her temper any. Once he had her in the set, he made no attempt to conceal his antagonism. Even worse, Damon was partnering Hermione in the adjacent set, his warm smile sending stabs of despair through Catherine's heart. He had not spoken with her since arriving.

"Can't you keep your feet away from mine?" growled Sidney, loud enough to draw the attention of nearby dancers.

She did not respond, but her reticence did nothing to dissuade her cousin.

"Devlin should have left you in the country where you belong," he groused.

"What concern is it of yours?" she murmured.

"Tricking him into marrying you will not guarantee your entry into society," Sidney shot back, again pitching his voice loud enough to carry. He had chosen a set next to the most vocal gossips. "Your manners are those of a servant, but why am I surprised? That is what you have been. Does your fancy lord know you have worked as a housekeeper since abandoning your place in polite society?"

"Having one's family claimed by the hereafter hardly constitutes abandoning society," she riposted. "And while I admit to sinking to a position as your poor relation, that hardly qualifies as joining the servant class." She lowered her voice. "But I understand that your feeble mind might be incapable of discerning the difference." *Please let this set be over!* Again he was deliberately ripping her up in public, and there was nothing she could do to stop him. What was his purpose? This went beyond his lifelong spite. She shivered.

"I wonder how you forced him into wedlock," sneered that horrid voice. "A simple compromise would not have done it—no earl will take a servant to wife for such a reason. Did you seduce him? Are you carrying a token of the encounter with you now?"

He stared at her waistline until Catherine thought she would faint. Someone tittered. *I must say something,* she repeated to herself, but her brain had frozen in shock.

"Cat got your tongue?" Sidney gloated.

"Not at all," she snapped. "I was merely wondering if your malicious lies are as obvious to others as they are to me. Perhaps I should allow Damon to call you out."

Fear flicked through Sidney's eyes, but he banished it in an instant. "Nice try, but the truth will out," he said.

"It certainly will—and the sooner the better," she agreed, the assurance in her voice causing more than one face to crease in sudden thought. Lady Beatrice was nodding nearby.

She wanted nothing more than to leave the ball, but Sidney's attack made it impossible. She tried pretending that she was enjoying herself, but she could see new rumors flying around the room and knew they concerned her. Each new group of gossipers turned speculative eyes from her to Hermione before breaking off to tell the tale to others.

She had champions, of course, starting with Lady Beatrice.

"That boy is a bad one," the gossip proclaimed to Catherine, her eyes fixed on Sidney. "You handled yourself with admirable aplomb."

"Thank you, but I wish I knew his purpose," said Cat with a sigh. "How can I counter him? It is like batting away a cloud."

"Perhaps he is in trouble and wishes to divert our attention. But do not despair, for I will discover the truth."

Catherine thanked her for the support, but she did not believe it possible.

Louisa, Edith, Lady Ingleside, and Lacy Sommersby also rallied around. Lord Rathbone questioned Sidney's motives. Damon denied the charges, but few believed him. Colonel Caldwell led her out for the next cotillion, it being the only dance she could manage that allowed more than light banter.

"It is false," he stated up front. "I know Damon too well to believe otherwise. But do you have any idea why?"

"That is the question of the hour. Sidney has always despised me. Lady Beatrice thinks he is diverting attention from some misdeed, but I suspect retaliation because Damon denied him a loan—not that I can offer that explanation to the world."

"I doubt it is the loan. He cannot be that badly dipped, for he is not a gamester. Just hold your head high. The truth will eventually emerge," he assured her. "I have witnessed this sort of attack before, so I know what you are going through. A lad once cried foul when he wagered over his head in a game I won. I nearly lost my commission before a friend forced him to confess the truth."

"Damon?"

"No. This happened ten years ago, before I met either Damon or Peter."

"What was his motive?"

"He was afraid to tell his father that he had gambled away half a year's allowance."

"Pride is a terrible thing."

"Very true." He finished the change and led her into the next figure, correcting her stumble when she turned the wrong way. "Braxton is not the first to create tales out of whole cloth, either. There was a similar campaign three years ago against another innocent girl. I helped expose that one. The culprit was a madman who became obsessed with the young lady and tried to destroy her when she turned him down."

"Did she recover."

"She is now happily married with her reputation intact. I have no doubt that you will survive this spate of malice as well. Society will see reason as soon as the novelty wanes, but you are in for a rough time until then."

"I expected no less."

By the time the supper dance concluded, the gossips had

each offered a theory to explain Devlin's marriage. Lady Beatrice swore that Hermione had done something unforgivable, prompting Damon to wed another in retaliation. She cited Damon's public cut as proof and vowed to uncover the specifics. Lady Debenham swore that Hermione was an innocent victim of Catherine's unscrupulous scheming, reminding society that Cat's own cousin admitted the charge.

Catherine was encouraged by the resulting debate. At least people were thinking, and many knew that Sidney was not a credible source. But since both theories were wrong, she tried not to expect too much.

Her biggest surprise occurred late in the evening. Lord James Hutchinson sought her out for a set of country dances and then remained at her side during the subsequent waltz, promenading about the ballroom. His pointed glare sent Sidney scurrying away.

He was dressed as Julius Caesar with a laurel wreath planted firmly on his black hair. It gave him an unexpectedly distinguished look, the short tunic and breastplate becoming him better than any of the other Romans at the masquerade.

"Why?" she asked after half an hour of light flirtation. He was more subtle than Rathbone, though just as expert, but she suspected he had a different goal in mind. The heat in the ballroom had driven them onto the terrace—in full sight of the doors.

He did not pretend to misunderstand her. "I cannot allow Braxton to succeed, my lady. He is deliberately trying to destroy you, as should be obvious to anyone with the tiniest intellect."

"Are you altruistic or do you merely dislike Sidney?"

"Both—and more. I have a bone to pick with your cousin, for he tried to fleece my youngest brother. I must clip his wings before he ruins anyone else."

"Do you really believe I am innocent?" Her voice wavered on the words and she wished the question unasked.

"Of course. I am considered an excellent judge of character—that alone will enhance your credit. Neither you nor Lord Devlin is capable of the behavior implied by your cousin. But you should be aware that the *ton* will enjoy speculating for some time before they relent and admit the truth that is already staring them in their addlepated faces. Until then, you will need all the friends you can find."

"Thank you, my lord. But what benefit will you derive other than embarrassing Sidney?"

Lord James suddenly seemed unsure of himself. "I am hoping to recapture the interest of a young lady," he admitted at last. "She is taking my admiration for granted. If she thinks she no longer holds my regard, she may examine her heart and discover that she really does love me."

"I see." Catherine smiled. "You wish to direct your attentions elsewhere but do not want to risk hurting an innocent party."

"Exactly. I can hardly endanger your reputation since I will be seeking to restore it. Enough people know I dislike Braxton to prevent unwanted rumors."

"I wish you luck in your own campaign, my lord."

"Thank you. Would you accompany me to the theater tomorrow—properly chaperoned, of course."

"I would enjoy that."

The music ended. Catherine had promised the next set to Lord Forley, so they turned back to the ballroom. Embarrassingly, her toe caught on the doorsill, knocking her off balance. She caught herself only after grabbing Lord James's arm with both hands, her knuckles making a loud thump against his breastplate that drew several eyes to her predicament.

"Careful," he admonished.

"Thank you, my lord. I nearly created a hideous spectacle," she admitted with a laugh. "How the gossips would love that!"

"It is I who would get the blame for tossing you about." He chuckled. "Relax and you will do fine. You are a diamond both inside and out, which everyone will acknowledge before much more time has passed."

"How dare you disclose financial information to others?" demanded Damon the moment he had chased Brigit from Catherine's room.

"What are you talking about?"

"Jack knows about Sidney's loan request. He could only have learned it from you."

"So what? We were discussing Sidney's spite and he asked about his motive. You said yourself that must be it. Should I have lied and claimed Sidney was retaliating because we pushed him into the stream when he was five years old?"

Damon glared. "You do not discuss money with people you barely know!"

"Jack is your closest friend. He will not spread the tale further. He is trying to protect me from Sidney's malice, but cannot do so unless he knows the facts. If you don't like it, perhaps you should disprove the rumors yourself!"

"No one can help you if you don't cease the top-lofty condescension, Catherine," he charged.

"What are you talking about?"

"Dancing. Refusing sets because the gentlemen aren't good enough for you will do you far more damage than anything Sidney might say."

"Well, pardon me for avoiding society for eight years!" she spat, fighting tears. "You never considered that I might not know the steps, did you? It is so much easier to accept the criticism of others without thinking too hard. I never thought you would turn into another mindless sheep who blindly follows the fashion of the moment."

She turned away to stare out over Berkeley Square, her tears now impossible to hide. Damon's own behavior was making the situation worse, but how could she explain that without dredging up Hermione? There was no way they could rationally discuss Sidney if she clouded the issue with his former betrothal. But before she could find the right words, the door slammed.

She groped her way into bed, muffling her sobs with the pillow.

Chapter Eleven

Damon spurred Pythias to a hard canter, grateful that the early riders were not yet out. He needed to think—something he could not do in bed, for nightmares had intruded every time he dozed off. Finally giving it up, he had headed for the park to blow away the cobwebs.

When had he lost control of his life? He hated scandal, yet for four days he had been caught in the center of one. Granted, it had not initially been Catherine's fault, but she was keeping the stories alive. Both her address and her behavior were sadly lacking. She either remained silent in the face of Sidney's charges or erupted in childish brangling. Her barbed comments had been overheard more than once. Repeating them made her sound like an arrogant fishwife.

And she continued to throw caution to the winds. The only way to counter the gossip was to demonstrate rigid propriety at all times. Instead, she had driven in the park with Rathbone—a renowned rake—and attended the theater with Lord James, a feeble-minded, posturing popinjay whose baggy pants and ridiculous cravats must make him a laughingstock. Neither action would have mattered in the normal course of events, but with her morals already suspect, she was pouring oil on the flames. Why couldn't she have chosen her escorts from those known for rigid propriety—Ashton, Norwood, or Rufton, for example.

New tales surfaced daily in the clubs, accusing her of vulgar language, continuing liaisons, and a blue education. This last did not bother him, for she had always been intelligent. If only she would apply her common sense to dealing with society! But revealing serious interests at this time was unfortunate, for proving one rumor lent credence to the others.

His friends understood his dilemma. Hermione's support

was all that had kept him from creating a scene at the masquerade when Sidney started his tirade. She had even offered to teach Catherine about society, not that he had accepted. It would be unfair to drag her away from her own activities and he doubted her parents would approve. But her concern had touched him. If only he had been able to follow his heart!

But he hadn't. And the current disaster was mostly his own fault. He had ignored his promise to Peter for years, allowing Catherine to suffer alone. Had he done his duty and personally checked on her welfare, he would have learned of the will and could have insisted on a Season. If he had visited her after selling out, there would still have been ample time to find a respectable suitor. But he had not. By the time he discovered the truth, the only option had been to marry her. But the mistakes did not stop there. He should have presented her to society himself instead of relying on Louisa. His presence would have kept Sidney under control. Yet that would have meant throwing Hermione to the dogs, making her pay for his desertion.

He pulled up under an oak tree to allow Pythias a breather, then moved on at a more sedate pace.

Reviewing how he had arrived in this mess was pointless. He must look to the future. Hermione's reputation would soon recover—she was again surrounded by much of her usual court—so he must start building a relationship with his wife. They had known each other all their lives, but that was part of the problem. He felt no lust for her. He had thought of her as a sister for so long that bedding her seemed almost incestuous. Yet she was a beautiful woman. He mentally ticked off her attributes—glossy black hair, violet eyes, creamy heart-shaped face, voluptuous bosom, slim legs—but he could not move beyond anger at the loss of Hermione, whom he had wanted to bed from the moment he saw her.

He frowned. There must be some way to resolve his problem. Perhaps he should try to recapture the warmth they had shared before he left for Portugal. Was he still capable of warmth? That naive young Damon had died at Vimeiro. Hardening his heart was all that had preserved his sanity through the carnage of war. Man was a brutal being, tamed by only the thinnest veneer of civilization. But that surface cracked easily.

He ruthlessly suppressed memories of the atrocities he had witnessed. He himself had done things that in the cold light of a London drawing room seemed almost bestial. He was hardened by seven years of fighting and now possessed too complex a character to revert to the simplicity of youth. But he must try. It was better than doing nothing. Another scandal-ridden public appearance could damage Catherine's reputation beyond repair.

"Good morning." Hermione's cheerful voice interrupted his reverie. She turned her horse to trot beside his, her groom dropping back out of earshot.

"You are in looks today," he noted, admiring the military style riding habit that drew attention to her curvaceous figure.

"Thank you, my lord. My modiste finished this yesterday and I could hardly wait to try it out."

"It suits you," he said gallantly.

"Are you trying to worm your way back into my good graces?"

"Is it necessary? I thought you had forgiven me."

"And I thought you wished to restore my damaged credit. Yet you ignored me at Lady Dickenson's Venetian breakfast yesterday and did not even attend Lady Durham's ball."

"You had ample escort, my lady, as you must admit."

"But you deliberately avoided me—which Lady Beatrice noted, of course. She cited that as proof that your recent attentions have been contrived. You know she is determined to blame me for your desertion. Four people cut me dead last night, and I danced less than half of the sets. You promised to help me. It is the least you can do after throwing me over so publicly!"

Damon flinched. "I always keep my promises, but I cannot attend every entertainment. If I follow you around like a puppy, people will impute even worse motives." Damn Lady Beatrice for an interfering harridan!

They rode in silence for a couple of minutes. The spring

birds were in good voice, each valiantly defending its territory with song. But his spirits refused to lift.

"You seem troubled," observed Hermione at last. "Perhaps you should send your wife home to the country until she learns to comport herself properly."

"It is not your place to judge her," he responded coldly, though the suggestion offered a solution to his immediate problem. Was that really the answer? But he could not send her home without accompanying her, which smacked of running away. None of the Braxtons were likely to behave civilly, and he knew from experience how little they followed convention.

"Of course not," Hermione agreed immediately. "I was quite out of line. It is just that I care for you. It hurts me to see what she is doing to your name, for you deserve far better. I understand why you turned down my offer, but someone needs to teach her."

For once her accompanying smile did not warm his heart. Instead, her continuing criticism irritated him. "What are your plans for this week?" he asked, pointedly returning to the subject.

She sighed. "It is difficult to start over this late in the Season. We will visit Vauxhall tonight with my cousins. Lord Gresham is including us in a theater party tomorrow—not that he is the least bit interesting. I may need rescuing from his ponderous prose by the first interval."

"I can't help you there. We are promised to Lady Peverell's musicale." But he could not avoid another wave of guilt. Restoring her reputation would be a harder battle than he had expected if the best escort she could find was a dullard like Gresham. Yet he could not abandon Cat, either, especially in light of Sidney's spite. Only his own presence promised any hope of deflecting the lad.

"What a boring evening for you," observed Hermione. "Perhaps you can slip away and call at the theater."

"I've seen *Hamlet* too often already," he replied shortly, again irritated but unable to decide why. "And you have an escort for the evenings. No one will think it the least odd that I am elsewhere. I will make a point of greeting you in the park during the fashionable hour, and I expect we will both attend the Stafford ball."

She nodded.

He made his excuses and departed. He would also be at Vauxhall, but Hermione did not need him. He planned to recapture some of the warmth he had once shared with Catherine. Only then would he have any hope of controlling her behavior. At the moment, the least hint of criticism was enough to trigger an argument.

Lord James was Catherine's first caller of the afternoon. Today's Cossacks were a lively green-and-gold stripe that appeared ludicrous below his impeccable cravat and form-fitting green jacket. She managed to keep from laughing until he pulled out a jeweled quizzing glass and minutely scrutinized her gown.

"Forgive me," she gasped at last. "That was abominably rude."

"My behavior or your own?" One brow lifted.

"Mine, of course."

"You disappoint me. Did you not realize that I was demanding your laughter?" An elaborate pout elicited new giggles.

"You are serious!"

"You feel better for the release, do you not?" She nodded and he grinned. "I have to occasionally poke fun at people's affectations, including my own. And you must concede that today's fashions are ridiculous. Consider Lord Pinter. One could run him through without inflicting injury, for most of him is false—calves, thighs, shoulders, even his hair. The lad is bald as an egg with a figure like a skeleton."

"Perhaps he should adopt Cossacks," she suggested.

"God forbid! I only wear them to distance myself from Brummell's imitators. They've hardly a thought amongst them. And no originality, for their latest fancy is to ape their youngest siblings."

"The lisping?"

"Of course. It's remarkably silly." He demonstrated, speaking in a high, girlish tone and fluttering his hands while he minced across the room, leaning forward on his toes until she was sure he would fall. "Tho thorry thothiety thinkth you a courtethan, my dear. You mutht be horridly dithtrethed!"

"Idiot!" she choked through renewed laughter. "Do you know that outfit resembles a skirt when you walk like that?"

"Naturally. It is meant to. Absurd, I agree, but one must keep *au courant*, though frankly I believe it a trifle much." He had reverted to his normal voice, though retaining the foppish mannerisms as he preened before a mirror. "Now admit that you feel better."

"If you insist."

"Stubborn, aren't you? But there is a lesson in this madness. Society's spite is merely another affectation that will be gone and forgotten after a few tomorrows. None of them really mean it, but they are frightened of being out of step."

More visitors arrived and she thrust down a spurt of disappointment. Having a friend she could laugh with was a luxury she had not enjoyed since Damon left for war. The dour man who had returned wasted no time on humor. She had not realized how much she missed the gaiety that had filled her childhood.

Lord James's claims were absurd, of course, his own affectations prompting most of them. But they gave her something to think about as she studied the posturing of her guests. And that kept her mind off her problems.

"I heard the most astonishing tale about Mr. Sidney Braxton," exclaimed Lady Beatrice an hour later. "Do you recall how he was injured while riding in Lord Gregory Mallowfield's curricle last year? It lost a wheel and careened into a tree."

Catherine raised her brows, for she had not heard of it, but the other guests were all nodding agreement.

"Lord Gregory was terribly upset," recalled Lady Debenham.

"He even called in Dr. Massington—and we all know how expensive he is—to treat young Braxton's back," added Lady Marchgate.

"That is not all he did," reported Lady Beatrice. "Lord

Gregory paid Braxton five hundred pounds to quiet his charge that the incident was a deliberate attempt to injure him."

"Preposterous!"

"That is a fortune!"

"Who would believe such a claim?"

Lady Beatrice snorted. "Lord Gregory's grandfather would. But that is not all. Mr. Braxton was seen in Kent—riding to hounds with Lord Hawkins—at the very time he was supposedly suffering back spasms in London. One wonders if he did not arrange the accident himself."

"Shocking!"

"Who saw him in Kent?" demanded Lady Debenham.

"Lord Hartleigh."

"A true gentleman," decided Lady Cunningham.

"If Braxton lied about the accident, can we believe him about anything else?" asked Lady Marchgate, looking pointedly at Catherine.

"I don't see how," declared Lady Beatrice.

"But one lie does not make all his claims untrue," insisted Lady Debenham. "I have confirmation from Sir Anthony Wilkins that Lady Devlin was seen publicly embracing Lord Rathbone several years ago."

A collective gasp filled the room.

"Under a kissing bough, no doubt," scoffed Lady Beatrice.

"Hardly. At a summer picnic when they believed themselves unobserved." She glared at Catherine.

"We all know Rathbone's reputation," said Lady Cunningham.

"At least you make the charge to my face," observed Catherine calmly. "How different it sounds in the telling. I was sixteen at the time. Lord Rathbone had just won a rowing competition against my brother. Since I had wagered a whole sixpence on that outcome, I was delighted enough to hug him." She let her eyes twinkle with mischief. "I admit that he had no objections. Even in those days he was a confirmed flirt."

Several ladies laughed. Lady Beatrice gloated. Catherine kept her composure, though she heaved a silent sigh of relief at having survived another inquisition. How many other tales from the past would these tenacious gossips uncover? Thank heaven no one knew of that stolen kiss! She had not even told Edith.

Catherine set aside her cares for the evening. She and Damon were to visit Vauxhall Gardens with Edith and Sir Isaac Peverell, Louisa, Sir Thomas Morehead, and Captain and Mrs. Hanson. She had not previously met Sir Thomas, who was one of Louisa's friends, or Captain Hanson, who had served on the Peninsula with Damon.

At first sight the gardens looked like a fairyland. The party had taken boats across the Thames rather than enduring the roundabout route required of coaches. Part of the glamour of Vauxhall was the inaccessibility that kept the riffraff from descending in large numbers as they had done at Ranelagh Gardens some years before, creating a crime problem that had driven away the upper classes and forced it to close. Many people were predicting a similar fate for Vauxhall once the Waterloo Bridge was completed, for its terminus was almost atop the gardens.

Thousands of lights led the eye from the wharf to the gates, with even more lanterns decorating the gardens themselves. Music wafted out to draw them closer.

"It looks like something out of *The Arabian Nights*," Catherine murmured as Damon led her down the main concourse toward the box Sir Isaac had reserved for the party.

"Not quite, but I see what you mean."

Vauxhall was not all that resembled a fantasy tale, decided Cat as the evening progressed. Damon was being remarkably attentive. Though the group stayed together as they wandered through the gardens, only Damon escorted her, his muscular arm resting beneath her fingers. He took delight in her delight, sharing her laughter at the puppets, her awe at the rope dancers, and her admiration for the cunning lighting that displayed trees and shrubbery to advantage. They danced, waltzing around the plaza until she was dizzy with exhilaration. And with hope. The caring brother she had idolized in her youth was back. And more. Shivers tumbled down her spine as he pulled her closer than was acceptable in a ballroom.

Not until they returned to the box for the usual supper of wafer-thin slices of ham and beef did his attention broaden to include others.

Edith took the chair next to Catherine, rolling her eyes at the gentlemen, who were caught up in discussing a pension bill for war veterans that had recently been introduced in Parliament. "That looks suspiciously like a betrothal party," she said, nodding toward a box across the plaza.

Mr. Jeremy Crenshaw, Miss Letitia Armstrong, and their respective families were raising glasses in obvious celebration. Several young men peppered the lanky Mr. Crenshaw with quips—ribald in nature if their expressions and raucous laughter were anything to go by.

"It took a few days longer than you suggested, but they are now settled," agreed Catherine, but she missed Edith's reply as her eyes snapped two boxes to the right. Lady Hermione was ignoring her own party to stare longingly at Damon. And he was staring back, oblivious to the conversation he had been enjoying only moments before.

Catherine shivered. To cover her confusion, she turned to Eleanor Hanson and was soon engrossed in the antics of the lady's nephew, Robby Mannering, now age two and a half.

"It is nearly time for the fireworks," announced Edith at last, interrupting a description of Robby's accident-filled excursion to the dairy.

Damon helped Catherine to her feet and led her toward the viewing area, but she was no longer enchanted by his notice. Someone must have castigated him for ignoring her, so he was playing the part of an attentive and caring husband. She must never again forget that his heart was not hers. This was only another attempt to salvage their reputations.

But she could not remain melancholy for long. Never having witnessed fireworks before, she had not known what to expect.

"Beautiful," she breathed as the first shell burst into vivid gold sparks above the river. Everything receded as she gazed in wonder at the glorious sight. Fireballs, waterfalls, wheels, rockets, and more, all in glorious color. Her eyes widened in mesmerized wonder.

Damon flinched at the first explosion, every muscle tensing to dive out of sight.

"My feelings exactly," whispered Captain Hanson as another fireball exploded overhead.

"How can anyone enjoy this, Daryl?" He grimaced as a larger shell popped.

"They have never experienced a battle." A series of smaller explosions had the captain fumbling for the pistol he no longer carried. "This is too much. I am going back to the box," he said, shuddering with remembered pain. "Care to join me?"

A rocket screamed across the sky, leaving a red river in its wake and raising images of the blood-stained ditch at Badajoz.

"Gladly." They slipped through the crowd, striding rapidly into the darkness.

Catherine sighed when the final shell faded.

"Was this your first fireworks display?" asked Edith.

"Yes. It is not something one finds in the country. I never imagined anything so exhilarating."

"Time to return to the box," observed Sir Isaac. "And I have two arms," he added, nothing that Damon and Captain Hanson had disappeared.

Edith laughed, laying her hand on his right elbow. Eleanor Hanson caught hold of his left. Louisa and Sir Thomas had already moved off, deep in conversation, so Catherine fell in beside Eleanor.

"I should have known Daryl couldn't stand the noise," said Eleanor with a sigh. "He hates fireworks, claiming they remind him too much of war."

Of course. Catherine berated herself for her stupidity. No wonder Damon had left. But it would have been nice if he had returned after the show. The jostling crowd forced her to slide in behind Sir Isaac as Eleanor laughed at something the baronet had said.

Six inebriated youths raced past, knocking Catherine off balance. She recovered quickly, but the moment's hesitation allowed another raucous group to cut in front of her. Pushing her way through the milling crowd, she discovered too late that her friends were moving in a different direction. Not that she was particularly worried. Sir Isaac was clearly visible fifty feet away, the ladies both convulsed in laughter. Obviously they had not noticed her separation. She sighed. The concourse was well lighted and she knew where their box was, but if anyone saw her alone, the tattle-baskets would pounce with even greater fury. She increased her pace as her friends rounded a corner.

"Where you goin' in such a hurry?" slurred a rough voice as a man stepped in front of her. He was dressed as a gentleman but was obviously the worse for drink. Ignoring his question, she tried to push past him, but he grabbed her arm. "You need an escort, m'dear.'

"I have one, sir," she snapped. Twisting away from his grip, she sidestepped a couple indulging in a vulgar public embrace and tried to circle the drunk.

But he was not so easily deterred. "Of course you do. Me!". His sneering voice turned coarsely suggestive. "Have you seen the hermit?"

She dodged away, cursing the skirt that prevented her from running. Why had she worn such a narrow gown tonight? No matter how foxed the fellow was, there was no hope of escape.

"That's right, lovey!" He laughed, satisfaction and excitement clear in the sound. "Down the second path. The old boy is well worth visitin'. I 'spect you'll be right grateful."

Dear Lord! Panic was beginning to interfere with thinking. Where was Damon? She could no longer see Edith and the concourse seemed narrower than she remembered. Had she taken a wrong turn? A larger group of people approached. She considered asking for help, but they appeared nearly as foxed as her pursurer. Her skirt ripped as she tried for more speed, but she ignored it, snaking through the crowd and dodging a groping hand. The drunk was momentarily blocked. Where was she? Which way were the boxes?

"Bitch!" he swore, his voice now dangerously irritated. Several men laughed.

Whipping around a corner, she abruptly changed directions to slip through a break in the trees. Another path opened on the other side, this one unlighted. Running lightly along it, she strained to hear any pursuit. That horrid voice swore again only a few feet away, but to her relief, he continued along the other walk, his footsteps disappearing into the distance.

Where was she? Turning toward where she hoped the boxes lay, she followed the new trail. But within twenty yards, an arm snaked out of the darkness to circle her waist.

"Delectable!" grated a new voice.

"Let go!" she demanded, fear breaking out anew.

"Why? Girls who venture alone down the Dark Walk want only one thing." He clasped her close with that powerful arm, latching his other hand onto her bosom as he opened his mouth and bent for a kiss.

"No!" She twisted her head so his wet lips landed on her neck. Digging her fingers into his face, she fought to escape, all the while screaming for help.

"The lady is unwilling, Featherstone," drawled a bored voice. A fist connected with her attacker's jaw, lifting him into the air, spinning him around, and dropping him to the ground. One shiny toe of a pair of tassled Hessians prodded the prostrate scoundrel.

"Lord Rathbone!"

"What on earth are you doing here by yourself?" he demanded incredulously, thrusting a handkerchief into her hand and pulling her against his shoulder when she burst into tears.

She was beyond thought and could do nothing but sob.

"Well?" he repeated when she finally regained some composure. His expert eye studied her appearance. She hardly noticed when he straightened her gown, tucked a stray lock of hair into her coiffure, and wrapped his cloak around her to hide the rip in her skirt. But she huddled into its welcome warmth as a shiver wracked her.

"We were walking back to the box after the fireworks when the crowd separated us. Then a drunken gentleman tried to drag me off to visit a hermit. I escaped him by ducking out of sight behind a tree. This path was there so I followed it, hoping it would lead to the main concourse. That's when Mr. Featherstone grabbed me."

"He's a lord, I fear, though not a gentleman by anyone's standards. You are lucky it was no worse. Come, I will escort you back to your party. In future, stay closer to your friends. Vauxhall is no place for a lone female."

Catherine placed her hand on his arm, mortified to discover she was still shaking.

"Where is your husband?"

"He did not view the fireworks with us."

Rathbone muttered what sounded like curses. "I will have a word with him. It is not the thing to bring a lady to Vauxhall and abandon her to her own devices. Too many people place a dishonorable interpretation on the words 'Pleasure Gardens.' "

"Please don't chastise him. He could not stand the noise. Nor could Captain Hanson. War leaves many scars. And this is my own fault for becoming separated from our group. I should have paid closer attention."

Rathbone frowned, but ultimately agreed. Within moments they were back on the brightly lighted concourse. Several people were near the entrance to the Dark Walk, but none paid them any attention. Thus she was able to appear calm when they reached the box.

"Where have you been?" demanded Louisa immediately.

"The crowd separated us," she replied with a shrug. "But Lord Rathbone noticed that I had been cut off and offered to escort me back. Thank you, my lord," she finished, turning a smile on him.

"Any time, Lady Devlin." He bowed over her hand, then took himself off.

"I am tired and would like to return home," she told Damon quietly when he and the captain returned five minutes later. He seemed about to protest, but Edith had heard the words and quickly agreed, so they headed for the quay.

Catherine wanted nothing more than to describe her terrifying experience to Damon. He would drive away the last vestiges of her fear. But the opportunity never arose. They were using Louisa's carriage and sharing it with Sir Thomas. Even when they reached Berkeley Square she had no chance. Simms handed Damon a thick packet that had arrived while they were out. He immediately retired to his study.

How dare he? she asked herself once Brigit had brushed her hair and left her alone for the night. Panic had returned, leaving her weak and shaking. Rathbone had a point. It was unconscionable that Damon had left her without escort in a place known to be unsafe for ladies. It mattered not that he was uncomfortable around fireworks. He should have made certain that she would be properly chaperoned in his absence. But he had cared only for his own convenience. It hurt.

She could not avoid comparing the two men. Rathbone always made her feel desirable and worthwhile, even after accepting that she wanted only friendship with him. But Damon made it clear that she was a worthless impediment in his life, something to be ignored as much as possible.

The tears came then, scalding her eyes. She wept long into the night, finally falling asleep from exhaustion.

Chapter Twelve

"Of course Lady Devlin trapped him! Once she discovered her condition, she was desperate for a husband!"

The reading room at White's disappeared in a red blur as Damon heard these words. The speaker must not have noticed who was ensconced behind the newspaper. But before he could set the man straight, Jack's voice spoke up.

"Calumny, Shelford! Base calumny. There is not a word of truth to any of those tales."

"Then how did they start?"

"Spite embroidering innuendo. Sidney Braxton implied an affair that never existed. Lady Hermione took it a step further by inventing consequences. The motive should be obvious."

Sheldon laughed.

Damon surged to his feet as Sheldon disappeared into the gaming room. The situation was worse than he had imagined if even Jack was heaping abuse on Hermione. No one would have dared do so before he had jilted her. "I ought to call you out for such slander," he hissed.

Jack raised his brows. "I thought I was correcting the slander."

"Blaming it on another innocent is not improving the situation!"

"Calm down!" barked Jack, holding up his hand. "Do you dare call me a liar? The gossips always provide provenance for their tales, as you should know. Lady Debenham readily admits that she heard that claim from Lady Hermione."

Damon drew in a deep breath and slowly let it out. "Then she is the liar. You know she will do anything to score a point on Lady Beatrice. After Lady Beatrice declared that Hermione drove me away, Lady Debenham had to counter in kind. She is trying to protect her cousin's credit by throwing Catherine to the dogs."

It was the only explanation, he decided as he headed for home. Attributing the tale to Hermione would give it more credibility, for people would believe she had the facts from him. Jack would agree once he had time to think it over. Why couldn't the gossips stay out of this imbroglio? They were only making matters worse. He would restore Hermione's reputation—and Catherine's—and he would do it without harming innocent bystanders.

Catherine paused in the doorway of Edith's drawing room to admire its Chinese decor. Red velvet draperies framed the windows, their color repeated in the red brocade upholstery. Silk wallcoverings above delicate green wainscoting depicted exotic birds in bamboo jungles. Cloisonné vases and lacquered boxes mingled with carved jade on tables and the mantelpiece.

"Good morning, Catherine," called Edith, smiling widely.

"You look excited," observed Catherine. She joined her friend on a gilded Sheraton couch and accepted a cup of tea.

"Nervous would be a better description. I always am on days that I entertain. So many things can go wrong that my imagination runs wild."

Catherine laughed. "You speak as if this were a grand ball. It is only a musicale, Edith, and you have engaged the most modish soprano and the newest harpist. You have an enviable talent for organization, and I cannot imagine you hiring an incompetent staff. Now relax!"

"Perhaps I am overreacting," agreed Edith with a sigh. "I am breeding again and Isaac always claims that I see disaster lurking behind every tree when I am in that condition."

"How wonderful! About your expectations, I mean. When?"

"Not until late October—which is why I am in town. If it were any sooner, Isaac would never have allowed me to leave the estate."

"He cares about your health," agreed Catherine with a

pang. Damon had not made the slightest effort to cosset her, from the frenetic pace he set during their journey from Cumberland to his abandonment once they arrived. Even his attentions at Vauxhall had been missing when she needed them. Not that his indifference was anything new. He had allowed her to accompany him as a child only after she proved she was one of the boys. But she pushed her thoughts firmly aside. Edith would notice if she became melancholy.

"I did not intend to talk about myself this morning. We must do something about these malicious stories."

"Has something new come up?"

"Not that I know of, but someone is keeping the charges alive. Normally, the talk would have died by now. Everyone knew it was nought but the usual speculation over a sudden marriage."

"This is hardly speculation, Edith. You have heard Sidney. He speaks with authority, for I lived with his family. Damon can deny impropriety from now until doomsday, but no one believes him, for he would do so regardless of the facts. Only time will refute the worst charges, but even that cannot erase suspicion. And no one can forget that I do not always act as I should."

"Fustian!"

"Not fustian," she countered. "There is no getting around the fact that I am untutored in the ways of society. When my parents died, I was still in the schoolroom, and I have had no opportunity to socialize since."

"You exaggerate," insisted Edith. "Your manners are excellent and you cannot have forgotten all that we were taught at school. Miss Grimsby would shudder to think that her efforts were wasted." They both laughed. "Your behavior is just fine. The problem is that someone is deliberately drawing attention to every minor deviation from rigid propriety and twisting it into scandal."

"I would hardly call discussing a tenant's lying-in a deviation," said Catherine. "Even I should have known better— especially with two young girls in the room. Lady Beatrice gave me a stare that would freeze Hades."

"But she did not rebuke you."

"Only because Lady Debenham would have scored a point had she done so."

"You are too hard on yourself. If you were single, it might have been construed as a serious breach, of course. But married women have more latitude. You were speaking softly to two dowagers far enough removed from the Misses Cathcart that they were unaware of your topic. The real problem is that someone is waging war against you."

"Your imagination is out of control, Edith. Why would Sidney stoop to harping on minor indiscretions when he has already implied such large ones? Besides, finesse is not his style, and he has no real quarrel with me. He should lose interest before much longer."

"Don't be a goose, Cat," snapped Edith. "Mr. Braxton has nothing to do with keeping the gossip alive. This pettiness comes from Lady Hermione. You must know her reasons."

"Damon hurt her badly."

"Ha! All she wanted was his title and wealth. She hated you even before she set eyes on you, for you won the prize she had been stalking. She cares for no one but herself and couldn't get rid of her court fast enough when he turned his eyes in her direction. Lord Devlin is well rid of her."

"That does not make sense, Edith. She has nothing to gain by vilifying me. Damon is the one who embarrassed her, yet she welcomes his company."

"There are times when you really are naive." Edith shook her head. "Her personal feelings mean nothing. You stole the position she wanted. There is no chance of finding its equal this Season—the Duke of Norwood has settled on Lady Emily Sterne—which means she must either accept less or spend another year under her father's roof. Of course she would seek revenge. It does not help that you are beautiful and sweet in a way that she can never hope to emulate. She is jealous, Catherine. And spiteful."

"Nonsense!"

"It is she who is keeping alive Sidney's charge that you are in the family way. And I also believe that she is behind the tales that you conducted affairs with servants and tenants."

"It makes no sense," protested Catherine again. "Perpetuating the gossip must hurt her more than it does me. I cannot believe she is that childish."

"She *is* childish. The girl is barely eighteen and has been spoiled all her life. But you are right about the effect. If she keeps it up, she will become a pariah. She should realize that very soon. Or we can find someone to point it out to her—someone she will listen to."

"And create a new charge to be bandied about town? No. Leave well enough alone, Edith." She refused to discuss it further. Edith was ignoring the only important fact—Damon had not chosen Hermione because of money and position. Whatever the lady's motives, his heart was engaged. And would remain so. Damon was the most loyal man she had ever known, which was why they were caught in this wretched coil in the first place. If Damon ever thought she was scheming against Hermione, even their lifelong friendship would not survive.

Damon leaned against the back wall in Lady Peverell's conservatory, hardly hearing the fluid notes that held the rest of the crowd spellbound. The first interval should be starting at Drury Lane. Was Hermione as bored as she had expected to be? He had not spoken to her at Vauxhall and still winced at the reproach that had blazed in her eyes the one time she had trapped his gaze. It had deflected him from his plan to recapture the camaraderie he had once shared with Catherine. Was it possible? The evening had started well, but by the time they had left for home, she was as coldly uncommunicative as ever. And it wasn't from tiredness. She had been even worse today.

What was he doing here when he would have enjoyed the theater more? Catherine wasn't even with him. He glanced across the room to where she sat, her attention focused on the soprano. This was how he had pictured her that day in the clearing—soft black curls framing her creamy face, those womanly curves caressed by shimmering silk that perfectly matched her violet eyes. Of course, he would never have placed that peacock, Lord James, at her side. His hands tightened into fists.

He should never have come. No one would have cared if he had gone elsewhere this evening. Many husbands refused to attend musicales, considering them dull and more suited to ladies.

The soprano ended her final aria and the crowd rose in search of refreshments. Damon deliberately avoided Catherine's eye, instead ducking down a hall. Was it too late to go to the theater? He could not make the first interval, of course, but he could be there for the second. Slipping into the library, he paced the floor in indecision.

What was the point? Hermione did not need his escort tonight and Catherine did. If he were not nearby to keep her from breaking one of society's myriad rules, she might inadvertently invite new rumors. The arbiters of fashion did not take ignorance or naiveté into account when condemning behavior.

He snorted. Even when he was present, he was unable to either control her behavior or turn aside Sidney's spite. But he would do nothing to add credence to the tales. For the time being he must dance attendance on her. Turning to the door, he prayed the harpist would be good enough to hold his attention. All this thinking was bringing on a headache.

Two giggling girls stopped just outside the library. He would have pushed past them, but their words stopped him.

"—like that scandalous Lady Devlin. She doesn't even care who sees her! Lady Comstock watched her emerge from the Dark Walk at Vauxhall just last night, disheveled and clinging to Lord Rathbone's arm. She is certainly no better than she should be!"

"So true. Miss Patterson was telling me only yesterday that Mrs. Bassington saw her return from the garden at Lady Wharburton's masquerade practically draped around Lord James Hutchinson. If ever a woman appeared thoroughly kissed, it was Lady Devlin."

"Well, what can one expect from someone so lost to good breeding that she would trap a man who was all but betrothed to another?"

"Too vulgar for words. And she treats her maid like a close friend. But that is all of a piece. I heard she was nought but a servant herself until her marriage."

"Shocking!"

They moved on, entering the lady's retiring room. Damon gritted his teeth. The insinuations were exaggerated and misinterpreted, as usual—at least he hoped they were. What had Catherine and Rathbone been doing in the Dark Walk?

Catherine lay awake, vainly trying to understand her husband. At Vauxhall he had been the caring brother she had once known, until after the fireworks, when he reverted to coldness. Following Edith's musicale—which he should have enjoyed—he seemed even grimmer. Yet the next morning he had joined her for breakfast, sharing the latest gossip, discussing her life with the Braxtons, and even flirting lightly. In the three days since, his attentions had blown hot and cold, confounding every attempt to understand him. He had driven her in the park during the fashionable hour, accompanied her to a ball, two routs, and a literary evening, and treated her with a warmth they had not shared in years. He had also snapped her head off for no reason at all, snubbed her for asking a personal question, deserted her to fawn over Hermione, and abandoned her at Hatchard's bookstore to accompany a friend to Tattersall's. She had been forced to take a hackney home. What game was he playing? It made no sense to think he was merely countering the continuing rumors. Being friendly in private could not affect society's opinion, and ignoring her in public made the gossip worse.

His secrecy also bothered her. It would be better to honestly talk—and not just about the rumors and his courtship of Hermione. She still had no idea what her uncle had done. But Damon eschewed discussion, and his abrupt mood swings left her hanging in uncertainty. Which Damon would she meet tomorrow? The friendly charmer? The angry accuser? The remote stranger? Were any of them real? He had been so quiet on the way home this evening that she was afraid he was on the verge of some new attitude.

She pounded a fist into her pillow. London was not a place in which she would ever feel comfortable. Nothing was real. People wore masks that hid honest emotion. Events were staged that seemed glamorous on the surface, but were nought but empty posturing. No one did anything useful. Perhaps her years of servitude had colored her thinking, but she did not enjoy waste. And that included waste of one's time—which was the perfect description of the London Season.

A scream from Damon's room interrupted her thoughts. He was suffering another nightmare. Sighing, she drew on her dressing gown and went to wake him. The closest they ever came to conjugal relations was when she shook him out of one of his dreams. It was becoming almost a nightly occurrence.

But this one was different. She froze in the doorway as his muttering resolved into words.

"Peter—" He thrashed about on the bed. "Too much . . . not even for you . . . Hermione."

Catherine gritted her teeth and reached out to grab his shoulder, but his next words stayed her hand.

"How can I live without you?"

Pain ripped through her chest at the plaintive wail. It was as she had expected. Damon loved Hermione with a depth that would never die. If only she had insisted on thinking over his offer. She should not have allowed him to force her into so momentous a decision without any consideration. Even the shallow courtship of a London Season would have given her more time. And why had he offered for her? An ancient vow to Peter should not have held precedence over the woman he loved. If that was truly his reason, why had he not claimed her when he sold out?

Leaving him to his dreams, Catherine quietly returned to her own room. But sleep was a long time coming.

"I've met the most delightful girl!" Peter spoke so fast the words tripped over his tongue. "You must come see her, Damon. Even you must agree that she is something quite out of the ordinary."

"Who is she?"

He frowned, agitatedly pacing the room, then shrugged. "Her uncle runs the confectioner's shop on George Lane."

"*Peter, you fool!*" Damon exploded. "*You don't dally with merchant's daughters—or their sisters or nieces!*"

"*It isn't dalliance I have in mind,*" he countered passionately. "*I love her. She is beautiful!*"

"*This is too much!*" Damon's fist landed on the table, knocking a wineglass to the floor. "*How does she differ from the Black Hart's serving wench you were in love with last week? Or the vision in pink muslin you saw in church last month? Rein in the emotions, Peter, or you will wind up in trouble.*"

"*This is different!*" insisted his friend, hands clenched in frustration. "*I want you to talk to Father about her. She is worthy of so much more than working in a shop. I need to dress her in silk, satin, and diamonds. You would not believe her glorious eyes, Damon. She should spend her nights dancing or singing for the sheer joy of living! I shudder to picture such perfection leading a life of drudgery.*"

"*No! Not even for you, Peter. You delude yourself—again. Your soft heart is notorious by now. Every chit in town makes a play for your attention. Come down out of the clouds and think for a change.*"

"*How can you judge without even meeting her?*"

"*But I have met her,*" said Damon gently. "*That confectioner has two nieces. Which one caught your eye? Agrippina or Hermione?*"

"*Agrippina.*"

"*As I thought. There's a schemer, or I've never met one. She has been meeting Wallace for weeks, hoping for hush-up money when she cries rape. Now I know why she has not already done so. In you she sees a bigger prize—a title.*"

"*No!*" Peter blanched, falling to the floor in a dead faint. Damon sprang to catch him, but they were no longer in Oxford. Portugal's hills were silhouetted against a setting sun as he cradled Peter's shattered body in his arms. Hope, love, and joy deserted him, flowing into the pool of blood below Peter's head. Great rending sobs tore from his throat. "*Dear God, Peter, how can I live without you?*"

Blue eyes opened, glittering in the fading light. "*You will find a way, my brother. And when you do, you will be happy again.*"

Damon bolted upright in bed, cold sweat trickling down his back. For once the dream remained clear in his mind. What was not clear was why that memory would return. Peter had gone through two years of instability before they left for Portugal, flitting from one pretty face to another, swearing that each was the love of his life. It had become Damon's duty to keep his friend from disgracing his name. Agrippina was a typical case. When her uncle discovered the liaison with Wallace—the girl was in the family way by then—he cried foul and demanded marriage. It had cost the lad's father a sizable fortune to buy her off and suppress a potentially ruinous scandal. If only Peter had learned to look beyond appearance to the character beneath!

He drew on his dressing gown and paced the room. The real oddity was that last scene, for it had no basis in reality. While he had seen Peter fall in battle, he had not been able to do anything for him. Why had his mind conjured up a fictitious confrontation? Was it because he still felt guilty over Peter's death?

He had no answers, but it was pointless to return to bed. He pulled on some clothes and went down to his study to ponder the latest figures from his solicitor.

Chapter Thirteen

Damon had already left when Catherine awoke. She ate, met with the housekeeper, then spent a desultory hour shopping. But melancholy banished all pleasure. She could not forget Damon's latest nightmare. Giving it up as a lost cause, she returned to Berkeley Square.

Why had Damon married her? If Uncle Henry had absconded with her dowry, there was little they could do to recover it at this late date. Any promises Damon had made to Peter seemed feeble in light of his courtship of Hermione.

Enough! She must distract her mind from this constant analysis. She retrieved her copy of Jane Austen's *Emma* from the library, pausing to smile at the room. Books were the greatest benefit of her marriage. Damon's library was extensive and he had accounts with every London bookseller, so she could read anything she pleased. Her eyes scanned the shelves—classics, poetry, philosophy, recent scientific advances, novels, estate management, and much more. Many of them had been purchased since his return. In that respect, he had not changed. He had always had an inquiring mind.

Her eyes caught the name Braxton on a paper atop the desk. She gasped, dragging her unwilling feet closer. It was her father's will.

She had been too distraught to attend its reading, having learned of Peter's death only that morning. She knew the provisions, of course. Uncle Henry had explained them a month later. After grants to several servants, the remainder went to the next baron—not that there was much to leave.

Why would Damon obtain a copy? There was nothing unusual about the document. Peter had died two days before their father, so his own will would not have affected the estate.

She scanned it, frowning over the arcane language solicitors seemed to love, but found nothing odd. A dowry was mentioned, but the money would have come from general funds. If those had been lost, her dowry would also have disappeared. Everything was exactly as she had expected.

Turning to the last page, she gasped, for it was a codicil dated two days after Peter and Damon had left to join their regiment. As she read the words, she could see her father furiously pacing the floor, anger and pain harshening his voice. For the entire two months before his own death he had ranted at Peter's ingratitude, his stubbornness, and his disregard of duty and common sense. The thirteenth baron could not ignore Peter's figurative slap in the face. Putting his life on the line was irresponsible, unfilial, and disrespectful, for Lord Braxton had already forbidden it.

The codicil made those points again, in excruciating detail, then declared his punishment. "I hereby bequeath the estate known as Ridgway House, along with its contents and attached farms, the London house at number 17 Curzon Street, and the sum of one hundred thousand pounds to my daughter, Catherine Anne Braxton, to be held in trust until the advent of her marriage." Here he included a diatribe belittling the ability of women to understand financial affairs, citing the eccentric Lady Hester Stanhope as a prime example of the stupidity of allowing females any control of their fortunes. The trust would be administered by his solicitor, Mr. Adams, and by his brother, Henry Braxton. Her father concluded, "If Catherine remains unwed at the age of five-and-twenty, the trust will revert to the fourteenth Baron Braxton."

Catherine stared at the paper as the truth dawned. Mr. Adams had died shortly after reading the will; thus Uncle Henry would have been the sole administrator. He had been right to claim that he had inherited little from his brother. The financial difficulties they had been suffering were real. But if he prevented her from marrying until she turned five-and-twenty, a fortune would be his—a simple matter if she were removed from society.

Shame engulfed her—shame that her uncle could treat her so shabbily; shame that she had been so easily manipulated; but most of all, shame that Damon should discover her family so lacking in honor.

Damon.

Shame immediately converted to rage. She had been naive indeed to believe that he had married her to rescue her. No wonder he had been in such a hurry. They had wed the day before her birthday. Thus he now controlled Ridgway House and a vast fortune.

It was exactly the wrong time for him to return home.

Damon strode furiously up the stairs. Every time he thought he had Catherine's trust straightened out, he discovered new misdeeds, and today had been no exception. Braxton had sold the Curzon Street house soon after acceding to the title, but the trust records were so confused that it had been difficult to trace the proceeds. Damon had now proven that the baron had diverted the money to his own use.

At least thirty thousand pounds had been missing even before this latest discovery, much of it openly paid to Braxton under the guise of exorbitant trustee's fees. Adams was lucky he was already dead. If he had lived, Damon might have strangled him for accepting such a sloppily constructed trust. Even if he knew that the codicil was only an angry gesture that would soon be abandoned, his dereliction to duty was inexcusable. Normally a trust would be administered by at least three men, with clearly stated provisions for replacing them. Braxton's heir should have been excluded from consideration. And all records should have been kept by an experienced man of business. But it was too late to repine. Catherine would be lucky to recoup half of her inheritance. He had already noted the mismanagement that had allowed Ridgway to slide into disrepair. It would take years of effort and a considerable infusion of cash before full productivity was restored.

He slammed into the library and stopped dead. Catherine was sitting at his desk, the codicil held in shaking hands.

"What a despicable blackguard you are," she spat.

"What?" Caught by surprise, he could hardly believe his ears.

"I despise fortune hunters."

"What are you talking about?" He dropped a packet of papers onto the desk before turning puzzled eyes to his wife.

"I am not stupid, Damon." Her voice rose. "You had no interest in marrying me until you discovered Father's will. But a fortune this large is hard to resist, isn't it?"

"It wasn't that way at all," he protested, thrown off balance by the charge. "Yes, we had to wed before that codicil expired, but only to protect you. Your uncle has been cheating you for years—nearly half of your legacy is missing—and I could not allow him to get away with it all."

"Of course not," she agreed scathingly, standing to glare at him across the desktop. "It was better to take it for yourself."

"Nonsense! I have no need of your fortune. My own is far bigger. But I cannot stand cheats."

"Considering that you didn't bother to tell me anything, I can only believe that you are also a cheat." She whirled away to look out the window.

"Don't you know me better than that?"

She glanced over her shoulder, tears visible in her eyes. "I don't know you at all, Damon. You've changed, and not for the better. The boy I played with and the idealistic young man you grew into would never have behaved so selfishly. It was bad enough knowing that you only married me because of some idiotic promise you made to Peter. But even that did not inspire you to the altar until you discovered that I was also an heiress."

She might as well have kicked him in the stomach. "Devil take it, Cat, you are becoming hysterical. Enough of this fustian. We will talk when you are calmer." His own temper near the explosion point, he turned his back, busying himself with lining up books on a shelf.

"I am not hysterical," she countered. "Postponing the truth will not change it."

"What truth? I never promised Peter to marry you."

"So you are a liar as well as a cheat," she sneered, circling in front of him so he had to look at her. "You admitted your vow to Colonel Caldwell."

"If you have been eavesdropping on my private conversations, then you should also know how guilty I feel for not checking up on you years ago."

"Why should I? I don't eavesdrop, as you would know if you remember anything about me. I only heard that one comment. If you are going to reveal secrets, you should not shout."

He took a turn about the room. It was only to be expected that she was upset. He had planned to discuss the trust with her as soon as he knew the full extent of her uncle's defalcations, but this was not the way he had pictured the disclosure.

"You are making a mountain out of a molehill," he said soothingly. "I would have told you sooner, but I have been too busy trying to find out how much your uncle stole."

"I am sure you have," she agreed, crossing her arms, her icy eyes freezing his thoughts. "What a shame if you gave up the marriage you wanted only to discover that the fortune you wed me for was gone."

"What?" His mind was again reeling. Surely she could not know about his courtship of Hermione.

"Did you think that people would protect me from your perfidy?" Her incredulity taunted him, for he had believed just that. "Any number of them, starting with Lady Hermione herself, have been eager to tell me about it. Your behavior is unworthy of the great war hero, Damon. I always believed that you were honorable. It is chilling to discover that you could discard even that in pursuit of a fortune."

"How dare you?" he snapped, grabbing her arms as his temper shattered. "How dare you impugn my honor?"

"So self-righteous!" She batted his hand aside, glaring into his eyes. "I do not hang on your every word like my idiot cousins. Nor can I ignore facts. You made a vow to Peter, yet did nothing to carry it out. You were often back in England, yet made no attempt to see me. You courted another, leading all of society to expect a betrothal until you discovered that I am an heiress. Then you jilted her to rush me into marriage, promptly abandoning me to dance attendance on her again. Don't you dare speak to me of honor and good intentions when any imbecile can see the truth!"

"I do dare, Cat!" he spat, holding her in place when she tried to turn away. Tears were streaming down her face, but he ignored them. "You have concocted a pretty tale out of half-truths and ignorance. Shall I judge you the same way? What am I to believe when the town buzzes with tales of your own dishonor?" Fury made his voice shake.

"How quick you are to believe spiteful insinuations, my lord," she observed coldly. "Is that how you justify your behavior?"

"Are they spite?" he asked softly. "You manage to create scandal every time you leave this house."

"I have done nothing of which I need be ashamed. Can you say the same?"

"I have to live in this town," he reminded her, ignoring the question. "That will be difficult if my wife is not received. Your only chance of improving your credit is to embrace propriety, starting with cutting all connection to Rathbone."

Twisting from his grasp, she whirled out of reach. "How dare you! I'll not cut one of the few people trying to help me."

"Help you? Into his bed, perhaps. The man is incorrigible, as you would know if you had any sense. And Lord James is no better. He does not care a whit for you. His attentions are merely a ploy to embarrass me. Quit making a cake of yourself and threatening both of us."

"Stop it, Damon!" Her foot stomped.

"Now you sound like a spoiled child," he charged. "I refuse to continue this discussion until you come to your senses."

"Isn't that too bad! You should have thought a little harder before you chose money over affection. After everything you have done to me, what you want is irrelevant."

"Think, Catherine! Once your reputation is gone, you will never recover it."

"Listen to the omnipotent lord! The great, infallible earl!

You might consider your own advice, Damon. I'm not the only one who notices how you drool over Lady Hermione." She turned to leave, but his voice stopped her before she could escape.

"Hermione at least is a lady. What am I to call you? More than one person saw you emerge from the Dark Walk that night." Icy contempt dripped from every word.

She had no idea who had seen her, but she was too furious to hold her tongue. "I suppose Hermione was there and immediately ran to you with the tale. And you believed her embellishments, as usual. It never occurred to you to wonder how I fared after you abandoned me to fate. But then listening to her malice is so much easier than thinking for yourself. Too bad you didn't stay with your original plans, Damon. Frankly, you deserve each other, for you are two of a kind—secretive, manipulative, and totally selfish. Neither of you cares a jot for anyone, and you revel in hurting people! You have done more to destroy me than Sidney and Hermione combined." Tears brimmed over and she stumbled from the room, slamming the door behind her.

Damon poured a generous glass of brandy and tossed it down. Things could not possibly get any worse. *Promise me . . . look after Catherine.* His honor had taken such a beating he doubted it could recover. She was half right. He had hurt her more than the Braxtons had. And he had harmed Hermione almost as much.

Where had he gone wrong?

He poured another drink. What a stupid question! Every decision since Vimeiro had been bad. He had not checked on her welfare after the accident despite being in England a score of times—for several months, he had been a courier between Wellington and the government. He shuddered at the memory of how he had coerced her into marriage. She had been exhausted, frightened, and cold. He had picked her up—as he had done so often in her childhood—dusted her off, soothed her fears, and demanded that she marry him. When she hesitated, he had pushed harder, lying instead of explaining. Before she had even had a chance to think, the deed had been done.

He should at least have prepared her for town. London

dowagers were ruthless. And they loved scandal. Of course they would have informed Catherine about his courtship. He had been in the army too long to remember that. But what could he have told her? *I am marrying you despite leading another lady to expect my offer last week.* The facts were too damning. And his treatment of Hermione was dishonorable. Knowing that, Catherine would never believe his protestations that her fortune was unimportant. He intended to put the bulk of it in trust for her, but there was little he could do to convince her that it had been his intention from the first.

Sighing, he downed another brandy and wearily massaged his temples. What had she been doing in the Dark Walk? She blamed it on him and claimed Rathbone was helping her. Neither assertion made sense, but Cat never embellished the truth. There must be something he didn't know.

Sidney Braxton frowned at the letter in his hand. It was from his mother, which was bad enough, for the woman always sent very long missives crammed with complaints and admonitions. But this one was so thick she must be furious.

He broke the seal and moved closer to the lamp, trying to decipher her crabbed writing. As his eye skipped down the page, curses filled the air.

Codicil . . . Ridgway House to Catherine . . . You must come home immediately . . . Your father disappeared . . . Devlin is demanding that we retire to Braxton Manor . . . Do something, Sidney . . . She continued through four crossed and recrossed pages, but he gave up squinting to make out her words. The disaster was worse than he had imagined.

Damn Catherine!

Chapter Fourteen

Catherine spent the next several days trying to escape the trap she had tumbled into. She was married to a man who did not want her. The Damon she had adored for seventeen years was dead. War had turned him into a selfish tyrant, destroying any hope that they could find happiness together.

But what could she do? Annulment was impossible. Without his consent, the church would never agree, and she would lose the inheritance if one was granted. Anything Damon could not keep would revert to Uncle Henry. Thus she had no money. And she had no place to go. Ridgway House now belonged to Damon. She would never be welcome at Braxton Manor. And she could not establish a separate town residence without creating an unforgivable scandal. So she must remain at Devlin House and pretend to be Damon's wife.

How could he have changed so much? Their confrontation haunted her. The old Damon would have told her about the codicil, described her options, and allowed her to decide which one to follow. It was what he had done the summer her favorite horse had to be put down. His trust had meant as much as his sympathy. The new Damon issued orders, offering no explanations and allowing no questions. Yet he expected instant obedience.

Something had to change, but she did not know where to begin. Nor could she discus it with others. Society had already censured them for marrying so quickly. Revealing their reasons could only make it worse. But the future looked grim. Damon was ignoring her, refusing even to exchange greetings. She could feel his regret. And who could blame him? She could never replace Hermione in his heart, a truth that made her feel more useless and degraded than any indignity Dru or Horty had inflicted. He would doubt-less set the lady up as his mistress as soon as she wed. But his wife must pretend that all was well.

"A new rumor is making the rounds," reported Edith as her carriage clattered over the cobblestones into Berkeley Square, heading for their first morning call.

"What now?"

"Specific charges, citing time and place, that accuse you of liaisons with Lord Rathbone, Lord Devereaux, and one of your grooms. The gentlemen are both notorious lib-ertines."

Catherine gasped. "There is not a shred of truth to that! Though Rathbone is an old acquaintance, I have never even met Devereaux."

"I should hope not! He is a dedicated lecher who delights in seducing wives. Few invite him to marriage mart affairs so I doubt you have seen him."

"That should be easy enough to establish then. Louisa accompanies me most evenings and can swear we've not met."

"Don't be a goose, Cat," admonished Edith. "No one in-vites others to an illicit meeting. And Lady Debenham cites your use of a chaperon as proof Lord Devlin doesn't trust you. One must never go out alone, of course, but a matron need take only a maid or footman."

"Then there is nothing to do," she concluded gloomily as the carriage rolled to a halt. "I might as well retire to the country."

"Fustian! It is not like you to give up without a fight."

"How? You said yourself that no one will believe me, so protesting my innocence can do no good."

"We need to go after the author of these stories. Is it Lady Hermione or Mr. Braxton?"

Catherine frowned. Hermione seemed unlikely. Innu-endo was enough to keep Damon's eyes on her, so she would hardly risk lying outright. . . . Sidney also preferred innuendo because details were easy to check—unless Dru or Horty had pushed him into it. They must realize by now that they would never see London. . . . Damon had already accused her of impropriety with Rathbone. Was he planning an annulment? A fortnight of marriage could have made the money look less desirable, and destroying her character might make it easier to obtain one. But if he were naming a second paramour, he surely would have chosen Lord James.

"I have no idea," she told Edith, loath to mention any of these possibilities. The footman pulled open the door and handed them out.

Catherine blinked, as she always did when entering Lady Debenham's relentlessly Egyptian dressing room. Twin caryatids supported a grotesque chimneypiece. Furniture legs terminated in clawed feet while arms ended in animal heads. A sarcophagus lid stood in one corner next to a crocodile settee. She shivered. Even the refreshments carried out the theme, with biscuits shaped like lotus blossoms and shortbread carved into cartouches.

"Lady Devlin!" exclaimed Lady Debenham maliciously. "Just the person I wanted to see."

"My lady." Catherine curtsied to her hostess. "I trust you are well."

"Quite well. Lord Pendleton told me the most astonishing tale this morning."

"Did Lords Oakridge and Seaton fight another duel?" she dared ask.

"That truly would be astonishing," agreed the gossip as several guests tittered. "Oakridge has not yet recovered from the first one. But Pendleton claims that Lord Devlin cheated your family by producing a forgery that assigns him ownership of lands and investments that rightfully belong to Lord Braxton, then threw them off the estate with not a feather to fly with."

"What a twisted tale!" declared Catherine, forcing herself to laugh into those predatory eyes. Sidney's hand was obvious, for Pendleton was one of his friends. "Someone's imagination is certainly working overtime. My father's will left me everything not entailed, including the estate on which we lived. My uncle—who was my trustee as well as my guardian—has been managing Ridgway House for me—you must agree that it is not a job I could have handled myself. Now that Damon has assumed the responsibility, Uncle Henry is free to return to his own estate."

"I suppose someone heard of the move and imputed sinister motives to it," put in Edith with a shake of her head.

"Sidney Braxton," announced Lady Beatrice from the doorway. "He started that tale last night, out of spite I've no doubt."

"Perhaps he did not know the details of the late baron's will," suggested Lady Debenham, resigned to seeing her tale quashed. "He was only a boy when his father acceded to the title."

"Fustian!" said Lady Beatrice. "Malicious lies are an integral part of his character, as you should recognize. I had a most illuminating talk with Lady Hawthorne—she has known the Braxton family all her life. Sidney has ever been a troublemaker and he bears long-standing grudges against both Lord and Lady Devlin."

Catherine opened her mouth to protest this washing of her family linen in public, but Lady Beatrice's eyes and Edith's elbow kept her silent.

"What crime did they commit against the poor boy?" asked Lady Debenham, ranging herself on Sidney's side.

"Not a thing," swore Lady Beatrice. "But he envied their friendship, so he did everything possible to get them in trouble, including deliberately damaging property and then blaming them."

"Lady Hawthorne exaggerates," declared Catherine desperately. "There was no evidence that Sidney was responsible for either cutting down the yew hedge or starting the stable fire. Visiting us was always frustrating for him, for there was no one his own age to play with. I am two years his elder and the boys another five beyond that."

"Was he an only child then?" asked Lady Horseley.

"Not at all," responded Lady Beatrice, forcing a nod of agreement from Catherine before continuing. "His mother and sisters never visited Ridgway House."

"They were always welcome," insisted Cat. "But my aunt is not a good traveler."

"Nonsense!" snapped Lady Beatrice. "I applaud your loyalty, my lady—especially in the face of their antagonism—but the truth must be told. Your aunt is a schemer who forced your uncle into marriage despite her common origins. I remember the scandal quite clearly."

This announcement drew exclamations from the younger matrons and resulted in the baring of Eugenia's birth and character. Though the disclosures hurt Sidney more than herself, Catherine could not help feeling ashamed. More than anything, she wanted to line up every member of society and scream at them to stop—stop vilifying her family; stop accusing her of immoral behavior; stop talking about her altogether. They had everything wrong, for she and Hermione were both innocent victims, and Damon was not the poor deluded target of some malicious plot. But her time was up, and she had to leave.

The factual portion of the day's gossip was good news. Her uncle had been told to move, so she need never see him again. With a better master, Ridgway was capable of producing a good income. She had several ideas for restoring its prosperity, but Damon was no longer talking to her.

If only they could retire to the country! Then maybe they could rediscover their old friendship and find some way to live together in peace away from the gossips who were driving them farther apart each day. And perhaps the tranquility of Devlin Court would allow Damon to finally set the war behind him and heal. Her heart bled for him every time she had to shake him out of a nightmare. How could he live with such horror?

Damon threaded his way through the crowd in Hyde Park, pulling to a stop next to Hermione. "Would you ride with me?" he asked. The question was rhetorical, for he was here by appointment. He had run into her on Bond Street the day before, to be met with a teary-eyed tale of how Lady Marchgate had just cut her because he had ignored her for two days. And so he had agreed to visit her box at the opera and to meet her in the park the next afternoon. But his temper was far from congenial. She was thwarting his efforts to ease her back into the marriage mart. She had been so obviously glad to see him at the opera that her escort had visibly abandoned all interest in her. Even her normally doting parents had looked askance on her performance. He was beginning to believe that her continuing problems with society arose more from her behavior than his own.

"How kind of you!" she exclaimed now, bidding a laughing good-bye to the gentlemen who had been flirting with her moments before. Her groom fell in behind them. Perhaps he had overreacted at the opera. Her manner today was everything proper.

"Your credit has improved, I see."

"Hardly. Those two are bores, but I must either pretend to enjoy their sallies or remain alone, thus reminding all the world of your perfidy."

"Enough!"

She turned tearful eyes toward him. "Forgive me, Damon. I should not vent my irritation on you. This is no more your fault than mine, and it must be horridly difficult. You cannot like hearing talk of Lady Devlin's affairs and speculation about where she and Rathbone will next appear."

"I said enough," he growled through clenched teeth. "My wife is not your concern. You will cease this constant harping and turn your mind to bettering your own position or I will wash my hands of you."

She gasped, her eyes glittering in anger. "Are you so blind that you cannot see what she is doing to you, or do you not care that your name is becoming a byword? I would think that any man would take steps to keep so unsuitable a wife away from society!"

"You overstep propriety, my lady, in every way. Good day!" Damon wheeled Pythias and cantered down a side road, leaving an open-mouthed Hermione behind. Damn Catherine for inspiring talk. And damn Hermione for repeating it! He cursed himself for providing yet another tale for the tattlebaskets—at least thirty people must have witnessed his abrupt departure.

He was about to return and apologize when he spotted Catherine in a perch phaeton with Lord James. His fingers clenched the reins. What would it take to convince her that only discretion would defeat the rumors? The dandy was far too attentive. As was that cur, Rathbone.

Catherine laughed, her silky voice clear above the din, her face lighting as he had not seen it in years. She was beautiful, clad in a stylish blue carriage dress and matching pelisse. Her black curls peeked out from a frivolous bonnet, reminding him of how soft they had been that night in Cumberland.

But another memory erased the scene—violet eyes flashing fire as she accused him of being a fortune hunter. Turning his back on the cream of society, he left the park.

Catherine tamed her laugh into a smile. "Rogue!" she charged Lord James.

"Hardly, but I had to do something to ease your gloom, even if it lasts only a moment."

"Thank you—I think." Another carriage passed with barely a nod from its occupants. She sighed.

"Your cousin has been busy."

"True, though what he hopes to gain from his latest lies is unclear. There is no question about the validity of my father's will."

"So I thought," he agreed. "But then I know his methods. Many do not. If his claims prompt an investigation, he expects Lord Devlin to buy his silence."

"He does not know Damon if he believes such fustian. And he cannot have read the will. It was written just after my brother bought colors against Papa's wishes. Anyone who met Papa during the next two months heard the identical tirade. He made no effort to hide his ire. My uncle would have questioned it eight years ago had he suspected its validity. Sidney hasn't a hope of legal recourse, and Damon is not one to shirk a battle, whatever the stakes."

Further talk was delayed when Lady Sommersby stopped to chat. She was succeeded by Lady Beatrice—who made a point of enjoying Catherine's company—and by Colonel Caldwell. They had just bid him farewell when Lady Hermione approached. Catherine braced herself, but Hermione's eyes darkened in fury and she rode by without a word.

"The cut direct," marveled Lord James, sounding pleased.

"I wonder why. She usually delights in barbs and setdowns." Catherine was more shaken than she wished to admit. Hermione's spite was becoming more overt, as was her possessiveness toward Damon, who was living in her pocket. This cut felt as though it had been delivered by Damon himself.

"I doubt that was aimed at you," consoled Lord James. "Lady Hermione is still a spoiled and willful child, but she will mature into a charming lady."

The truth was staring Catherine in the face. "She is the one you love? You poor man!"

"The situation is looking brighter," he countered. "She is inordinately jealous because you have stolen two of her beaux."

She stared as if she had never seen him before. "What a despicable cad! You used me! You two deserve each other, for neither of you can see beyond your own selfish whims. Don't you understand that you have increased her spite? But what do you care? What are a few more rumors when set against so many?" Tears trembled in her eyes.

Lord James pulled into a nearly deserted side road and drew his horses to a halt. "Dear Lord! I never intended to harm you, Lady Devlin. Yes, I used you—I admitted as much at the masquerade. And I misjudged how far Hermione would carry her pique. But I have never condoned the rumors and have worked to expose them as lies, as anyone in town can attest."

"No one believes the protestations of a man many consider my lover," she replied with brutal honesty.

He paled. "No one sees me in that light! Admittedly there are tales of liaisons that name you, but I have never figured in them."

That explained Devereaux, realized Catherine. Hermione would never admit that one of her suitors had defected, so she substituted Devereaux for Lord James. She sighed, motioning him to resume their drive. They were bound to cause new talk if they remained in serious conversation, but she was curious about what had happened.

"Did she turn you down?" she asked as they approached the horse guard barracks.

He sighed. "I first met Hermione last fall. She was exactly what I want in a wife—beautiful, intelligent, and accomplished. We both prefer London to the country. She will make an outstanding society hostess. If I accept one of my father's seats in the Commons, she will make an even better political hostess. Her only fault is conceit—a tendency fostered by adoring parents who deny her nothing."

"Not an uncommon situation among well-born beauties," agreed Catherine with a sigh.

"Unfortunately. But she will outgrow it once she is removed from their influence. After all, she is barely eighteen. We get along well and I believe she cares for me, but she was not ready to settle for someone lacking a title—there are too many brothers and nephews between me and the marquessate to ever consider the possibility; I was eleventh in line at last count. I spent Christmas with her family, hoping to press my suit, but her cousin brought Devlin home. In her youthful naiveté, she could not see beyond his title. The fact that he was a war hero added another cachet."

"Yet you still love her."

"I cannot help it, and she does not have deep feelings for Devlin. I hoped that jealousy might turn her eyes back to me. After all, he is out of reach and they have little in common. He will spend most of his life on his estate. I doubt even the pleading of a beautiful wife could change that."

"True. He can be exceedingly stubborn."

"Her actions confirm that she is upset by my apparent change of heart. She will begin to examine her options any day now. Her tantrum over Devlin's defection—for that is what prompted her attempt to hurt you—will no longer seem necessary, at which point I will return to pick up the pieces of her broken fantasies. In the meantime, a little competition could awaken Devlin to the treasure he holds."

"Don't count on it. Damon is not the sort to be taken in by games. He is more likely to suspect you of seducing me in retaliation for stealing Hermione's affections. He will harden his heart and swear he doesn't care. I have no fondness for games myself, Lord James. And I do not believe in manipulating people, for it sets all parties up for disaster. You have already goaded Lady Hermione into increased vitriol, destroyed whatever trust Damon had in my judgment, and damaged my reputation and your own—despite men's claims to your face, your name is indeed linked with mine. It is time to call a halt. I wish you luck, of course, but in trying to force Damon to abandon Hermione you failed to consider that he truly loves her."

"Then why did he marry you?"

"Not for any reason society has suggested, and it is not relevant to this discussion."

"But he cannot know Hermione if he believes she would suit."

"Enough! You do not know everything either. Love does not conform to logic." She deliberately turned the conversation to neutral topics until he returned her to Devlin House. Damon was out, which was the first good news she had received all day.

"What is this?" demanded Catherine, bursting into Damon's study the next afternoon.

"It would appear to be the *Times*."

"How dare you sell my home!" she hissed.

"What would we want with a second house so near our own?" he countered sharply. "You seem to forget that your home is now Devlin."

"Devlin will never be my home!"

"Devlin will be your home for the rest of your life. Like it or not, we are married."

"Selfish brute! You care only for yourself, don't you? It matters not that I have lived all my life at Ridgway or that the tenants have been dependent on my family for generations. All you want is to reduce my inheritance to cash as quickly as possible so that you can indulge in your own affairs."

"The tenants are not the issue," he declared. "I have already instructed my steward to see after them. Whatever improvements are needed will be completed within the month. But I have no need for another house. Your aunt will be gone next week. Whatever personal effects you wish to keep will be transferred to Devlin."

"I see." She stared as if seeing him for the first time. "You will remove all trace that Ridgway House ever existed—strip away the farms, then sell the park to some jumped-up cit to use as his country residence. How dictatorial you have become, my lord. It never even occurred to you that I might like a say in the disposition of my own property."

"Catherine—"

But she interrupted. "Of course, it is not my property, is it? I have no rights in the matter at all."

"Surely you must agree that it is ridiculous to keep two houses so close to each other. Why would you want the house to sit empty? If you love it so much, you should be glad that someone will be using it."

"I am not stupid, Damon. You would never have inserted this particular advertisement if the goal was only to sell the house. 'Late Elizabethan park and manor both in need of considerable renovation or replacement . . .' Even the most hen-witted simpleton can see that you wish to destroy all trace of Ridgway. Why would you do so unless you feel guilty about stealing my inheritance and want to remove any reminders?"

Damon paled. "It is not like that at all," he protested. "I never considered it in that light."

"Of course not. I am such a worthless impediment that my feelings don't count, and you have become so hard a man that embarrassment must be alien to your nature."

Her bitter voice cut deeply into his heart, severing the last vestiges of control. "Damn it, Catherine! Why must you pick fights every time we meet?"

"I? Since when is asking questions about my own affairs considered picking a fight? Perhaps it would have been better if you had died in Spain. You have changed so much I can't believe you are the same man. The Damon I grew up with would never have run roughshod over me this way. Have I had a voice in one thing that has happened since you returned? Have you told me anything? Your every action has been calculated to show me how little you care. Yet you accuse me of picking fights."

"What am I to do?" he moaned to himself, on the verge of collapse. Everything he did was wrong. He was so tired of carrying the burdens alone. If only Peter were here to josh him out of this mood. But Peter was gone. Forever. He laid his head in his hands and fought back tears.

Horrified at his reaction, Catherine tentatively touched his shoulder. "Damon?"

Her soft voice was the last straw. He broke into choking sobs.

"What is wrong, Damon?" she murmured, her own tears close to falling. She gathered him into her arms so that he could sob against her shoulder. It was a familiar position, though usually it was her crying on him. One hand gently brushed back his hair.

"I can't do it, Cat," he choked. "I can't keep Ridgway. He is there. Everywhere. It is bad enough at Devlin."

"Peter." Sudden understanding broke. There had been a bond between Damon and her brother that defied comprehension. Too wrapped up in her own grief, she had never really considered how Peter's death would have affected him.

He nodded, his arms closing around her back. Sobs tore from his throat, convulsing him until she feared he would crush her. Dizziness nearly overwhelmed her as everything she thought she knew burst apart, settling into new patterns. Gone was the demigod. Gone was the lionhearted protector and omnipotent mentor. She was left comforting a man broken from years of experiences too horrible to endure and burdens too heavy to carry.

"I can't stand Ridgway," he continued soberly once his sobs finally ceased. "Perhaps if it changes enough, he will no longer haunt me."

"I don't believe that, Damon," she countered. "And neither do you. Peter is gone. You have to come to grips with that, and the fastest way to do it is to go there and confront him."

"You are naive." He pushed her away.

"And you are blind. I had to live there after he died,

Damon. Day after day. Week after week. For nearly eight years. Perhaps your bond was stronger than mine, but not by much. He was everywhere—riding through the park, laughing in the gallery, fishing in the stream, flirting with the gatekeeper's daughter, and doing a host of other things. I wanted to die to escape the constant agony—my God, I must have seen the two of you riding off to war a thousand times—but eventually it grew easier. I can now relax in the clearing because I have made peace with him."

"Catherine—"

"Try it, Damon. If he is haunting you, then you must find out why. Perhaps it is guilt over that idiotic vow. Or it may be something else about which I know nothing. But he will not depart until you reconcile with him and with yourself. The house is irrelevant, and I really do not want to sell it."

"I will think about it," he conceded finally.

"Thinking is a start, but you also need to talk. And not just about Peter. The war still bedevils your mind. You often shout when in your nightmares, so I know you are troubled by memories of Badajoz and Waterloo." She laid a comforting hand on his shoulder.

Damon opened his mouth to send her away, but found himself describing the last eight years instead—the horror of war; battles fought; friends who died; even atrocities he had seen. She listened, asking pertinent questions and sharing his shock and pain. But soon his narrative changed, dwelling now on humorous events, things that Peter would have included in letters to brighten her day. He was amazed, for he had never paid attention to such things himself. Now he described the goat that had pulled down a clothesline and paraded around camp with a lady's corset dangling from one horn; the contest Tucker had arranged with other batmen to see who could concoct the most savory stew, and the lengths they had gone to to top one another; the stray dog that had adopted his regiment, performing the most amazing tricks in exchange for food; and many more. His voice lightened, their laughter filling the library, creating an atmosphere he had not experienced since Peter had died.

*   *   *

Damon stared at his empty desktop long after Catherine left. Something had changed. He had not realized how dictatorial he had become, and he did not like the image Cat's angry words had painted, but that was not what held him frozen in place. He had last cried after Vimeiro. It would have been better if he had not broken down, but the incident had produced one positive result. Catherine had neither condemned him nor spurned him, instead abandoning her tirade to comfort him. Their discussion left him feeling better than he had felt in years. Perhaps the future was not as bleak as he had imagined. And he had one more hope— Cat had felt good in his arms.

Chapter Fifteen

Fog clung to the trees and whispered along the grass as Catherine turned through the gates of Hyde Park. These early-morning rides were the only time of the day when she could truly relax. Pegasus was another benefit of her marriage. Damon had purchased the gelding the day after they had arrived in London. He was a perfect steed, spirited and powerful yet biddable enough that she had no qualms about her rusty skills, for she had done little riding since Uncle Henry sold her father's stable. Though he had replaced the horses with his own sorry slugs, there had been no mount for her.

Pushing Pegasus to a canter, she pounded past the Serpentine. Other riders were also out for morning exercise, but she recognized no one through the mist. When she pulled Pegasus back to allow the horse to cool, dampness seeped through the heavy wool of her habit, chilling her to the bone. She probably should have stayed home.

An errant breeze swept the fog aside, providing a clear view of the copse a hundred yards ahead. Deep in conversation, Damon and Hermione rode side by side, Hermione's hand resting intimately on his arm.

Catherine gasped, nearly crying out, but the fog closed in so swiftly she could not be sure that she had seen them. Perhaps her mind was playing tricks on her. Damon had not mentioned taking morning rides and she had never seen him here before. But that meant nothing.

She had expected their frank discussion to reinstate their former openness, but he obviously did not share that delusion. Did he regret his moment of weakness? That would explain his refusal to escort her to the opera last night. His breakdown might even make things worse, for he would despise his loss of control. Hermione played the helpless innocent to perfection—just the act to restore his confidence.

"Damn them both," she muttered viciously, then jerked Pegasus to a halt as pain knifed her chest. Pegasus turned a reproachful eye on his rider, but she ignored him. The wretched truth left her breathless. She was in love with her husband. Again.

How humiliating. And how stupid! Seething with frustration, she headed for the gates.

She had first fallen in love with him the year she was fourteen. He had come home from school looking more handsome than ever, his broad face, amber eyes, and tawny locks sending chills down her spine. Unlike many young men, he did not turn his back on those he considered children, continuing to offer help and advice—which she had sorely needed that year, for she had been experiencing an awkward growth spurt. Her parents had had eyes only for each other, and Peter was off in the clouds with no time to waste on her. But Damon was always there—her advisor, her friend, and her great protector. She had kept her feelings secret, knowing even then that he would never return them. She was merely his little sister, someone to be alternately comforted and ignored. And her love had been uneasy, almost as if it really were incestuous.

It had faded, of course. By the following summer she was hopelessly infatuated with Sir Mortimer's son, Toby. The next year it had been Lord Rathbone, who had spent several weeks on Toby's estate. By the time Damon bought colors, he was again her stalwart older brother, and she hardly recalled her love.

He had retained that status. His return to Devlin Court and the way he rescued her from Braxton Manor echoed their lifelong relationship as he comforted her fears and soothed away her pain. How stupid of her to allow her feelings to grow beyond the bounds he had always set. Despite marriage, nothing had really changed. She was still the hoyden whom he allowed to tag along at his heels.

Her outburst the day she had found the codicil had been shameful. If she had been allowed time to absorb the shock, she could have discussed the situation rationally. Instead, she had given her temper free rein and killed even his brotherly affection, forcing him more firmly toward Hermione. Even yesterday's rapport was unreal. She had indeed been naive. Thoughts of Peter had shattered his composure. He must have confused the time and place, turning to her as he would formerly have turned to him. It was but a momentary aberration that meant nothing.

Pegasus suddenly jumped straight into the air and twisted completely around, exploding into a jolting gallop the moment he hit the ground. Caught by surprise, Catherine tried to hang on, but her balance had been too badly compromised. Her leg slipped off the horn, throwing her into the air.

Tuck your head and roll, ordered her father's groom. *Land on your feet,* yelled Peter. *It will hurt less if you relax,* advised Damon as he plucked her out of a hedge on her eighth birthday.

Her hip slammed against the horn, jerking her other foot loose from the stirrup. *Tuck! Feet! Relax!* She tried to relax and twist her legs under her, but before she could do more than think about it, she hit the ground. Pain exploded through her head and the world went black.

"Where is that damned carriage?" demanded a harsh voice.

"It cain't possibly get here yet, sir," protested her groom.

She tried to move, but failed. Was she dead? Yet this hardly sounded like heaven. A lurid course burned her ears before the first voice continued.

"Of course. It has been barely ten minutes."

Colonel Caldwell, she identified groggily. He sounded less in control than she would have expected of a Wellington aide. Fingers gently prodded her head.

"At least nothing is broken."

"Who would do such an 'orrid thing?" demanded the groom.

"You are sure it was a dart?"

"Look." A tense silence followed. "I found it on the ground just where 'er 'orse spooked. An' there's an 'ole in 'is flank. I saw nobody, but we was by them trees, so there was ample place to 'ide.''

"Do you really believe that someone hid in the trees, waiting for Lady Devlin to pass so that they could cause an accident?" asked the colonel incredulously.

"Could be. We ride 'ere most every day at just this time—even when it rains. 'Er ladyship loves t'exercise.''

The argument continued above Catherine's head, but she was no longer listening. Her head throbbed as new pains joined those already holding her motionless. Damon. There had been two people by that copse—her husband and the woman he wanted to wed. She would never have believed that he would stoop to murder, but she had misjudged him more than once. The Damon who had returned from the Peninsula was a harsher man than the boy she had known. And he was inured to death. How many people had he killed in the last eight years? To have achieved his heroic stature, the number must be high. One more would hardly matter.

Blackness returned, spiraling her into unconsciousness.

The next time she awoke, she was in her own bed in Berkeley Square.

"Thank the good Lord!" Brigit exclaimed, rushing to offer a drink to her mistress. "Lord Devlin will be relieved. He's been frantic about you."

Right! she scoffed silently, gagging on the bitter liquid as the details of her morning ride returned. "How long have I been here?"

"Most of the day. It's nearly dinnertime. I must tell his lordship that you are awake."

"No!" She struggled to sit up, but pain forced her back. Brigit squeaked in alarm.

"You will tell him nothing," said Catherine more calmly. "And you will not allow him in this room. He caused my accident. His anxiety is because the fall did not kill me."

"You are delirious, my lady."

"Not at all. My groom knows that a man in the copse of trees we were passing deliberately tried to harm me. I saw Lord Devlin in that copse. How badly am I hurt?"

"Nothing is broken. You have a badly bruised hip, a concussion from landing on your head, and a cut on your thigh where the horse kicked you. And you were unconscious so long the doctor had to bleed you. It will be a week before you can rise."

Catherine groaned.

"He left some powders to help the pain."

"Good. I cannot think clearly right now, but promise me that you will admit no one to this room. And make sure you personally pick up my trays in the kitchen."

"If you insist," agreed Brigit doubtfully.

Catherine took one of the powders and slipped back into sleep.

"She what?" demanded Damon.

"She believes you caused her accident," repeated Brigit. In a few words, she told him Catherine's tale.

"Surely she knows me better than that!" he snapped before bringing his voice under control. The maid looked terrified. "She is wrong, of course, but I will not annoy her. It is more important that she rest and recover in peace."

"Thank you, my lord."

"You will keep me informed of her progress."

"Of course."

Once Brigit left, Damon paced furiously around his study. His initial reaction was to strangle her for suspecting him of so base an action, but he had to admit that the evidence was damning. And what had really happened?

He had been riding in the park, trying to figure out what to do about Ridgway in light of Catherine's opposition to selling the place. So intent was he on his thoughts that he almost missed Hermione's greeting. He had stopped to talk to her—it could not have been for more than a minute—then left her by the copse and continued on his way. The news of Cat's accident had greeted him on his return home. It was his first hint that she had been in the park.

Who would wish to harm her? While there were plenty of people who might be irritated at her—starting with her family and Hermione, he had to admit—none of them had a sufficient grievance to justify an attack. There had been incidents in recent years of violence against the aristocracy, but he did not believe it in this case. Women were rarely the target.

But perhaps it was aimed at him. Could someone hate him enough to strike at him by injuring his wife? Hardly. He had always retained the respect of his men. In fact, the losses among his own troops were lower than in other battalions, something his men were inordinately proud of, for they had seen just as much action and been through just as desperate a fight. His estates had been well run in his absence, so his tenants had no complaints. It was true that he had instituted some changes on his return, but most had been suggested by the tenants themselves, who were better educated than most and proud to be keeping up with new techniques.

Aside from his neglect of Catherine, the only toes he had trampled were those of Lord Braxton. His marriage had thwarted the man's plots. But Braxton had fled the country and Sidney's pique had been lessening in recent days.

He would have to talk to Jack. The colonel had come upon Catherine almost before she hit the ground, sending his own groom racing to Berkeley Square to fetch a carriage. He might have seen who else was in the vicinity. And he must talk to Hermione. The culprit could have passed her while making his escape.

Catherine shifted to a more comfortable position.

"Let me rearrange those pillows," offered Edith, already performing this service. "You look a little peaked."

"I should not. There is nothing wrong with me outside of a few bruises."

She had relaxed her orders when Edith called, admitting that boredom was a larger enemy than her unknown assailant. She had not revealed the cause of the accident, claiming that Pegasus had spooked in the fog. Part of her reticence arose from ambivalence. Though the evidence pointed to Damon's guilt, she could not really accept it. Her injuries had led to two days of feverish delirium that made it difficult to separate fact from fantasy. Surely not even war could change him that much! She knew him better than any other living person. Could she have been so wrong in her estimation of his character?

"Lady Jersey's rout last night was quite exciting," reported Edith, settling back into a chair.

"An exciting rout?" quizzed Catherine. "Surely not!"

"Exciting," repeated her friend. "Everyone was buzzing with the latest news of Brummell."

"What did he do now? Make up his quarrel with the Prince?"

"Never! After three years, neither of them would consider it. But you know that Brummell has been plunging very deep of late."

"True."

"Well, two nights ago he admitted defeat, leaving the theater during the first intermission to slip away to France. They say he owes thirty thousand pounds."

"Good heavens!"

"His fall has prompted the younger bucks to cease imitating him."

"And just as well. None of them approach his flair."

"True. The best-dressed gentlemen set their own styles. But Brummell's departure was not the most thrilling event of the evening. Miss Josephine Huntsley returned to town, making her first public appearance in years."

Catherine frowned. "The name is not familiar. Should I know her?"

"I forgot that you were not here. She first came out in 1810, proving to be the most inept, unprepared disaster I have ever witnessed. She was barely seventeen at the time and had no training as far as I could tell. Frankly, I cannot imagine how Lady Jersey came to invite the girl to her rout, for she had long since banned her from Almack's. It was what drove her from town."

"The poor thing."

"Save your sympathy. That was the final caper of a week of shocking behavior. She was so clumsy that she routinely knocked things down, including at least one gentleman in the middle of a country dance. She managed to ruin six gowns and three of Weston's jackets by tipping over a punch bowl and spattering everyone nearby. And somehow

she tore her own gown so badly on Bond Street that she
was bare from ground to bosom."

Catherine stared.

"Yes, shocking. I am amazed that her parents allowed
her near London. They must have known of her problem. It
is even more amazing that she is back."

"Has she improved in the interim?"

"Not that I noticed. Her father has doubled her dowry,
but even the fortune hunters shy away. Who would accept
so disastrous a wife? After bumping into Lord Hartford, she
staggered into the Countess Lieven, ripping the flounce half
off the lady's gown."

"Dear Lord. She's a patroness!"

"Precisely. But instead of apologizing, Miss Huntsley
fled the scene, knocking over a pedestal supporting what
used to be a priceless Chinese vase. Then she tripped,
falling down the stairs and taking four ladies and two gentlemen with her. Lady Haliston will be confined with a
twisted ankle for at least a week."

"Gracious! Is she really that clumsy or is she so terrified
of making a spectacle of herself that she does just that?"

"Who knows? But the resulting talk drove all earlier gossip from everyone's minds."

Something in Edith's voice put Catherine on her guard.
"What were the earlier tales?"

"There are hints that Lord Devlin was responsible for
your accident."

"What?" Catherine's mind raced. She doubted that the
servants had repeated her suspicions. They were loyal to
Damon and would never do anything to hurt him. Damon
would certainly not voice the thought. "That is preposterous!" she said now, automatically jumping to his defense.
Whatever the truth, she would not fuel rumors.

"Of course it is," Edith agreed. "But you need to be
aware of the stories. He would not be the first to be ruined
by innuendo."

They spoke no more of it and Edith left a short time
later. Catherine remained deep in thought. Perhaps someone had witnessed the attack but did not dare speak up—a
servant, for example. But if Damon was innocent, the tale

was another attempt to cause trouble. It could only have come from the culprit. Those who had been nearby— Colonel Caldwell and Lady Hermione—would never spread such stories.

Damon had also heard the rumor, likewise refusing to believe that his servants were responsible. Even Brigit considered him innocent. But that bolstered his theory that someone was striking at him through Catherine. The only credible culprit was Lord Braxton. Had the man returned?

He needed answers before Catherine left her sickbed. Protecting her was impossible if he did not know who threatened her. He waited until he and Jack were walking toward Berkeley Square after an evening at White's, then laid out his fears and lack of evidence.

"I suspect Lord Braxton may have pushed Sidney into recklessness," he concluded. "Sidney is too harebrained to concoct these stories and too cowardly to act on his own."

"Do not be too sure of that," countered Jack. "His friends are very crafty, and he has learned much from them. More than once they have lured cubs into scandal, then agreed to hush it up in exchange for a generous settlement."

"Damn! Why did you not tell me about this before?"

"I thought you knew. Sidney's reputation has never been good."

"I had no idea. You know I avoid town as much as possible. But what was Braxton about to let his heir fall in with a set of sharps?"

"I suspect he didn't care."

Damon stared at his friend, his mind racing. "That might explain that very odd caller at Harte's office two days after—"

Two men jumped out of the alley leading to the mews. Both brandished knives. The fight was brief, but intense. Damon's walking stick sent one weapon clattering to the ground. Jack managed to twist the other loose and hurl it into some shrubbery. Ignoring the gentlemanly tactics taught at Jackson's saloon, the two military men waded in and soon had the thugs on the run.

"You're hurt," observed Damon once he caught his breath.

"It's only a scratch." Jack was already tying up his left arm. "The cutpurses and footpads get bolder every year. Where is the damned watch?"

"You know the Charlies are worthless against scum like that," Damon reminded him. "But I doubt that pair will be back. Come in and let Tucker look at that arm." He led the way into Devlin House. "And that's an order."

"At once, Major Fairbourne, Lord Devlin, sir!" barked Jack, saluting smartly.

"You forgot *retired,* Jack."

"And you forgot that I outrank you. I ought to call you out for insubordination."

Laughing, they headed for the library.

What was Sidney up to now? wondered Damon. Jack's disclosures had shocked him more than he had admitted, putting a different complexion on the problem. Was Sidney stupid enough to believe that Catherine's inheritance would revert to her family if she died without issue? Or was he trying to extort money?

He pulled out his solicitor's report on Sidney's finances. The boy was deeply indebted to moneylenders, with no chance of covering even the interest. He had already received two warnings. The next step would be a beating. To make matters worse, he had recently dropped a bundle in Watier's and another at a hell on South Audley. He must be growing desperate.

But Sidney was not the only problem. Though Damon had traced the most vicious tales to Cat's cousin, others arose elsewhere. One had originated with Lady Debenham, but he could not believe so canny a lady would risk multiple fabrications. Thus he had another enemy whom he had not yet identified.

Chapter Sixteen

True to his word, the doctor kept Catherine in bed for the full week. The moment he let her up, she sent for Louisa, determined to resume her social schedule and try to deflect the gossip that had burgeoned in recent days. Some even charged that Damon had locked her up, then fabricated a tale of injuries to hide that fact. Edith had laughed at the cub who had made that claim, but those who loved scandal preferred lies to the truth. So she would attend the Cunningham ball and brave the dance floor despite the bruises on her hip and thigh. Lady Cunningham's entertainments were always sad crushes, hosting the cream of London society.

Like so many balls, this one was held in rented facilities, for only the largest homes could host such a gathering. But the decorations were opulent—banks of flowers and ferns; silk swagged around the walls; extra lamps augmenting the elaborate chandeliers; and even statuary and paintings brought in from the Cunningham residence. People surged in an ever-shifting mob, greeting friends and exchanging *on-dits,* their voices drawling in bored affectation. Jewels sparkled, gold and silver embroidery glittered, and eyes glowed.

The day had been warm with a thick mass of sooty air blanketing the city, allowing London's stench to creep into Mayfair. The press of humanity in the ballroom added new smells that assaulted her nose: Lord Oldport's heavy musk failed to mask the fact that he never washed; Lady Enderly's cloying rosewater nearly obscured Miss Bentley's delicate lavender—really!—the woman must bathe in perfume, for she smelled like a courtesan; Lord Forley's sandalwood fought with Lord Hartleigh's spice as they argued over government reform; Lord Fantail minced past wearing an entire summer flower garden; and the refreshment room exhaled delectable aromas to entice the throng.

Music swirled as Catherine plunged into the conversation, accepting congratulations on her recovery and ignoring the sarcasm that underlay many of the voices. "It was my own fault for riding in the fog," she explained many times. "Pegasus shied at a ghostly image—I think it was that odd-shaped shrub where the carriage road veers away from the Serpentine. Fortunately neither of us suffered any lasting harm." She then deftly deflected the subject to Brummell and other *on-dits*. Miss Huntsley's accidents always made humorous telling.

"You look much better tonight," observed Edith when they managed to find each other.

"And feel better," agreed Catherine with a smile.

"Lady Beatrice and Lady Debenham had the most amazing argument this afternoon—or as near an argument as either of those stiff-rumped gabsters would condone in public. Lady Beatrice's cutting tongue neatly sliced Lady Debenham to ribbons, but Lady Debenham was not cowed. She used the most saccharine tones to imply that Lady Beatrice's advanced age made it difficult to see what was under her nose."

"Good heavens! What was it about?"

Edith sighed. "You, I fear, which took some of the delight from the scene—they were standing in Lady Marchgate's drawing room in front of twenty witnesses. Lady Debenham laps up every foul tale Lady Hermione tells. Her determination has pushed Lady Beatrice into supporting you more stoutly than I could have imagined, for she deplores any hint that her judgment is lacking."

"As do we all. And I can only bless Lady Debenham. If she had not put Lady Beatrice's back up, I would doubtless be home by now with no hope of returning."

They shook their heads over the vagaries of fate and turned their discussion to clothes. Louisa left them when Sir Thomas Morehead arrived. She rarely remained at Catherine's side, for matrons did not need the constant supervision necessary for young innocents.

"Did you finally admit that you had milked your injuries

long enough, cousin?" asked Sidney, joining them as soon as Louisa was out of earshot.

He is deliberately courting a public fight, Cat warned herself. "Still in town, cousin?" she retorted. "A dutiful son would be helping his family."

"They have no need of my assistance," he lied. "A dutiful niece would thank us for eight years of support instead of turning us out in the cold."

"You forget that we were living on my estate, supported by my income," she riposted softly. "Shall we make that fact public?"

His face slipped into a scowl. "We will discuss your delusions later. Partner me for this country set."

"I have already promised it." It was not a lie. Mr. Johnstone arrived at that moment and she joined the dancers.

Two sets later she was finally relaxing. After several sessions with a dancing master, she no longer had to worry about the steps, allowing her to converse with her partners, particularly during waltzes and quadrilles. Lord Rathbone was regaling her with *on-dits.*

"Miss Huntsley is growing worse, poor thing."

"I heard she made a cake of herself again," she agreed.

"In Lady Horselcy's drawing room this morning. She had barely arrived when she bumped into a footman, knocking a tray of pastries into Princess Esterhazy's lap." He whirled her through a dizzying turn.

"So she has now insulted yet another Almack's patroness. Are there any left?"

"I don't think she has done anything to Lady Sefton, but Miss Huntsley must know her situation is hopeless. She succumbed to hysterics on the spot. It took two footmen to carry her from the room."

Catherine sighed in commiseration, though there was nothing that anyone could do. Society did not condone deviation from its rules.

The dancers shifted, offering a glimpse of Damon across the room. She had not spoken to him since the attack and had not known he was at the ball. He was unusually handsome tonight, his deep wine jacket making his hair and eyes appear lighter. Or maybe it was the laughter that lit his face as he twirled Lady Hermione. She had not seen him so carefree since before Portugal.

"Lady Haskell told me the most farcical story this morning," Rathbone said as the music came to a close.

She responded automatically to a ridiculous tale involving twin boys, a dog, and a monkey, but she would have wagered anything that he had sensed her plummeting spirits and was trying to jolly her out of a fit of blue-devils. It wasn't working. As she laughed at the havoc wrought in Lady Haskell's drawing room, her voice sounded forced even to herself.

She did better in the next set, flirting lightly with Lord Hartford, but her mind was contemplating her bleak future. Living with a man who preferred someone else would never work. It had been bad enough when she merely considered him a friend. Now that she loved him, it was intolerable. But what choice did she have?

Two more sets passed before Louisa finally deflected her chaotic thoughts. She looked like a cat who had been at the cream. "What happened?" Catherine demanded the moment her partner left. "Did you give Lady Debenham the set-down you have been swallowing for the past month?"

Louisa actually giggled. "No. The poor woman will get plenty of them from Lady Beatrice when the truth emerges."

"Then why the smirk? Have you been snatching kisses in the garden?" she asked facetiously, then widened her eyes as Louisa blushed. "Heavens! You have!"

"No!" protested Louisa, but her color deepened. "I just wanted you to be the first to know that I accepted Sir Thomas's offer. The announcement will be in tomorrow's papers."

Catherine shared her pleasure. Louisa had been widowed nearly twenty years before, following a ten-year marriage that had produced no children. It was too late to rectify that, but at least she would no longer live in lonely solitude. The news lightened Catherine's spirits for a while, but it did not last. Her own future promised a full measure of loneliness.

An hour later her face was stiff from her forced smile. Her hip throbbed in pain. Lord Forley claimed a waltz, but she lost track of his conversation when she again spotted Damon dancing with Hermione.

Twice. Damon had led Hermione out twice. It was not unusual, but tonight it was the last straw. He rarely partnered his wife even once. She missed a beat, throwing Forley into a stumble. He only recovered after they had bumped into another couple, catching Cat's skirt and tearing the flounce.

"Forgive me, Lady Devlin," Forley begged.

"It was entirely my fault," she admitted, noting that the loose flounce was dragging on the floor. "But I must fix this or we will both fall. Excuse me." She slipped quickly from the ballroom.

Even more than repairing her gown, she needed to think, so she located an empty antechamber and thankfully sank onto its couch.

She couldn't do it. She couldn't face months and years of watching Damon dance with Hermione, ride with Hermione, flirt with Hermione. She couldn't face the gossip, the scorn, or the pity. And she definitely couldn't face a lifetime of cold, lonely nights wondering who he was with. But if she could not tolerate life with him, then she must leave.

She had already considered the possibility, so she knew what obstacles she would face. Would he grant her a portion of her inheritance so that she could live independently? Not at Ridgway, of course. It was too close to Devlin Court. But she could be happy in a cottage. Barring that, she would have to support herself. Her hands pressed against her throbbing head as the enormity of her decision registered. Working for a living would sever all connection to her own class. But it might be her only option. She had sufficient experience to become a companion or a housekeeper—eight years of practice. She would have to change her name, of course, for no one would hire a runaway countess. The only problem would be producing the necessary references. She could never ask Aunt Eugenia. But perhaps she could write one for herself. A distant cousin had recently died. She knew little of the lady except that she had lived alone in the wilds of Cornwall. No one could check a note from a dead woman. It might do.

She was choosing a new name when Lady Hermione walked in.

"This room is occupied," said Catherine.

"I know." Hermione shut the door and glared. "It is time you faced facts, my proud lady. And it is more than time that you ceased spreading slander about me."

"What are you talking about?"

"Don't play the naive innocent, for you are too old to get away with it. I don't know how you keep Lady Beatrice in your pocket, but the tales you are feeding her must stop."

"A clear case of the pot calling the kettle black, for we both know how many lies and exaggerations you have started. But you are mistaken. I have not spoken of you to Lady Beatrice or anyone else. If she has taken against you, it is your own fault, for she is using your misbehavior to spite Lady Debenham. All of society knows where that lady gets her falsehoods."

"Enough!" snapped Hermione. "You cannot bury the truth under innuendo. All of society knows you tricked Damon to the altar—was it for money or for social position? But dear Damon will make you pay. He loves only me—something your manipulative plotting can never change."

"I fear your youth has betrayed you," countered Catherine, refusing to admit the truth of Hermione's words aloud. She was pleased that her voice remained steady. "Damon has always admired beauty—which you have in abundance—but do not confuse that with love. It was not you he chose to marry."

"Chose?"

"Chose! As you would know if you were as close to him as you claim."

Hermione laughed. "You cannot hurt me, so quit trying. Even your pathetic attempt to win his sympathy by faking an injury did not work. He is quite eloquent in his contempt, you know. You should have heard him last night."

"The injury was quite real," said Catherine, trying to decipher Hermione's real purpose. Damon knew the truth and

would never have uttered such lies. "But it would not surprise me to learn that you were responsible. I saw you near
that copse only moments before my horse shied—a fact my
groom can confirm."

"Enough of your fantasies!" snapped Hermione, her face
no longer set in a smile. "You cannot excuse incompetent
horsemanship by inventing an attacker. Nor can you ignore
the fact that Damon loves only me. You may have seduced
him into marriage, but he despises being tied to a country
widgeon who does not even possess basic social skills. His
preference is obvious to the world. He will not even dance
with you for fear of sustaining a crippling injury from your
clumsiness. How we laughed when you tripped Forley just
now! Damon is mortified at your vulgarity and appalled
that you can never be the hostess he needs. Ostracism will
soon banish you to the eternal boredom of the country, but
don't expect him to stay there with you. Crushing *ennui*
would send him back to the society we both love, leaving
you to rot. That wedding ring will never bring you a moment of peace. The one unalterable fact remains—Damon
loves me and can only rue that he is stuck with you."

Catherine said nothing. What was to be said, after all?
Hermione was right. It was a fact that she had already accepted. Suppressing tears, she rose to leave.

"Cat got your tongue?" taunted Hermione.

"Not at all. You speak of social skills, but if this is an example of society manners, I can only rejoice that I was not
raised to that standard. It is you who have succumbed to
fantasy, my child. Take advice from someone both older
and wiser. Damon's affections are irrelevant—as are yours
and mine. Marriages in our class are contracted for financial and dynastic reasons—a fact your governess must have
taught you. Money and breeding may have bought you a
high place in society, but your very obvious spite and over-
weening conceit are fast eroding your image. You make a
further cake of yourself by publicly dangling after a married man. People are beginning to question your morals.
Consider your future and cut your losses before you destroy
your reputation."

Fury flickered in Hermione's eyes, but Catherine felt no

pleasure at the sight. Love might not be a normal part of society unions, but she was trapped in a tangle of misplaced affections that was likely to destroy all three of them. Slipping out of the antechamber, she sent word to Louisa that she was tired, then returned home.

Damon escorted Hermione back to her mother and thankfully escaped. She was thwarting his efforts to ease her back into the marriage mart. He had more than fulfilled his obligations to her. Three weeks was long enough to stifle gossip. In fact, her refusal to consider other suitors was harming her far more than his defection. Her possessiveness also disturbed him, for she had been charmingly conformable during their courtship. Now she followed him with her eyes when they were not together, and her tongue had developed an acidity he deplored. Had she changed? Or had he not seen her clearly?

He looked forward to the end of the Season when he and Catherine could return to Devlin. Events had unfolded too fast for either of them to make the necessary adjustments. With more time, he could have courted her, learning to see her as a wife. Society would have welcomed both her and their match. If only he had assumed his responsibilities earlier! But he had not, forcing them into scandals and distrust that had propelled them far down a road of confrontation. Backtracking would be difficult, if not impossible.

In the meantime, he had just recalled that Lord James had a genuine grievance against him. If not for Damon, the gentleman would have married Hermione. Retaliation would explain his attentions to Catherine and could also explain the pettier of the rumors.

"What do you know about the latest gossip?" he asked bluntly when he reached Hutchinson's side. "I am tired of people attacking my wife."

"So I am your latest candidate," observed Lord James, his eyes blazing with anger. "How so cloth-headed an imbecile survived seven years of war is beyond my comprehension. You could use a few home truths, Devlin, but this is not the place."

Damon was already itching to plant a fist in the dandy's face. "After you." He gestured toward the door.

They slipped through the crowd, dodging knots of chattering chaperones and several sets of country dancers until they finally escaped the ballroom. A footman directed them to an antechamber.

The corridor was empty, so Lord James began even before they reached the room. "Despite your suspicions, I have tried to deflect the gossip. If you had done the same, this would have blown over in days."

"What nerve!"

"Think, Devlin! When you spend all your time dancing attendance on Lady Hermione and ignoring your wife, what are people to conclude?"

"But how could I stand aside and allow an innocent to bear the blame for my own mistakes?" Damon countered sharply. Yet the question put his behavior in a different light. Again he had chosen the wrong course. And again it was Catherine who was suffering for it.

"Altruism is not the impression you are leaving, Devlin. But if that is your reason, then perhaps you are ready to hear the truth." They turned a corner, passing the retiring room. "Your most determined detractor is Sidney Braxton. He has a history of dishonor, including a plot to fleece my brother that I foiled just last month."

"Damn! I only recently discovered his penchant for sharping. Is your brother all right?"

"He will recover, though I hope his pride remains bruised for a while. But my interference cost Braxton an expected windfall. He is badly in debt, which must be driving his current scheme—backing you into a tight enough corner that you will pay him to recant his charges."

"Never!"

"Catherine swore that would be your answer."

"She knows of this?"

"We have discussed it. All of her friends have been working to help her. It was not difficult to identify the culprits, for only two have any real grievance. Braxton started the truly malicious rumors. The petty sniping originates with Lady Hermione."

"But—"

"She is selfish and willful," continued Lord James, refusing to allow the interruption. "Your marriage triggered a childish tantrum. She cares not a fig for you personally, but she really wanted that title. Since she can't have it, she is determined to make you both miserable."

"I thought you cared for her." Damon was reeling, though part of his mind was unsurprised and another part berated him for not accepting the truth sooner.

"I do. I love her more than life, but I am not blind to her faults. My only hope is that she will accept my suit when her pique runs is course—which I expect to happen soon. She is damaging her own credit far more than yours. Lady Beatrice is furious with her. Believe me, you would have been miserable with such a wife." He shut the anteroom door behind them and took a seat, motioning to the second chair.

"Damon loves only me," a muffled voice declared in the next room.

Hermione, Damon immediately identified, struck dumb as her taunting invective continued. He almost missed the soft murmur that finally responded. *Catherine!* Pressing his hands to his temples, he fought to control his rage. Hermione's diatribe was even harsher than her public claims.

"Well?" whispered Hutchinson, glaring at the connecting door. "You are up at bat."

"She deserves a set-down," frowned Damon.

"Agreed," said Lord James with a nod. "Make it a good one. I would not mind if she collapsed in hysterics. Perhaps it is time for me to pick up the pieces. She will make the perfect wife for the life I enjoy."

Damon examined the dandy, from his elaborate cravat to his ballooning Cossack pants, and admitted the truth. Lord James loved London's glitter, and Hermione was the same. "I wish you luck in your quest. And joy in your future," he said, holding out his hand.

Lord James grasped it firmly. "And you."

"Thank you. I misjudged you, it seems. The affectations make it difficult to take you seriously. Hermione may have made the same mistake." Without waiting for a response, he set his face in a grim smile and opened the door. Catherine was gone.

"Damon!" Hermione looked as if she would throw her arms around his neck.

"My lady," he responded coldly.

She gasped before turning her most enchanting smile on him.

"Forget the wiles," he ordered. "You seem to be laboring under a misconception. I do not and never will prefer you to Catherine, and if you do not cease slandering my wife, I will expose your spite to all of society."

"But you love me," she protested.

"You delude yourself." He stared at her until her face reddened in mortification.

"Then why did you court me?" she whispered.

He shrugged. "I was told that Catherine had married some years ago. With the deaths of both of our families, we had lost contact with each other, so I had no way of discovering the truth. Having lost the one person I could truly love, I fell back on the time-honored tradition of choosing a convenience from the current crop of candidates. You should know that love plays little role in the marriage mart, Lady Hermione. I looked for a young, conformable girl who would quickly learn not to interfere with my ways. All I needed was an heir and a housekeeper for Devlin Court. A peaceful life in the country demands no more. It is lowering to discover that my judgment was faulty, for you are nothing like I imagined. Fortunately, I learned that Catherine was unwed before I could make a grievous mistake. I have tried to remove the blemish my actions placed on your reputation, for I owed you that much, but I will not tolerate your vulgar, ill-bred, and childish spite. There is no excuse for it. You know full well that you never cared for me. Your only hurt was to your considerable conceit, for you possess not a shred of heart."

"You understand nothing!" she spat. Her hands spread into talons, as they had done in one of his nightmares. "How can I hold up my head when an earl, of all things, leads the *ton* to expect a betrothal and then jilts me? You

have harmed me more than your puny mind can compre-
hend. I hope she makes your life miserable for the rest of
your days! I hope your heir resembles your groom! I
hope—" But tears overcame her, and she collapsed onto the
couch, sobbing in despair.

"Good-bye, my lady," he said formally. "If there is any
taint attached to your name, you are responsible. Few
would have considered your reputation besmirched for
more than the proverbial nine days if you had not made
such a Cheltenham tragedy of it. Perhaps you will eventually grow up enough to realize how ridiculous your behavior appears to adult eyes." Turning on his heel, he strode
out of the room, leaving a sputtering Hermione behind. As
the door closed, her contrived sobs exploded into hysterics.

"Good work," murmured Lord James, peeking out of the
next room. "You needn't concern yourself with her again."

"I won't." He glanced back to the room where Hermione
still wailed, raising one brow.

"I'll let her cry awhile. I can't abide hysterics. Besides, it
will do her good to start fearing for her future."

Damon nodded and left. His words to Hermione had
been true, though he had chosen them only to make a point.
He loved Catherine—had loved her all his life. Though he
had long thought of her as a sister, his feelings had changed
before he left for the Peninsula. He had not noted it at the
time—indeed he was not even sure exactly when it had occurred. But it had happened. It was why the promise to
Peter had been unnecessary. Somewhere deep in his mind,
he had pictured himself always caring for her. And how
was he to do so without marrying her?

Stupid, he condemned himself. If only he had had time to
think before proposing. Now he was a month into an unconsummated marriage during which he had done little but
argue with her. *Idiot!*

"Have you seen Catherine?" he asked Jack, running his
friend to ground in the refreshment room.

"Not since before supper. Might she have left?"

Damon sighed. "I will go see. Hermione rang a peal over
her head. I never realized how childish the girl is. I have set
her straight, but Cat has to be distressed. She only rose

from a sickbed today. If you find her here, would you escort her back to Berkeley Square?"

"Of course. And it is time someone exposed Lady Hermione's spite to the world," dared Jack.

"Not yet," begged Damon, defusing his friend's exasperation by adding, "I believe she may shortly change her tune. Let me know what happens when she returns to the ballroom. If she publicly recants her tales, she deserves forgiveness and support."

Taking leave of his hostess, Damon turned his feet toward home. But a further shock awaited him. Catherine had returned from the ball and had immediately ordered out the traveling coach. She was gone.

Chapter Seventeen

Catherine climbed down from the carriage and dismissed her driver, ordering him to return to London. She waited until he was out of sight before picking up her valise and setting off along the Ridgway House drive.

Pain and grief had plagued her for two days as she floundered in an interminable hell of memories. Her eyes saw only Damon's carefree smile as he waltzed with the woman he loved. Her ears rang with taunts, rumors, and innuendo. Her half-healed injuries throbbed harder with every jolt from the road.

Hermione's attack had been the last straw. She could not tolerate another moment of society's censure. Damon's coachman was out when she returned from the ball, a bit of luck that prompted her immediate departure. Brigit also had the night off, but Cat had refused to wait until the maid returned lest delay lead to another battle with Damon. She was not up to arguing that night. So she ordered a groom to harness the traveling carriage.

Ridgway was merely a temporary shelter until she could decide what to do. Very temporary. She must be gone before Damon returned to Devlin Court. For now, she would claim that she was inspecting the house. The Braxtons had inflicted enough wear and tear to keep the servants from asking questions for several days. Damon would remain in town until the end of the Season, leaving her safe for a time.

She had noticed nothing during her walk through the park, but she frowned at the front door. No one answered her knock. Even more shocking, it was unlocked.

"Dear God!"

The great hall was in shambles. The suit of armor that had always stood against the curve of the stairs was scattered across the floor in twisted, barely recognizable pieces. Chairs and tables were reduced to kindling. Gouges marred the paneling and chips disfigured marble tiles. Her eyes stung as she moved from room to room, the story the same in each—broken furniture, ripped upholstery and draperies, wallcoverings damaged beyond repair. Glass crunched under her half boots as she crossed the dining room. Slashes savaged portraits, especially the picture of her father. Upstairs she found shredded mattresses, cracked mirrors, and debris littering floors. At least the destruction was limited to the public rooms and family sleeping quarters. An older wing was untouched.

Spite. She had been subjected to too much of it lately. This could only be the work of her family, who must have also turned off the servants. Her head shook. So much beauty destroyed. The paneling alone was over two hundred years old. No matter how much of her fortune had survived her uncle's depredations, she doubted it would cover the cost of restoration.

She finally reached the room that had been hers for the last eight years. The pillage was worse here than anywhere else. Belongings that she had kept since childhood had been meticulously destroyed—pages ripped out of books and then shredded; the china figurine her mother had given her on her tenth birthday broken and rebroken until no piece larger than a pea survived; clothing cut to ribbons. Even her shoes were slashed. Huddling in the corner, she succumbed to wracking sobs.

Dusk was falling by the time she pulled herself together to examine the room more closely. The condolence letters in her desk were gone, their hiding place exposed when her cousins smashed the desk itself. She shook her head over part of the cover from her copy of *Cinderella*. She had often pictured herself in that role, especially during the months immediately after the accident. But she no longer felt any kinship with the girl. Prince Charmings did not exist in the real world. Even heroes had problems and flaws. It would have been satisfying to help Damon forget the trauma of war, but she would not have the opportunity. At least Peter did not have to live with such horrifying memories.

Peter. She stared at the wardrobe, almost afraid to look. She had never trusted her cousins, so she had hidden his letters as soon as she moved to this room. Shaking hands removed debris from the wardrobe bottom. Lifting the loose board at the back, she again burst into tears. They were still there—letters from Eton, from Oxford, and six from the army. Resting on top was the book of poetry that Damon had given her two weeks before he left for war.

Clutching the surviving mementos of her childhood, she headed for the kitchen. Her cousins had probably destroyed her personal possessions the moment they heard of her marriage. The rest was a more intense version of their usual temper fit, triggered because they had to leave the estate. They would have waited until the last minute, first throwing out the servants, whose loyalties lay with Catherine and the house.

As expected, the kitchen was untouched. Dru and Horty avoided anything related to menials. They were higher in the instep than the most haughty matron. Sighing in relief, she found ham, cheese, and apples in the larder. There was even a loaf of bread that was still fresh.

She next turned her attention to sleep. The unused wing had not been occupied in over a century, but at least the beds were intact. Another place her dear cousins had missed was the linen closet, so she had clean sheets. Slipping Peter's letters and Damon's gift under her pillow, she emptied her mind of problems and succumbed to the arms of Morpheus.

Damon returned to the ball as soon as he discovered that Catherine had fled.

"She left for Devlin Court an hour ago," he told Jack. "I will follow at first light. Has Lady Hermione returned?"

"Not yet." But his voice died as the lady in question appeared in the doorway on Lord James's arm.

"My, she looks rumpled!" exclaimed Lady Beatrice, who was standing near Jack. "And her eyes!"

"You don't suppose—" began Lady Marchgate, but she stopped as the pair approached. All eyes swiveled from Hermione to Damon.

Hermione curtsied to Lady Beatrice. "I must beg your forgiveness for my childish behavior this Season," she began in a shaky voice, avoiding Damon's eyes. Silence rippled across the ballroom. Even the orchestra fell quiet.

"What precisely have you done?" demanded the gossip.

"I exaggerated Mr. Braxton's lies to create scandal for Lady Devlin," admitted Hermione. "When you did not cut her, I made up new stories of my own. None of it was true."

"Why?"

"That is the most shameful part," said the girl, turning to ignore Lady Debenham's furious gaze. "I was angry at her for exposing my older lies." Gasps echoed all sides. Even Damon had not expected that. "I had coveted a title, you see," she continued in a small voice that nevertheless reached every ear. "When Lord Devlin smiled at me last Christmas, I threw myself at him, claiming more interest than he had actually shown. He was too polite to contradict me so I was able to make him appear infatuated. I continued this dishonorable course in London, hoping that public pressure would force him to offer for me. But he refused. And he was right. My behavior was unworthy of my breeding. I have learned my lesson and only seek to repair the damage my plotting caused."

"Very prettily said," replied Lady Beatrice, but everyone saw the triumphant look she directed at a teeth-gnashing Lady Debenham. "We can forgive a youthful mistake—as long as it is not repeated."

"It won't be," promised Lord James. "Lady Hermione has done me the honor of accepting my hand."

"Thank you, my lady," Hermione said, curtsying again before turning to accept congratulations from the crowd.

"That wasn't necessary," Damon murmured when it was his turn.

"It was to me," she countered. "It was the best way I could think of to make amends."

"Let that be the last fabrication," he urged, then resumed his normal voice to offer his regards.

Lord James waited until Hermione was speaking to Lady Marchgate. "Thank you, Devlin," he murmured. "She, too, underestimated me. Perhaps it is time to adopt more sober attire. My father has granted me a seat in the Commons."

"Then you have much to celebrate."

Damon rolled over, but the bed was just as uncomfortable in his new position. Where would Catherine have spent the night? It had been midnight when she left, so she was unlikely to have gotten far. How much money did she have? That was another worry, for she had no idea of travel costs. Two nights at inns and several changes of horses would leave her in dire straits by the time she reached Devlin. Of course, Gordy may have gotten funds from Simms. It was a question he should have asked earlier, but he had not thought of it.

He again shifted, trying to fall asleep, for he faced a grueling journey if he could not catch up with her in the morning, but sleep was impossible. He tossed and turned through what was left of the night, memories and fears warring in his mind. If only he had met his responsibilities! He had left her unprotected after her family died and again after their wedding. If he had ignored his troops to such an extent, they would have been cut to ribbons—which was exactly what society had done to Cat.

He finally gave up and summoned Tucker.

"She what?" he repeated incredulously.

"She left 'er maid behind," repeated Tucker. "And Gordy."

"Then who is driving?"

"Barney."

Damon glared.

"The 'ead groom. 'E's capable enough."

"And how did that come about?" he asked in an ominous voice.

" 'Twas Gordy's night off."

He sighed. There was nothing he could do about it except to order Brigit to accompany Tucker in the baggage coach. As dawn brightened the sky, he tooled his curricle around Berkeley Square, dodged several gentlemen weaving their way home to bed, and headed for Somerset.

The day brought both good and bad news. She was

headed for Devlin, as he had expected, but she had not stopped for the night. Nor was she stopping for meals, opting for food baskets that she could eat while on the road. He should have suspected as much when he discovered that Brigit was still in London. What else could she have done without a maid to give her countenance? He cursed her haste and cursed Barney for allowing such abuse.

And he worried.

Why had she left? Did she hate him? He could hardly expect otherwise. He had never understood Mayfair. Though he had often been in town, his sojourns had been too short for him to really become part of society. He should have known how the *ton* would react. His ignorance had allowed Hermione to manipulate him into hurting Catherine, who might never forgive him.

Was that why she was in such a hurry? Or had something besides Hermione's vitriol driven her from town? Surely the urgency could not be so great that she had to push a servant to total exhaustion. It was not like her to misuse the staff. But perhaps she did not have enough money for inns.

His own exhaustion was growing. By evening—which arrived early due to a heavy cloud cover—he could no longer sustain the pace. Though every thought screamed to continue, he knew that it was foolish to do so. He had made up at least half of her lead, but he risked driving into a ditch if he followed his heart.

And so he halted. But despite the sleepless night and hurried journey, he could find no rest. Catherine's charges mocked him—*arrogant, dictatorial, selfish*. And she had a point. His treatment of her since his return was not what she was accustomed to expect from him. He had forgotten that she was an intelligent girl with a strong will. One did not coerce Cat. One persuaded.

Like the summer she was fourteen. Her favorite horse had broken a foreleg. Any horseman knew that the injury could not be mended; the only remedy was to put the animal out of its misery. Peter could not face breaking the news, so the job fell to Damon. He had taken her aside, explained the injury, and described the pain the horse would suffer. He had told her how badly the horse would limp even if they managed the impossible and got the bone to heal. She had cried, of course, and had been saddened at the loss, but in the end she had agreed that no other course was possible. It was typical of the way he had helped her through the trials of childhood. Why in God's name had he not remembered that sooner?

He rolled over on the lumpy bed and buried his head in the pillow. He had not offered one word of comfort or explanation since his return. Instead, he issued orders and expected her unquestioning compliance—as if she had been one of his subalterns. He had not yet made the switch back to civilian life. On the Peninsula, instant obedience was essential, often marking the difference between survival and death. But Catherine would resent being treated as a servant—especially after spending so many years in just that capacity.

Somehow he would have to make it up to her, and he must start by telling her exactly what he had done and why. It was too late to change the decisions he had made, so he could only pray that she would agree once she had all the facts. If not, his enemies could gloat over the unmitigated disaster he had made of his life. Now all he had to do was find her.

He did not catch up with Catherine the next day, and stopping to ask questions took time. It was nearly midnight when he finally arrived at Devlin Court.

She wasn't there.

She had never been there.

Too tired to think, he collapsed into bed, postponing further action until morning.

Chapter Eighteen

"Where am I?" Heart pounding, Catherine jerked upright in bed, but one look at the dusty room brought memory surging back.

Ridgway was in ruins. Her prayer that the vandalism was less than she recalled died when she entered the drawing room. It was hopeless. Even the ceiling was damaged. She kept her eyes grimly on the floor as she crossed the great hall and climbed the stairs. Another view of the desecrated paneling would turn her stomach.

The library was better. Its furniture was intact, though the globes were ruined. Books had been dumped off the shelves, but they were in good condition, as were the ledgers. Her cousins had no inkling of how important the records were to the estate's future.

She set to work straightening the books. Most lay directly beneath their accustomed places, so sorting was easier than it might have been. Her cousins lacked all sense. They had destroyed furniture that was already falling apart yet left intact a library that included many valuable first editions. She smoothed the cover of a 1612 copy of *The Tempest*, Shakespeare's last finished work. What fools!

She was halfway around the room when she picked up a slipcased volume that was lighter than its size suggested. Puzzled, she pulled out the book. Its center was hollow but far from empty, containing the paperwork for investments totaling nearly fifty thousand pounds, recorded under the name Henry Graveston. A bag held over a hundred gemstones, with ten thousand pounds in large banknotes tucked underneath.

Plopping into a chair, she stared at the fortune spread across the desktop. It had to be the money Uncle Henry had stolen from her trust. He was wily enough to have made plans in case his scheme was exposed, but why had he not taken these when he fled? Not that it mattered. Her own situation was now very different. She need not enter service after all. Placing everything into a secret drawer in her father's game table, she set the hollow book on the shelf and continued her work.

An hour later footsteps echoed in the great hall. Hoping the servants had returned, she hurried out to the minstrel's gallery. Sidney Braxton looked up, his face set in a satisfied smirk.

"Some inheritance," he gloated. "My sisters know how to repay insults."

"Aided and abetted by their brother, I presume. It is a small mind that stoops to spite."

"So your sudden rise to the aristocracy has turned you into another judgmental harridan. You would not have sung such a tune before."

"Why are you here?" Anyone would decry a crime of such magnitude, but there was no point in starting a fight when they were alone.

"You destroyed my expectations. You owe it to me to undo the damage."

"Air-dreaming again? I owe you nothing."

"That's not how the moneylenders see it. I need something I can pawn or they will make an example of me."

She laughed. "Help yourself, Sidney. Your loving sisters destroyed every valuable in the place, and your father robbed me of all but a rundown estate. What do you think has been supporting you all these years? I couldn't give you more even if I wanted to."

"You lie!" His voice turned shrill as he mounted the stairs. "I got nothing from you. My allowance was too small to cover even tradesmen's bills." Something in his eyes had changed when he realized that nothing was left. His face now wore the look of an animal at bay. "You always considered yourself better than us, didn't you? But you will sing a different tune from now on. His bloody lordship will never trust you after your antics in town. Not that he will have time to think about them. Society suspects him of attempted murder. The authorities will keep him busy for years."

"It was you, wasn't it?" she said coldly. One of Sidney's few skills was deadly accuracy with a dart.

"Of course. Not that you can prove anything. If it comes down to my word against yours, no court will believe a female whose scandals titillate all the world."

"But they would certainly believe me!" Damon's voice had all the warmth of an iceberg.

Sidney whirled around to lean over the railing, his face twisting into fury when he saw Lord Devlin striding across the great hall. "What are you doing here?"

"Cataloging the damage to my wife's property," he answered calmly, joining the others on the gallery. "You will remove yourself from Ridgway and not set foot here again."

"You cannot control me. I will produce a witness to your assault and see you off to Botany Bay."

Damon actually laughed. "You haven't the brains God gave a flea, Braxton. Do you seriously believe anyone swallowed your lies? More than one man traced the tale to your lips and informed society. You are already on the verge of ostracism. If I publicize my father-in-law's will, you will never again be welcome in town."

"You would, too!" His face flushed scarlet with fury. "You always hated me. You all did. All three of you!"

"What fustian is this?" demanded Catherine. "No one hated you."

"You lie! You even forbade Mama and the girls to visit you."

"Whoever spread that tale is the liar," she said. "They were always included in invitations, but your father refused to bring them lest your mother's vulgarity reflect poorly on him. Now leave before you do something stupid."

Sidney appeared ready to explode. Damon stepped up to throw him out, but Catherine stopped him with her eyes, suddenly able to communicate silently with him as they had done in their youths.

Sidney's shoulders eventually slumped in resignation. "What can I do?" he murmured to himself.

"That depends on which problem you are pondering," said Catherine softly. "You are young enough that your recent tricks may be excused as wild oats if you reform. I don't know the extent of your indebtedness, but perhaps Damon can arrange financing to get the moneylenders off your back."

"You would do that?" demanded Sidney incredulously.

"If you are serious about turning over a new leaf," agreed Damon cautiously. "I told you to return once you knew the true state of your affairs, you might recall."

"He lies, Sidney! He will destroy you as he has me!" Henry Braxton appeared from the direction of the library, and Catherine gasped. He carried the hollow book, his face livid with fury.

"What are you doing here?" demanded Damon, gingerly stepping between Catherine and the Braxtons. "I thought you were in France."

"I had to leave once your damned solicitor showed up, but I only removed to London. There were things to do before I could consider going abroad." He glared at Catherine.

"It is too late," she advised, understanding why Henry's cache was still there. Once he had dodged Damon's solicitor, he would have had to wait until his family moved out or risk being seen. Her eyes again commanded Damon's silence. "I found it yesterday and sent it to London. It's gone."

"Nice try, but you cannot have gotten here before this morning. You were at the Cunningham Ball." Henry sneered.

"Too bad you don't command the loyalty that inspires your servants to travel around the clock," she goaded him.

"Someone should have killed you years ago."

"You planned the attack on Cat, even if Sidney actually carried it out," concluded Damon ominously.

"What attack?" Henry frowned. "I've no real quarrel with her—or didn't until today. My hatred is reserved for you, my lord."

"So you were responsible for that pathetic attempt to rob

me the other night." The quiet voice brought a new grimace to Braxton's face.

Catherine nearly demanded an explanation, but she caught herself in time. Damon did not need distractions. She had never considered Henry dangerous, but even a timid man might strike out to gain the sort of fortune she had found that morning.

"You robbed me of my inheritance," charged Henry, ignoring Damon's conclusion. "If you hadn't meddled, my stupid niece would never have gotten a penny."

"My interference started only after you had been systematically cheating her for years."

"Balderdash! You know very well that my half-witted nephew would never have bought colors without your pernicious influence. He would have died with his father and that devilish codicil would never have been written. I had to put up with eight more years of that vulgar harridan and her greedy daughters because of you."

"You knew nothing of Peter if you believe such tripe," said Damon, shaking his head sadly. "He was army mad from early childhood. It was his idea to join, though I tried to talk him out of it."

"You lie!" Lord Braxton's roar reverberated around the vaulted ceiling. "You deliberately destroyed me. The only recompense is your lives. A boat is waiting for me just across the hills. I will ransack Devlin for a stake to replace what you stole. Your servants won't protect a dead man's house when it means their own demise."

"You are serious!" Surprisingly, it was Sidney who spoke.

"I had enough put away to make a new start, but your cousin stole it," declared Henry.

"Don't be his puppet," Catherine begged as Sidney started toward her. "He wants your help now, but he will abandon you the moment he leaves. He was planning to walk out on the lot of you the day after my birthday. He would have shipped your family to Braxton, sold Ridgway, and absconded with the lot."

"You lie!"

"She tells the truth," swore Damon. "He invited a buyer

down to look over the estate. Fortunately, the man did not arrive until after the codicil was known."

"Think, Sidney!" urged Catherine. "You cannot trust his words. How often has he promised Seasons to your sisters? But you heard his opinion of them just now. He can never allow them near town. They would blacken your name for all time with their antics. Miss Huntsley is a paragon in comparison."

Sidney turned blazing eyes toward his father, but Henry overrode his words. "Can you believe a chit who stole your patrimony and spread lies about you all over town? Society is buzzing with condemnation and laughing at your problems. It is true that I never meant to bring out your sisters, but I would not ignore my heir. Let us rid ourselves of these pests, take what we need from Devlin, then travel the Continent together."

Sidney still hesitated.

"Many is the time these two carried malicious tales to me," hissed Henry softly. "I knew the complaints for lies, but think of all the unjust punishments meted out by my brother—the same man who conspired to rob us both. That infamous codicil was devised solely to keep everything out of our hands."

It was the last straw for Sidney's precarious temper. Catherine screamed as the Braxtons attacked Damon. She tried to help, clawing at Sidney when her cousin grabbed Damon's throat. Sidney let go, smashing her into the wall. Too stunned to catch her breath, she lay gasping on the floor.

Damon had managed to turn his back to the wall, restricting his attackers to a frontal assault. He landed a solid punch in Sidney's stomach, then planted a facer on Henry. But Lord Braxton's rage had left him numb to all feeling. He grabbed Damon's arm and swung him toward the railing that overlooked the great hall. Damon hit it low and bounced off, but he lost his balance. In trying to stay on his feet, his guard fell. Sidney landed a heavy blow in his midsection even as Henry snapped his head back.

Catherine lurched to her feet, eyes frantically searching for a weapon. The struggle was growing fiercer, with

Damon twisting to kick Henry and nearly taking a header over the rail when Sidney knocked him sideways. The remains of a chair lay in the corner. She broke a leg free from the wreckage and dashed back to the melee. Sidney had fallen to his knees while her back was turned. Roaring, he scrambled up to launch himself in a murderous dive intended to push Damon over the side. She slammed the leg into Sidney's shoulder, pushing him off course. He crashed into his father, their combined weight falling heavily against the railing, which broke, dumping them both into the great hall. But Henry again had hold of Damon's arm.

"No!" Catherine's scream was lost amid the shouts of the men and the crash of bodies that echoed through the rafters. It took a moment to realize that someone had caught hold of a surviving baluster post.

She dove for the edge. "Thank God!" Damon was grimly hanging on, chest heaving as he tried to catch his breath. Without looking at the stone floor fifteen feet below, she grabbed his other hand, then braced herself against the unbroken section of rail while he swung his leg onto the gallery. In another minute, she had pulled him to safety and burst into sobs of relief.

"It's all right, Little Cat," he crooned, drawing her into his arms to muffle her tears. One hand gently stroked her hair. "They shan't hurt you again."

Comfort washed over her as it had so often done in the past. Perhaps their friendship was not dead after all. Was it possible that they could live together in harmony?

Her tears finally died and she pulled back far enough to look him in the eye. "Are they—" She could not complete the question.

"I don't know. But if you are recovered, I will see."

She nodded and he let her go.

Damon spent a hectic hour minimizing the damage. Though Ridgway's servants had accompanied him to the estate, the fight was over by the time they rushed up from below stairs. He sent Ned for the doctor and set the others to straightening the great hall and an adjacent antechamber so the Braxton crimes would not become neighborhood gossip. Henry was dead, his head smashed against the floor. Sidney had landed atop his father, breaking several bones. He seemed surprised when Damon suggested the fall was an accident, but readily agreed.

Damon finally joined Catherine in the library, setting a tea tray on a table at her elbow. He had no idea what to expect. By avoiding Devlin, she had confirmed his fear that she hated him. She must have believed Hermione's claims. And who could blame her? He studied her, trying to gauge her mood. Her eyes were puffy from another bout of tears, but she seemed under control.

"I am sorry about the damage to Ridgway," he began hesitantly. "It is partially my fault. If I had not called Hortense a trollop—and worse—she may have been less vindictive."

"You did?" Her eyes widened in surprise.

He grimaced. "Yes, though that is hardly my usual style. But she had just tried to compromise me, and I lost my temper."

"You?"

"I'm afraid so. Even those of us known for common sense and prudence get angry, Cat. You, of all people, should know that, for I've lashed out at you more than once lately. It is all of a piece. Nothing I've done in years has turned out right. I should have protected you better."

"Of course," she interrupted bitterly. "Peter would have expected it." Her cup slammed onto the table. "Quit living your life according to what my brother might have wanted, Damon. Hasn't that caused enough trouble?"

He winced. "The contempt is well deserved, though a trifle misdirected. But that is also my fault. I have been less than truthful, my dear, often attributing my actions to Peter's wishes instead of admitting that they are also mine."

"Why?"

Setting his own cup on the mantel, he paced restlessly about the room, sidestepping heaps of books that still littered the floor. "Peter was always wildly emotional, relying on me to keep him in line. After years of playing the wise counselor, it was impossible to admit that I had feelings of my own. I might have grown away from that extreme after he died if I had not been in the army. But in battle, emotion kills, for it leads to carelessness. And thinking about what one is doing can break the mind. So I banished all feelings. When I could not do so, I coped by attributing them to Peter."

"What are you trying to say?" She glared suspiciously at him. The emotionless man he was describing was nothing like the sensitive friend she had known.

"While I was thrashing about the other night, terrified for your safety—travel is dangerous for a woman alone—I finally admitted where I had gone wrong. I should have told you the facts from the beginning. You tried to tell me that, but I wasn't listening. I was in the army too long, Cat. Years of issuing orders and expecting blind obedience has gotten to be a habit. That is essential in war, but you cannot have enjoyed my dictates."

"True, so suppose you explain," she suggested. Hope flickered across her face, but he didn't see it as he continued to pace.

"Half of me died with Peter," he stated, not for the first time. "The other half died two months later when your uncle told me that you were betrothed to another."

She jumped, for he had admitted no such feelings that day by the stream. Or when he had proposed, for that matter.

"I was so blue-deviled already that I hardly noticed the pain," he continued. "I convinced myself that everything was all right. Your uncle was looking after your interests, and you had a glorious future ahead. It allowed me to return to war with a clear conscience. But I never inquired about the details, except to send a note when mourning was over, wishing you happy."

"Uncle Henry must have destroyed it, along with your earlier ones and those I wrote you," she said wearily. "And every other communication to or from a personal friend. The only condolences I saw came from distant friends of my parents."

He nodded. "Even after I sold out, I never asked about your marriage. If I had discovered that you were unhappy, I would never have forgiven myself. Discovering that you were happy would have been worse, not that I consciously thought in those terms. Yet I still had responsibilities to the title. And after ignoring them for so long, I could no longer postpone securing the succession, so I set about choosing a bride."

"You needn't apologize, Damon. I would never condemn you for that."

"I sought out a girl who was as unlike you as possible, though I didn't realize it at the time." He stopped to stare out the window before resuming his pacing. "I tried to convince myself that I loved her, but that was merely a salve to my conscience."

She gasped at the implications.

"Fortunately fate stepped in and brought me home. It hurt to find you in servitude, Cat, but I was so certain of my own future that the logical solution never dawned on me. When I realized that your uncle had lied about your dowry, I planned to investigate, but not until he spirited you off to Braxton Manor did I begin to suspect a larger deceit. When I found your father's will, I could have strangled the man. But there was no time if I was to save you from his plots. I did what was necessary to thwart him, but without giving any real thought to either your feelings or my own. I should at least have explained."

"It is done, Damon," she said on a long sigh. "It would have been better if I had known about it earlier, but we cannot go back."

"But we can go forward," he said, kneeling before her chair to look deeply into her eyes. "I never loved Hermione, and after the way she has treated you, I cannot even like her. She has publicly admitted her lies, by the way, and will not trouble you again."

Catherine looked up in surprise. "How did that happen?"

"Lord James heard her talking with you at Lady Cunningham's ball. They are betrothed now."

"Wonderful!" Her radiant smile caught his breath, eliminating another worry. "He truly cares for her."

"And she for him. They would have been betrothed last Christmas if I hadn't interfered—another lapse in judgment to lay at my door. But enough of Lady Hermione. Your reputation is intact—too many people understand Sidney to lend credence to his words—so the next time you venture into London, you will find yourself the darling of the *ton*. Though just out of curiosity, what *were* you doing in the Dark Walk with Rathbone?"

"He rescued me from a lecherous drunk," she explained.

"One more crime to set to my account." He sighed. "Thank God he was on hand to help you. How will I ever atone for all my misdeeds?"

"I wish you would cease allowing a misplaced promise to rule your life, Damon. Peter is dead. Start thinking and acting for yourself."

"I do, but you have much to forgive, Cat," he insisted. "Even when I was trying to help you, my actions usually hurt your feelings. It is true that Peter demanded that I look after you, claiming that his own peace of mind was threatened unless I agreed. It was the night before Vimeiro. Maybe he had some presentiment of the disaster that would befall, for he was frantic about your future. I only mentioned it to Jack because it was something he would understand, and I had not yet examined my own motives for marrying you. But that vow was a meaningless formality for me, Cat. I would have done it even if he had demanded otherwise."

"Why?" Her heart was pounding so high in her throat that she could barely force the single word out.

His fingers lightly caressed her cheek. "I love you, Catherine Anne Braxton Fairbourne. I loved you even before I left for Portugal, though I did not admit it until recently. My feelings have not been brotherly for a very long time."

She laughed. "Good, for mine are not even remotely sisterly. I love you, Damon."

He pulled her into his arms and kissed her, a deep kiss of love and tenderness and growing passion. There was nothing brotherly about the way his groin tightened with painful, urgent need. And there was nothing sisterly in the way she arched into his embrace or in the moans that started deep in her throat.

Catherine's fear and anger floated away as his hands caressed her body. Every touch ignited heat and longing. This was a dream that had haunted her nights for years, she realized as his fingers untied the tapes of her gown and slipped it off one shoulder. His lips trailed downward until they reached her newly bared breast. She sighed and threaded her hands into his hair, pulling him closer.

This was hardly the ideal place to make love to his wife for the first time, Damon admitted dizzily as he slid her gown off and laid her gently on the carpet. But he could not stop. She loved him. Her words swept away remorse and anger. He felt her fingers sliding across his back and realized that she had pulled his shirt loose. Too bad the door was unlocked, he noted as he tossed his clothes aside. It was his last coherent thought for a very long time.

He was home at last, home where he had always belonged. And Catherine was with him, her fingers brushing away the lingering pain of war, her kisses banishing years of guilt, and her sighs cracking the shell that had protected him from feeling anything for so long. Happiness bubbled through those cracks—and love, excitement, heat, light, and more—in a growing eruption of emotion that finally burst into a cataclysm of sparks.

Catherine sighed with pleasure, surrendering to Damon's touch. His hands erased the pain of his attentions to Hermione, confirming with each tender stroke that she was loved and cherished. His knowing lips created sensations she had never imagined, building heat and intimacy. He truly loved her. She could see it in his tawny gaze, feel it in his every touch, hear it in the words he murmured between breaths that grew shorter and more frenzied with her every caress. There would be time later to hear about the scars he bore on his back and thigh. For now the time for thinking was past. The feelings he inspired spiraled out of control in a way that would have terrified her if he had not been Damon. Higher and higher she soared before her spirit exploded into a million pieces and the world went black.

She opened her eyes and blinked. She had never dreamed that making love could be so earth-shattering. Damon smiled and pulled her closer. "I love you, Cat," he whispered.

"A dream come true," she murmured in reply. He raised a questioning brow. "I fell in love with you the summer I was fourteen."

"The year we had to put Black Satin down. I never suspected. How I wish I had come home after the accident."

"We cannot remake the past, love. We can only let it go."

"Profound and true. But first, what was Henry babbling about? I know you were fibbing." He chuckled. "Even by pushing poor Barney unmercifully, you could not have gotten here much before sunset last night."

She laughed and scrambled to her feet, unembarrassed by her state of undress. A moment later she dropped her discovery into Damon's equally naked lap.

He stared at the cache in wonder. "My God! This is every shilling he stole from you!"

"He always was a pinchpenny, which made it hard to believe he could have wasted so much. It is what I meant when I told Sidney that Henry was about to abandon them. He intended to use my inheritance to build a new life for himself. Siphoning it into a different identity was his insurance against my unlikely marriage. His only mistake was in keeping everything at the manor." She joined him on the floor and unself-consciously snuggled into his embrace.

"The irony is that he could so easily have gotten away with it. If he had spent even a fraction of the cash on bringing you out, no one would have questioned him."

"Exactly. I suppose that was his real mistake. He was too clutch-fisted to let even a farthing slide through his fingers. And so he forfeited everything."

"I'm glad. I would have lost you if he had chosen otherwise." He pulled her closer for another heady embrace. The impropriety of place and time finally prompted him to set her gently aside. Wiggins would soon summon them to luncheon.

"There is another victim of your uncle's greed," he observed, exchanging her chemise for his socks.

"Who?"

"Sidney."

She nearly exploded, but the look in his eyes stopped

her. "He made his choice," she reminded him. "Can you really feel sorry for him after he tried to kill you?"

"You know how easily he can be manipulated. His father played him like a harp. And desperation does funny things to people. I have been checking his finances. He is at least ten thousand pounds in debt, but much of it arose from ignorance rather than profligacy. His so-called friends lured him into several unwise investment schemes. His only goal was to augment a woefully inadequate allowance so he could stay in London. And he appears chastened after today's revelations."

"So you want to pay his debts," she observed with a sigh, retrieving his cravat from the desktop.

"Yes, and I think we should give him enough to set Braxton Manor to rights. Then he is on his own."

Catherine frowned, but finally nodded. "Doing so will keep all this from becoming public. But he won't be grateful, Damon. And I doubt he will suddenly become an upstanding gentleman. He is easily led, and his friends are excellent leaders unburdened by noble impulses."

"I know, but whatever pitfalls he encounters in the future will be entirely his own doing. And he is now Lord Braxton. Neither your father nor Peter would have liked to see the holder of the title in debtors' prison."

"All right. Living with his mother and sisters will be penance enough."

"Such a sensible wife I have," he murmured, nibbling on her ear while he reached for his shirt.

"Are you still determined to sell Ridgway?" she asked, stroking down his still-bare chest with one finger and watching in fascination as his manhood stirred to life.

"What would you prefer?"

"It might make a wonderful home for your heir once he marries—close enough to keep an eye an him, yet allowing him to manage an estate. But if you truly cannot stand the memories, I will understand."

"They no longer bother me. I have made my peace with Peter. It was not he who was haunting me, but my own conscience."

"Good. Then you must realize that you and Peter were

not really opposites. Just as you embody the emotional nature that Peter never bothered to control, he inherited a good deal of sense. He just didn't use it, preferring to rely on your guidance."

"What is the point?"

"If Peter was really the other half of your soul, he is not dead. He merely moved into his other body."

"More likely he moved into yours."

She raised a questioning brow.

"You offer the same stability and companionship I got from Peter—and so much more." He grinned. "Either way, I am now complete."

"Perfect, in fact."

Her smile drove all thought of Wiggins from his mind. Tossing his shirt aside, Damon pulled his wife closer, proving that even perfection was capable of improvement.